The Willow Still Sings

A Story of Grace, Forgiveness, and the Strength of a Mother's Love

by Sarah Schwerin

Wow, what an awesome book! I'm blown away by such depth and range of emotion. Florence's life-changing journey will have you turning pages far into the night while keeping your box of tissues close by.

- Jennifer Hallmark
Author of *Smoking Flax* and *Jessie's Hope*

Sarah Schwerin's debut novel offers a look into one of America's most trying times—the devastation of polio. The reader follows a 1950s housewife, torn between caring for a daughter stricken with polio, while trying to hold together the remainder of her family, and carrying a misplaced guilt over her daughter's illness. Schwerin gives us characters that touch our hearts and some that stir our frustration, but everyone sticks with us after the cover is closed. A well-done story that pulls you in and doesn't let you go, leaving you with a memorable must-read that should find a spot on your nightstand.

- Cindy K. Sproles
Best-selling author of *Coal Black Lies* and *This is Where It Ends*

Sarah Schwerin has written a story that will touch the heart of readers everywhere, showcasing the strength of a mother's love, endurance, and hope when living through those life journeys that bring us to our knees.

Donna Mumma
Author of *The Women of Wynton's* cozy mystery series

As a fellow author who enjoys being in a critique group with Sarah, I can attest to the hard work and dedication to accuracy from her pen. Every word of this novel has been carefully chosen and prayed over. Sarah Schwerin's work never fails to entertain, educate, and excite.

Eva Marie Everson, CEO
Word Weavers International
Author of *Miss Beth Bettencourt*

Abundance Books

ISBN: 978-1-963377-53-8 (print)
ISBN: 978-1-963377-70-5 (ebook)
ISBN: 978-1-963377-71-2 (audio book)

Abundance Books
Kalamazoo, Michigan
www.abundance-books.com

Printed in the United States of America

10 9 8 7 6 5 4 3 2 1

"Amazing Grace" (Traditional). Words by John Newton (1779).
Music: "New Britain" (1835). In the Public Domain.

Cover design by Amber Weigand Buckley, Barefaced Media
Interior design and layout by Taryn Goliher

Contents

Chapter 1

Michigan, 1952

Florence slid her hand over the stained and faded cover, where splotches and spills ran into one another. Clear tape reinforced the broken spine. The thin pages fluttered open to the frosting section. Years of home-cooked scents embedded in the pages merged with the faint aroma of oil and flour wafting through the air. In the margin, her mother's slanted handwriting transported her back to another kitchen.

Florence savored a deep breath of the past each time she took the old cookbook from the shelf, not because she needed it, but because she wanted it near her. Painful and comforting memories swirled together.

While she blended confectioners' sugar into the chocolate mixture, her mother's voice echoed across the years. "Add a little at a time until you have the right consistency."

The frosting formed stiff peaks as she stirred and mixed in the vanilla. Dipping a spoon in the dark goodness, she sampled it. Perfect. Her tension fled in the past's embrace.

The front door slammed.

"Willie, is that you?"

"Can I have some now?" Her disheveled twelve-year-old son stood in the doorway, tossing a baseball in the air.

She paused mid-swirl, a little frown tugging her forehead. "Why did you wear your new pants? When you came home after school, I told you to change into something old."

"Sorry." He wandered to the table and jiggled a grass-stained knee. Eyes wide with practiced innocence, he leaned over the cake. "Mm, Mom, that smells sooooo good." Rumpled hair crowned the back of his head.

She finished icing the top, cleaned the knife with her finger, and set it in the double sink.

"No ball in the house." She retrieved the mixing spoon and tapped off the excess. "You can lick this."

He took it, still rotating the ball in his other hand. "Why are we having cake? Is it someone's birthday?"

"We're celebrating the first full week of school." Florence ran warm water into the sink and added Joy Dish Soap. "How was the game?"

"We won. Our team got two home runs, and I hit a double." Pretending that the spoon was a bat, he swung and made a cracking sound as if he had hit the imaginary ball. "I could help the Tigers get out of their slump. If I keep practicing, I could be the next Ted Williams."

She took the spoon from him and patted his batting arm. "I'm sure you could be, but even the Detroit Tigers wash their hands. Get cleaned up. We'll have dinner as soon as your father gets home."

He bounded into the hall and up the stairs to his room.

She glanced at the stain-marred corner of the page, then closed the cookbook. A celebration called for something sweet, not a bitter reminder of her failure. Her husband and children were her focus now—the perfect family she'd always dreamed of.

The aromas of chocolate cake and baked ham mingled in the warm kitchen. When she opened the side door, the late-day breeze cooled her. Forecasting the coming change of season, the oak's green leaves fluttered. The gray sky signaled that summer's heat was dwindling away. Soon, pumpkins and mums would scent the Michigan air.

Seven-year-old Jane trudged across the freshly mowed lawn to the swing that hung from the willow tree and lifted her face to the late afternoon sun. Brown braids trailed behind her. Florence remembered the many times her mother had braided her hair when she was seven.

The excitement of fall always brought a subtle dread when she was young. Harvest on the farm meant hours of canning and preserving—endless work. Her family had depended on the garden and crops to get through the winter. Now in the Detroit suburbs, the garden simply supplemented her husband Howard's paycheck. She anticipated the coming school festival and the winter holiday season. Finally, the dreaded polio summer would end.

Jane sat on the swing, digging her toe into the ground and scrutinizing something in the grass. Never would her daughter have to worry if they'd canned enough.

Like the neighbors, their wide backyard had a sprawling garden that extended the length of the chain-link fence. The day's wash fluttered nearby on the clothesline. But unlike the neighbors, Howard had enhanced the area with flower beds, a rock garden, and a sandbox.

Jane twisted the swing tight, then lifted her feet to spin in a circle, pressing one toe of her shoe into the ground until she halted. She shook her dizzy head and caught sight of her mother. "Can we go to the park tomorrow?"

"I think it's still closed."

"Mrs. Fields said they reopened the parks because the polio danger has passed, but it's too cold to open the pools. I hope they won't be closed next year. I miss swimming."

While striding toward the swing, Florence muttered under her breath. "First grade teachers know everything."

Jane picked up an acorn and twisted off the cap.

Had she just shivered, or was that Florence's imagination? "Are you cold?"

"No, I'm hot."

Her weary tone struck a discordant note in Florence's mind. "How do you feel? You're not as energetic as usual."

"Just tired. We ran races at recess and played tag. First grade is fun, but it's hard. We had to do a bunch of writing. My hand's sore." Her fingers wiggled in the air, and she hopped off the swing. "I can check the garden for tomatoes."

Inside the house, the timer dinged, drawing Florence into the kitchen. The old cookbook had stirred up memories of her mother's sickness, but illness couldn't lurk around the corner of this home. Her family was healthy.

While lifting the ham out of the oven, her stomach growled. They'd not had baked ham with pineapple since Easter. She gave the mashed potatoes a final stir and washed the dishes. Folding the newspaper so the headline wouldn't show, she stowed it in the corner behind the white Tupperware canisters. If Howard didn't already know the latest report about the Korean War, there was no sense in him seeing it when he first came home.

William returned with his wet hair slicked tight to his head. He held up still-damp hands that looked fairly clean. "I'm ready to eat."

"Good. Put the ham on the table." Her eyes narrowed in a warning look. "Don't sample it."

"Aww." He took the platter to the dining room.

Florence knew he'd position it close to his plate. She added a dollop of butter to the potatoes and green beans as the side door opened. Jane slouched in and put two tomatoes on the counter. "There's still a green one left." Pinpoints of sweat dotted her forehead and darkened her bangs.

"I guess that will be our last one this season." She studied her daughter's red cheeks. "Do you feel okay?"

Head drooping, Jane slogged across the kitchen. "I'm tired."

A spark of worry flared, but she tamped it down. Jane had simply had a full day. "Get washed up for dinner. We have chocolate cake for dessert, your favorite."

Jane grinned.

"Hey, sis." William passed her as she left, but she walked on without comment.

"What's wrong with her?" He carried the green beans to the table. When he picked up the potatoes, he pressed his face a little too close and sniffed the starchy scent.

"Oh, no. Don't even think about sticking your finger in those potatoes. Your sister is just exhausted from first grade." Florence took plates from the cupboard.

William laughed. "She doesn't know exhausting. Junior high is much harder than elementary."

The front door opened. "What smells so good?" Howard stretched his shoulder blades beneath his dress shirt and let out a small groan, pressing one hand against his lower back.

Glad that everyone was under one roof, Florence stood on her tiptoes, kissed his cheek, and gently squeezed his shoulder. "You seem really tight. You must have had a bad day."

He sniffed the air. "Is that ham I smell?"

"With pineapple and chocolate cake for dessert." William slid across the hardwood floor on his socked feet.

Florence shook her finger at him and gave him a warning glance, then faced Howard. "So, how was work?" His back pain was his barometer, and his stretch indicated he'd had a long day. The farm injury flared up whenever he felt stressed.

"The traffic was horrible. I should have been here fifteen minutes ago. There's been rumors that production at Dodge Main has been slowing down, but the work seems to have increased." He hid his grimace with a grin. "How was your day?"

"If you're in pain, wear your back brace like the doctor told you."

He shook his head. "What would the fellas at the plant think? They look up to me. I'll take some aspirin after dinner." He hung his coat in the hall closet, then eased down onto the couch. "I'm working another shift tomorrow. Then afterward I'm going out with some of the fellas for a drink, so I'll be home late."

"But tomorrow's Saturday. I thought we could go to the park or do something together as a family." She couldn't remember the last time the four of them had an outing.

"Go with Olive. You girls always have fun together."

She frowned at the dirt that he'd just tracked in, her lips pressed tight. She got the broom and dustpan, then swept from the front door all the way to the kitchen. Though the new Hoover vacuum and stove were nice, affordable because of Howard's extra pay, she'd rather spend time with him. She missed the early, exciting days of their marriage.

Her shoulders tensed. Being in management at Hamtramck's assembly plant seemed just as grueling as when he worked on the line. "You said that when you were promoted to foreman, you wouldn't have to work on the weekends. We don't really need the extra shifts, do we?"

Howard hissed a sigh while he removed his shoes. "I know you like the extra money, and I could be in the running for another pay raise." He winked at her, then disappeared into the dining room.

In the kitchen, Florence hung up her apron, one she'd made as a newlywed. It was comfortable, like their house, not too big or small, but cozy like a hug. When she joined Howard at the table, William's grin slid from them to the ham. He drummed his fingers on the yellow and chrome table.

Howard had bought the table and six matching chairs for their third Christmas at a time when he still thought of her first. The two unused chairs collected dust against the wall, taunting her with the unfulfilled dream of more children. They'd waited ten years for William and another five for Jane. Hoping and trying hadn't made babies magically appear. Maybe her punishment for the past was getting only two children.

Jane slunk into the dining room.

"No happy-to-see-you hug?" Howard pretended to cry.

With a giggle, she embraced him, then slid into her chair.

"So, how was school?" Howard glanced between William and Jane, then forked a slice of ham onto his plate and passed the platter to Florence.

"Good," William mumbled with his mouth full of potatoes.

Jane shrugged, fingering her napkin.

"Mrs. Fields must have worked you hard this week. You usually have so much to say. All summer you told us how many days until the start of school. Then, every day this week, you've talked nonstop about this girl or that boy or something Mrs. Fields said. Now you have nothing to say?"

"I'm just tired, Daddy."

Biting her lip, Florence studied Jane's face, trying to read the thoughts behind her eyes. Her mother's and sister's sickness couldn't resurface. Not in this day and time.

"Charlie said we're going to win that war in Korea, just like we won that one in Germany." William slid a large slice of ham onto his plate. "I can't wait until I'm old enough to fight."

Florence flashed glances from her exuberant son to Howard's face, where a scowl settled. Making her voice as low as possible, she said, "William, no war talk at the table." What would make him comprehend how upset his dad got about the war? He was too young to understand Howard's humiliation of being rejected for service in World War II. The topic made him feel like a failure. It never mattered to her, but Howard's father hadn't let him live it down.

Howard cleared his throat, but seemed to relax when he reached for the ham. "Next week, I'm meeting with Wilks. He mentioned something about a promotion. If I'm lucky, he'll invite us over for dinner some Sunday. Won't that be fun?"

Her nod accompanied a tight smile. One more dinner with near strangers. She scooped potatoes onto Jane's plate and hers.

While they ate, William gave his father a play-by-play of the Friday sandlot game with the neighborhood boys. Florence tried to regain her calm, comforted that her family was together.

Howard reached for another slice of ham, but caught sight of Jane's downcast face. "What's wrong?"

She mixed her green beans with her mashed potatoes. "Nothing." She sniffed and wiped her eyes.

Florence shared a worried look with Howard. "Did you have some kind of problem at school?"

"No. May I be excused? My stomach hurts."

"They probably had to do the duck and cover drill today. Same as our school." William took another piece of ham, trailing juice onto his fabric placemat. Florence sighed. That would have to be scrubbed soon before the stain set.

Howard cleared his throat, glared at William, then turned a warm gaze on his daughter. "They want you to be safe. We have to be ready."

"I don't want the bomb to burn me." Jane lowered her head into a sob.

A gleam in his eyes, William chewed. "That's why we should get a fallout shelter. The Johnsons are getting one. But if we get 'em first, it won't be a problem. We could blow those—"

Jane shrieked and covered her ears.

Howard pounded the table. The water in their glasses sloshed up and over the edges. "Stop scaring her. Your mother just said no discussion of war at the table!" He unclenched his fists and flattened them. "Sorry for yelling, but Willie, you shouldn't scare your sister. You'll give her nightmares."

William slid down in his seat and crammed a couple of green beans into his mouth. He lightly elbowed Jane. "Sorry."

She sniffed and hiccupped.

"Eat up dear, it's almost time for dessert." Florence hated when William picked on Jane, especially during mealtimes. Didn't he realize how lucky he was to have a sister? And Howard was rough on William, like his own father had been on him. Couldn't he see the similarities?

Jane pushed a green bean around her full plate. "I'm not hungry. Can I go to my room?"

An alarm rang in Florence's head. Usually, chocolate cake made both the kids feel better. Placing the back of her hand on her daughter's forehead, her pulse quickened. "Howard, she's warm."

He swallowed, still unconcerned. "She's worked herself up. It's been a big week. She'll perk up in the morning."

Florence nodded, though her throat threatened to close. "I'm sure you're right. Why don't you go lie down, Jane? I'll be up in a little while."

Without a word, she left.

"More cake for me." William shoveled potatoes into his mouth, only slowing down when his cheeks bulged.

"What if she's sick, Howard?" Her deepest fear thudded like the beating of her heart. Warm foreheads could turn into major illnesses and might progress to …

He lowered his fork. "She's probably overtired from school. You worry too much. Eat something. It'll make you feel better."

Although Howard and William had two slices of cake each, Florence couldn't eat anything else. Her stomach burned and her mouth felt dry. Sipping water didn't help. Howard and William played catch outside while she washed the dishes, attuned to any sounds from upstairs, fighting the fear that arose when anyone in the family got sick. Spanish flu wasn't a threat anymore, but other diseases could be just as deadly. Florence finished the dishes, then drew the shade over the dark backyard. Turning off the downstairs lights, she went to check on Jane.

She lay curled into a ball, fast asleep. When Florence pressed her lips against Jane's warm forehead, the scent of earth and shampoo haloed her. Florence closed her eyes and sighed over a memory of a younger child. Soft, downy curls framed a round baby face of the girl they'd waited so long for. The miracle baby they cherished after thinking they'd only have one child.

Howard met her in the hallway, his brow raised.

"I think she has a low-grade fever." A light peeked from under the bathroom door and the water spray of the shower started. Her heart thumped and the old worry resurfaced. What if she couldn't keep her children healthy?

"It's probably a cold." Howard led her into their room. "Kids get sick all the time and then they get better. Don't worry so much. Death and disease aren't around every corner. What happened to your mother and sister won't happen to Jane."

Florence sat on the bed and closed her eyes, listening to the familiar sounds of Howard's nighttime routine. Instead of comforting her, the noises acted like the yeast in bread and her anxiety grew. He never seemed to worry. She clung to a sliver of hope. Howard had to be right. The illnesses of her past could not revisit her present.

Chapter 2

"Ma, Ma…" In the dark of the bedroom, William shook her, his eyes wide with fear.

Howard sat up and groaned. "What is it?"

"Jane's real sick."

Her son's ashen face and troubled words propelled Florence down the hall. Howard grumbled at her heels. Disease names flashed through her mind and her throat tightened. She'd been right to worry.

"I heard her crying. She didn't want me to wake you, but when I had to help her walk to the bathroom, I knew I had to." William pushed in front of them and picked up her covers from the floor.

Sweat dripped from Jane's forehead down her cheeks. "I'm okay, Mama." She shivered as her brother draped the soft pink blanket over her. "I'm just tired and cold." Closing her eyes, she rubbed her head and draped the other arm across her stomach. "My tummy hurts too."

Florence took her small hand.

Howard patted her shoulder. His husky voice betrayed worry. "It's probably the flu."

The flu wasn't that bad these days, not like during her childhood. It *had* to be the flu, not anything worse. She'd been so careful. They hadn't gone swimming or even played in the sprinkler. There'd been no local outbreaks since last summer.

William kneeled next to her. His tousled hair made him seem younger than his twelve years. He tipped his face up. "She's bad sick, isn't she?"

When Florence smoothed the covers, heat radiated from Jane. "She's burning up. We need to call the doctor."

Howard rushed down the hall and bumped into the phone table. Items clattered to the floor, startling Florence. He'd never fixed the uneven legs of his high school shop project.

Florence reached for one of Jane's books as Howard's curses floated down the hall. Then, she heard him flipping through the phonebook pages and mumbling, "Doctor, doctor, doctor, pediatrician—"

She called, "It's on a card in the back. It should be sticking out."

"Oh, I found it." The rotary phone dial click, click, clicked with each numbered spin. "Doctor …"

Florence opened up *Little House in the Big Woods* and began to read. If they escaped into Laura Ingalls Wilder's world, maybe her own nightmares wouldn't come true.

Halfway through the second page, Jane tapped her leg, then reached toward the dresser and whispered, "The picture, Mama."

"What is it, dear?" She smoothed her daughter's wet hair away from her forehead. She couldn't lose her.

"Can you hand me that?" A shaky finger pointed.

Florence got the picture from the dresser. The image showed a young Jesus between his mother and father. His hands securely held in each of his parents, a perfect family. A smile of contentment and health filled his round face. Jane had chosen it from a calendar that Aunt Mildred had sent. Enamored with the image of a boy Jesus who was about her age, she tucked it next to herself each night. For her birthday the previous year, Florence had it framed. Through the glass, the creased corners were visible.

Jane reached for the picture, but her hand fell onto the sheet, inches away. Florence's heart thudded. It couldn't be. It had to be something easy, a virus, the flu. Tomorrow, every-thing would be better.

"Let me hold it for you." Tears threatened while Florence gripped the frame.

"It looks like Jesus is talking to me." Jane closed her eyes. "He wants to play with me. He can stop the bomb. Can I have a doll like him? I want a doll like *that* Jesus. He'll make me feel better."

"I'll get her a doll like that." William stood in the doorway.

Florence shook her head at him.

"Not now, son." Howard patted William's shoulder, then leaned against the door frame as if to hold himself up.

"I've got some money saved." William straightened and pushed his chest out.

Jane smacked her lips. "My throat's sore and I'm thirsty. Would you get me a drink?"

William scurried to the kitchen for a glass of water. Howard sat on the small chair by Jane's dollhouse, a giant in the pink, frilly room. He gave Florence a tired smile. "The doctor should be here soon."

When the doctor arrived, Florence felt a mixture of relief at his presence and dread over his possible diagnosis. Taking small, hesitant steps, she retreated to the back of the room and let him sit in the chair beside Jane.

After setting his bag on the floor, he smiled at her fevered face, but spoke to her parents. "What are her symptoms?"

Jane moaned, her eyes still closed. "My head hurts."

"Fever, sore throat, upset stomach, and she's weak." Even as Florence said the words, she knew what he'd say.

The doctor shook his head. "Jane?"

"Yes." Her eyes cracked open.

"I want you to bend your chin to your chest. Can you do that?"

Jane lifted her head half an inch from the bed, then cried as it fell back. "That's all I can do. Is that okay?"

The doctor flashed a weak smile. "You did good, sweetheart." His somber voice told Florence that Jane didn't have a routine childhood illness. He motioned Howard and Florence into the hall. "Let's talk."

Florence didn't hear his next words. A buzzing filled her head, and her heart hammered. Memories and feelings from over thirty years earlier returned. Her failures replayed in her mind.

William froze, his mouth open, glassy-eyed. Howard stood pale and motionless.

Then the doctor turned to her. "Don't take her to the hospital down the street. Go to the Sister Elizabeth Kenny Polio Center at the Oakland County Contagious Hospital. "

"Mom, Mommy." Jane cried and rolled her body a little. "I want to get up, but my legs don't work right."

"I can call an ambulance to transport her." The doctor took his bag and stepped back, as if he feared Jane's contagious disease.

"I'll take her." Howard scooped her up, her body small in his powerful arms.

The buzzing continued, and time moved in slow motion. Florence stared at the discarded picture of Jesus, safe with his parents.

Jane had polio.

How long had it been since they whisked Jane away? Florence tried to follow the stretcher, but an orderly held up his hand. "You have to wait here."

Every chair was filled in the spacious waiting room. Most of the visitors yawned and exchanged anxious looks. A woman cried soundlessly into her hands. Down the aisles, a white-haired man paced. A mother read a book to a sleepy-looking boy on her lap.

A nurse appeared, adjusting her white cap, and called out a name.

The crying woman rose from her chair and followed the nurse. Her heels clicked on the shiny tiles.

Howard stared out the window, pressing his hand against his lower back. A man in a military uniform walked under the streetlight. Howard sighed. She'd never been able to convince him it didn't matter whether he served. He always wanted to provide and protect. Now, Howard withdrew a piece of basswood from his pocket and whittled over the white handkerchief he'd spread on his lap to catch the shavings. His fingers flew as his knife chipped away at the block of wood.

Florence sidled up to him. The wood smell made her feel like she was sixteen again and watching him whittle on the porch. "What are you making?"

He shrugged. "A crown for our princess. Maybe a baseball for Willie. Not sure."

She leaned against him. The hospital brought reminders of the past, but his presence comforted her. "Those are very different things. And that piece of wood doesn't seem big enough for either one."

He stopped whittling and returned the items to his pocket, folding the cotton around the wood flakes. "I never know what it's going to be when I start. That's the fun part. Watching the creation take shape. Just like with your baking." He wrapped his arms around her.

Leaning into his embrace, she exhaled all her tension. "I always know what I'm baking."

"I know. You like plans. But this will turn out okay, Flo. You'll see. Jane's a fighter. Many people fully recover from polio. She will too. On Monday, she'll be running into the school building and telling us about her adventures during dinner."

Florence let his words quench her worries. "You could make her a crown. She'd like that. Or something for her dollhouse." Howard had built Jane a dollhouse years ago, and he loved surprising her with handmade furniture for it.

He stifled a yawn. "Why don't we find an empty chair and sit?"

A different nurse appeared and called out another name. A couple followed her down the hall. Howard and Florence crossed the room and took the vacated chairs. Across from them, a man spoke quietly into a payphone.

The chair leather squeaked when Florence shifted. She put her hand on the metal armrest. "Should we call William?"

"He's probably sleeping. He knows to call Olive if there's a problem. It'll be okay. Why don't you rest your eyes?" He put his arm around her.

Her eyes were so heavy. She yawned and laid her head against him.

An hour later, Howard shook her awake. "We can see her."

A nurse studied her clipboard, tapped her foot, and looked in their direction. "Mr. and Mrs. Miller, are you coming?"

Howard hurried toward her, leading Florence with light pressure on her arm.

"The doctor will talk to you now." The nurse pointed. "He's with your daughter at the end of the hall." When an alarm blared, the nurse scurried toward the sound before they could ask her any of the dozens of questions that crowded their minds.

Iron lungs lined the hall. Amplified by the high ceiling, the deafening roar of the mechanized breathing filled her ears. Whooshing in and out, the machines breathed for each person. The respirators were like metal coffins. Was her daughter encased in one now?

"Florence." Howard tugged at her hand.

"Why are they in the hall?"

The boy closest to her had dark, wavy hair. He looked younger than Jane. Stopping, she placed a hand on the warm metal. She wanted to brush the thick hair away from his forehead. To reach into the machine and comfort him. He moaned.

Howard led her away. "An attendant said there's been another outbreak. They must have run out of space."

A nurse in a crisp, white uniform rushed past them into a room. The brief opening of the door revealed more iron lungs lining the walls. Her chest tightened. With the summer over, why was this still happening?

"Come on, Flo. They said she's at the end of the hall. She won't be in one of those."

How could he be so sure? Still, she followed him into the cavernous whiteness, holding in her most demanding thoughts. What would this disease mean for them, for Jane? Would the dreams she'd made for Jane need to be packed away, like the summer clothes stored in the attic?

When they reached the end of the hall, Florence pressed her face against the large glass window. A doctor studied a chart.

Nurses in masks and gowns hurried from bed to bed. So many patients. So much sterile coldness.

"I don't see her."

Howard pointed. "She's in the second bed on the right side."

But the small, still figure couldn't be her energetic daughter who never stopped moving. Florence started to say, "You're mistaken," when a doctor approached. He took off his white gown, gloves, and mask and deposited them in a tall bin. Then he stepped into the hall.

"Excuse me." Howard cleared his throat. "What can you tell us about our little girl, Jane Miller? They just admitted her."

Florence eyed the door. She needed to get in there. Jane would be frightened to wake in unfamiliar surroundings, so far from her family and their warm home.

The doctor flipped through the pages on his clipboard. "Ah, here she is. Poliomyelitis. Paralyzed from the neck down." He stopped reading and peered at them. "She's one of the lucky ones."

"Lucky?" Howard scoffed.

"Her lungs aren't affected right now. She's young. I'm sure movement will return to some muscles, if not most."

"What do you mean *right now*? And what …" Florence moved closer to the door. All the doctor's words jumbled in her mind, not making any sense. She clutched the sides of her dress to stop the shaking in her hands and her rising panic.

"We need to let the virus run its course. All you can do is go home, wait, and make sure you burn or clean anything that might have been contaminated. Pay special attention to bedding and toys."

She gaped at him, wondering if the disease could still spread to Jane's lungs. What damage would it wreak by the time it finished its destructive path? Then, another thought hit her … "William!" Florence gasped. Could he get polio, too? What about Howard? She reached for the doorknob. She needed to comfort Jane.

"Stop." The doctor crossed in front of her, and raised his arm to block her, concern on his face. He glared at Howard. "Your wife can't go in there. It's not safe for you or the patients."

Florence backed up, then edged closer. "I have to see her."

He continued to bar the way. "You can't. She's highly contagious and will have to be isolated until the virus runs its course. These outbreaks are serious. You'll need to be isolated, too. The board of health will bring a quarantine sign to your house."

Florence wanted to push him aside. After all, he was thin, and only an inch or two taller than her. Howard grabbed her arm when she moved. "Don't." He ushered her down the hall. The doctor's information reduced his earlier fear, replacing it with a calm resolve. "We have to go. Think about William."

She followed with stunted steps, attracted and repelled by the overflow of iron lungs, and the mesmerizing rhythm of breath, of artificially sustained life. *Whoosh. Whoosh.* In and out. In and out. The March of Dimes advertisements rushed through her mind, images of children in wheelchairs, braces, and crutches. At best, polio would cripple her daughter for the rest of her life. At worst…

"No." Her feet stopped moving. Howard pulled, but she shook him off. "I'm not leaving her."

Even when he held her, the pressure of his rough, tear-stained cheek failed to console her. All her strength evaporated with the memory of Jane's feverish cries and the smell of sickness that surrounded her. She sobbed into his chest. "I can't leave my baby."

Chapter 3

The next day, Florence opened the window and coughed when smoke gusted inside from the belongings Howard put in the burn barrel. The acrid smell made her stomach clench. Wiping her hands on the apron that had become a full-time uniform, she turned from the upsetting destruction to the work she still had to do.

Jane's sweet room, now bare, taunted her. Gone were the pink sheets, the dollhouse Howard had built, and all her toys. She dipped a cloth in a bucket of warm, soapy water and washed the bed frame. Howard had convinced her they didn't need to burn the furniture.

The toilet flushed in the hall bathroom and a door banged open.

"William, come here."

A moment later, he appeared in the doorway, with red eyes from crying, or maybe from lack of sleep. "Are you feeling okay?"

"I already told you I'm fine."

She wiped her hands on her apron and motioned him over to feel his forehead. It was cool. "Go wash your hands. I didn't hear the water."

"I did." He groaned. "See, they're still wet." He held them up.

"Well…" They appeared wet, but how could she be sure there weren't millions of polio germs crawling on his skin right now? "Wash them again, with soap, then dry them. After that, go downstairs and get the bucket on the kitchen table. It has soapy water in it. You need to clean your entire room."

He frowned and headed toward the staircase.

"Hands." She narrowed her eyes and pointed to the bathroom. They couldn't be too safe.

He stomped out his obedience.

When the water ran in the bathroom, she went back into Jane's room. Crouching, she swiped the bedframe with the cloth, her knees protesting the prolonged kneeling on the wood floor. A flash from the silver frame of Jane's favorite picture caught her eye from under the bed. She stood and studied the image. Halos shone around the smooth white faces of Jesus and his parents, who glowed with health. No one could be that perfect. Why did Jane love this picture so much, and talk to it like a dear friend?

Florence hated the cherubic faces that seemed to silently mock the tragedy that had struck. She gave a short, frustrated scream and slammed the picture down on the dresser.

"What's wrong?" William stood in the doorway, rubbing his hands on his dark denim pants.

"Bug." She spun toward him, hid the frame behind her back, and lied. "I thought I saw a bug, but it was just dust. Sorry."

His gaze traveled around the room. "It sure looks different in here."

She had to offer hope. "Jane will be home soon. Get the bucket and clean your room."

Guilty thoughts pounded in her head like fists pounding bread dough. Her fault, her fault. Her mother, dead. Her sister, dead.

Now Jane had polio.

The guilt pulled her down, and she grabbed the wall to steady herself. How could she have been more careful?

And she couldn't bear to tell William he might never see his sister again. Through the web of cracks in the frame, Jesus still smiled. His kind eyes searched and saw her guilt. Maybe she deserved this, but no one in her family did. Florence shoved the broken image back under the bed.

After she finished, she crossed the hall. William ran his hand along the pennants in his room and spun his globe a couple of times. He dusted the shelf above his bed, taking his time to fiddle with the pirate ship his father had whittled for him. Then, not seeing his mom in the doorway, he twirled the dust rag in the air as if it were a lasso. He gave a quick swipe to the dark wooden bedframe, then wiped the matching dresser with little enthusiasm. Picking up the rag to twirl it again, he sneezed.

"Are you okay? Do you have a fever?" She rushed to him and felt his forehead. Still cool. A dreadful pattern filled her thoughts. Death followed illness. Her mother, then her sister. Now Jane. She couldn't bear for William to get sick too.

"Geesh, Mom. Stop. I'm okay. It's the dust." He crossed his arms and sneezed again.

"Tell me if you feel sick."

Dropping the rag back into the bucket, he sat on his navy bedspread and straightened his baseball cards.

Sighing, she tapped his foot with hers. "Wipe the dresser and bedframe again. I'll strip the bed and wash the sheets. Make sure you clean everything."

He raised his eyebrows and looked up from his cards. "What?"

"Put those away and clean." Taking the cards from his hand, she put them in her apron pocket. "You can have these back when you're finished."

She took his bedding down to the washer, moving ever closer to completion. Later Howard shuffled inside, smelling of smoke, his face streaked with soot. "What are you doing?"

Her legs and back ached. Going to bed would feel so good. "Getting rid of germs. Protecting us the best I can. I've done upstairs. Now I have to finish down here."

"Leave it until tomorrow. It's time for dinner."

"I can't. I have to finish the entire house. Let me warm up some soup."

While she swabbed surfaces around them, Howard and William ate from her mother's old chipped bowls. Howard thought she should throw them away, but her mother had always told her, *one flaw doesn't ruin the bowl's purpose.*

When she fell into bed after midnight, she stared at the ceiling, mentally reviewing every room and surface. Maybe she should re-scrub the toilet. Could that be how the polio had entered? Last week's newspaper had an article reporting they'd found the disease in fecal matter. Should she get up and give the bathroom another once over? It would have been better if she'd contracted polio. This was like her childhood, when disease struck a loved one and left her picking up the pieces.

Careful not to wake Howard, Florence slid out of bed and padded downstairs. Taking the thick cookbook from the shelf, she opened to a section in the back. She ran a finger over the title of the dog-eared page—Recipes Especially Prepared for The Sick. Even though the recipes had never helped her mother or her sister, maybe they would help Jane.

With the mail and newspaper in hand, Florence stretched her arms over her head and inhaled the crisp September air. The maple next door had begun turning a brilliant red. The morning sun made the world seem full of possibility.

Dressed in a stylish black dress belted at the waist, her neighbor, Olive O'Malley, strode down the street. Her heels clicked on the sidewalk, while her daughter, Alice, skipped a few paces ahead.

Florence waved and called to her. "Olive."

Olive stopped, glanced at Florence, then grabbed her daughter's hand, and rushed Alice across the street into the Thomas' house. Florence waved the mail and newspaper as if to sweep away the strange behavior. Olive was the one who had introduced Florence to the morning coffee group. Every Tuesday, a group of six or seven neighborhood housewives gathered at someone's place for coffee and conversation. Olive had become her best friend and Alice was Jane's. Many days after school, Florence watched Alice while Olive worked. Then after work, they'd talk over day old croissants with the sound of their girls' laughter in the background. Why had her friend acted so strangely?

When Florence turned, the board of health's quarantine sign leered at her. Realization struck. There'd be no more coffee groups. Others would fear for their family's well-being too. Fall's promises made her forget that her promised future had changed, and that part of her heart had gone missing. If the situation was reversed, Florence would have at least talked to Olive and explained. Talking across the street wouldn't make anyone sick. She'd listened to Olive after her husband passed away.

Dragging herself inside, she laid the paper in front of Howard. Then the Iowa return address and the familiar scrawl on the letter in her hand registered. The recent affront faded, and she smiled.

Howard glanced at the front page of the paper, an article about uranium mining out west. "Is that from my sister?"

She nodded and slit the envelope. At least one person still cared. If Mildred were here, she would have marched down the front steps and confronted Olive like the deer who had infiltrated her garden. She skimmed the first paragraph, an amusing story about one of their pigs.

"Sometimes, I think I'd like to be a farmer in Iowa. Get away from here." William, still in his pajamas, dipped his toast into his egg yolk and took a big bite. Nothing seemed to curb his appetite.

Florence raised an eyebrow at him. "Move away from the city? You know there aren't a lot of big cities in Iowa." Strange comment. Like his dad, he loved the city and spending time with his friends. She remembered how Howard's eyes had sparkled when he told her his dreams of moving to Detroit, away from the country. He was going to make it big and drive the fanciest car money could buy.

William shrugged off his own words and grinned. "It's just a thought. I'm sure I'd get bored."

Florence laughed. "You know I was raised there. Your dad and I both. We were never bored. Playing in the hayloft, swimming in the pond, picking wild berries. There's lots to do in the country."

He drained his milk. "I'm too old for those things, Mom."

Howard turned a page and grunted his amusement.

She winked at William. "They have baseball and girls out there too."

He grimaced. "Girls?" He shoveled the rest of his food into his mouth, then shot her a questioning look. "How come we don't go there? Aunt Mildred, Uncle Henry, and Peggy come visit, but we never go there."

A lead weight lodged in her stomach, causing her to cough. She couldn't tell him. He wasn't old enough to know what she'd done and what she'd left behind. "It's far and …"

He arched his eyebrows in disbelief.

Howard peered over his paper. "Farm life isn't that great. You wouldn't like the chores. Every day. The jobs are here. Put your dishes in the sink and get dressed. Give your mother some quiet."

Florence met Howard's gaze for an instant, but then focused on a stray breadcrumb on the table. They knew who had decided to avoid their hometown.

William set his dishes in the sink with a loud clatter, then fled the room when his father lowered the paper and gave him an annoyed stare.

"That boy," he mumbled while still reading. Without looking up, he asked, "So, how are my sister and her family?"

She skimmed the letter for an interesting tidbit to tell him. She'd reread it later tonight. "Peggy grew another inch again." Florence missed seeing her only niece grow up, but she couldn't go back to Iowa. Too many memories and too much opportunity for new heartache.

At the sight of the next sentences, tears welled in Florence's eyes.

We are all so sorry to hear about Jane. We are praying for her healing. You're welcome here anytime. Let us know how we can help. We can hop on the next train to Michigan if we need to.

"Florence?" Concern etched Howard's face. "Is something wrong?"

She folded the letter and stowed it in her apron pocket. Crying now would solve nothing. "No. They're all doing great."

He gave her a skeptical look, then returned to his paper.

She pushed her eggs around her plate. *We are praying for her healing.* As if prayer could change anything. Her past proved that God didn't care about her or her family. Peeking over the coffee cup rim, the heading on the back of Howard's newspaper glared at her. It listed those who had contracted polio, as bitter a record as her unpleasant, cold coffee. She'd forgotten the milk.

"Are you finished?" She grabbed Howard's plate and stacked it on hers, assuming his mumble meant yes.

The spray of hot water filling the sink and the gentle clink of dishes were the only sounds in the kitchen. Breathing in the scented steam of the dish soap brought her a fraction of release, while she mentally compiled a list of the rooms she'd cleaned. What remained? Jane had played in her bedroom closet a couple of weeks ago. And she must do the downstairs coat closet and under the bed. She rubbed a nonexistent stain from a plate.

"Are you listening to me?" Howard asked.

"I'm sorry, I didn't hear you. What did you say?" She faced him with her full attention, drying her hands on a towel.

"Nothing." He folded the paper and stood.

"I'm sorry, Howard. I didn't mean—"

"I know, you were busy—cleaning."

"But that's what the doctor said to do. I don't want you or William to catch polio." She followed him into the living room where William lay upside down on the couch, his head resting on the carpet, his denim-clad legs in the air. Didn't Howard realize how serious polio was? He was acting like nothing had changed, when in reality, everything had.

"You've cleaned enough. The smell of ammonia is making me sick." Howard focused on William. "What are you doing? The blood is rushing to your head. That isn't good for you."

William sat up. "I'm bored." He stood and wobbled a little on his way to retrieve his discarded ball mitt.

Florence eyed his flushed cheeks. "Are you okay? You look—"

"Oh, my goodness. He's fine. His face is red because he's been upside down." He pointed William to the backyard. "Go outside. I'll be out in a bit so we can practice your pitching."

William turned, but then faced his parents again. "You know if we had a TV, we …" He met his father's glare and retreated from the house, slamming the door on the way out.

"Do you think he's okay? I don't want him to overexert himself."

"Stop cleaning and worrying so much. Everything will be fine." Howard patted her shoulder, then left.

While Florence vacuumed the living room area rug, she mentally replayed Howard's criticism of the time she spent scouring the house and worrying. He hadn't even talked about Jane for the past few days. When her name came up, he talked about work. He'd missed the meeting with Wilks and expected someone else to get the promotion, showing more concern about his job than their daughter. Maybe that helped him cope. He was more like his father than he admitted, and he couldn't see it. Both men were gruff and hid their emotions. Probably why Howard and William clashed.

Her hand brushed the letter in her pocket, and she took it out. Mildred's familiar words always contained an invitation, an urging. She didn't understand Florence's reluctance. Even during their short phone calls, Mildred asked her to think about going home.

Home. Her first home with her parents and sister had been a safe space. The two-story farmhouse smelled like the bread her mother loved baking year-round. Laughter bounced off the walls that her father had built himself.

At twelve, she'd leaned against the counter and sighed.

Her mother continued kneading the bread dough. "What's wrong?"

She sighed again. "Nothing." The thought of Mildred's older brother, Howard, made her feel shaky and gave her weird, unfamiliar feelings.

After studying her for a moment, her mother pointed to the dough. "Did you wash your hands?"

Florence nodded.

"Then help me knead."

While working with the dough, the yeasty smell calmed her. "He wanted to talk about sports and cars, but when I mentioned the church social, he ended the conversation." She pounded the dough. "Boys are so selfish."

Her mother checked the open cookbook and began chopping vegetables. "Men and women think differently. We have different wants, different needs. A lot of women are nurturers. They're good at taking care of children and the home. Most men need jobs to do. They enjoy providing for their family."

"And they're selfish." Florence pounded the dough again.

Mom finished chopping the vegetables and slid them into a pot. "Not necessarily. Your young man may have felt too embarrassed to talk about the church social. Give him time. He'll come around." She studied Florence. "You know what might sweeten the deal? Brownies. You know that cooking is the way to any man's heart, don't you?"

Florence gathered the brownie ingredients, and her mother finished the bread. While she mixed the batter, Howard's dark eyes danced in her imagination. When he tasted her brownies, he'd sweep her up in his arms and … A niggling thought interrupted her musings. Was he worth the trouble? Brownies were her favorite. A moan stopped her thoughts.

Her mother stirred the soup with one hand, the other hand wiped sweat from her forehead. "It's warm in here, isn't it?"

"Are you okay, Mom?"

Saying nothing, her mother washed her hands, then went to the couch and stretched out. "I just need to rest for a bit."

"Mom?" Worried about her mother's sudden weakness, Florence kneeled next to her. Unsure of what to do, she asked, "I still don't understand. Why do men and women think differently? Why can't we all be the same?"

"God made us different." Her mother tugged at the worn quilt, and Florence tucked it around her. "Can you shut the window? I'm cold."

"Of course." Florence rubbed her forehead in confusion. It was fall and her mother was sweating and shivering at the same time.

Mom closed her eyes. "Can you finish the dinner and watch your sister?"

Florence kissed her mom's cheek and returned to the kitchen. Her mother's words carried on the warm breeze that floated through the open windows. "You're such a good girl, Florence."

Even now, as a grown woman, Florence saw her mother on the couch, sweating, and recalled helping to cover her. Trying to ignore the memories that traveled across the years, she put the vacuum away and went outside. Though no longer a twelve-year-old in an Iowa farmhouse, questions still swirled in her head. If she'd been able to fulfill her mother's last wish, would sickness stop visiting her?

On the porch, cool air filled her lungs. Was Jane struggling to breathe? Would she meet the same end as Florence's mother?

That day she set the table and put the soup and bread in the center. She was about to call her sister in from playing in the backyard when her mother's labored breathing changed her direction. Years later, the exact sequence of events eluded her, but the smell of burned brownies mixed with the salt of her tears.

Brownies were no longer her favorite.

Florence went to the backyard where William wound up and threw the baseball to his dad. Howard winked at her as he caught it. Then he threw a quick one back and William caught it with a whoop of glee.

Maybe not everything was so terrible. She didn't want to keep replaying the loss of her past. Instead of concentrating on cleaning and worrying, her family needed to be her focus. Howard loved lemon cake. She'd make it for him. The citrus scent would drive the memories of the past away. And after cooking, she'd call the hospital to check on Jane. History couldn't repeat itself. Maybe God would hear her this time. *Please don't let Jane die.*

Chapter 4

The sun had not risen when Florence looked out the kitchen window. But she didn't need the light to know who was missing from the backyard. Rocks lined the garden's perimeter. Jane's small hand had placed each one. William had picked the last tomato. Now wilted plants and weeds cluttered the garden's neat rows. The willow tree swing hung still and silent. Florence turned the light on, then rubbed Jergens lotion into her chapped, scrub-roughened hands. She stowed the bottle in her bag. Jane loved the cherry-almond scent.

"Are you ready? I have to be there early. We have some new hires I need to train. Besides, I told Don I'd pick him up. His car's in the shop." Howard waited in the doorway, his hands on his hips. "Do you really need to go? They haven't allowed you to visit her for the past month. Today won't be any different."

"She might get released to the recovery ward." She shoved the waxed paper-covered sandwich in his lunch pail and resisted the urge to slam the lid. "I can't miss a chance to see her." Staring through a window was better than nothing. If she lingered nearby, maybe Jane would sense her presence.

"They said they'd call when they transferred her. I'm sure the nurses are taking good care of her. Going constantly is a waste of time and bus fare. Stop and think about William and me." He studied his appearance in the hallway mirror. "Do you think I used too much Brylcreem?"

"No." She kissed his cheek and playfully patted his head. He had overdone the hair tonic, but she liked the smell, and he looked okay. Handing him the metal lunch pail, she started toward the staircase. "Let me wake Willie. I don't want him to oversleep."

"He's twelve, Flo." He opened the front door and tapped his foot. "He can get himself ready for school. I heard him earlier rustling around in the bathroom."

A soft thump came from upstairs. She wanted to hug her son and convince herself he was still healthy. Instead, she consoled herself with the fact that he walked to school with a friend, and she would be back by the time he came home. She got her bags and followed her husband into the crisp morning air.

On the way to the car, he muttered. "When I was his age, I was practically running the farm." He shivered. "I better get my coat. I think a cold front's coming in." He hurried back inside.

While the first rays of sun lit the empty street, peace settled around her. Florence loved the sight of the evenly spaced houses. The two-story homes had identical white siding and wide porches. Bushes framed each large, well-kept lawn. The sameness soothed her. The shantytowns and foreclosed farms of her Iowa childhood still haunted her nightmares. Instead of poverty and desperation, their neat street spoke of prosperity. Soon the war in Korea would be another memory and … her heart sank. She'd let herself forget about Jane while she imagined a happy, safe future. None of this meant anything if Jane wasn't home.

Across the street, a door closed. Florence craned her neck to see Olive O'Malley descend the porch steps of the Thomas' house. She waved. "Olive."

Olive's quick glance showed concern. She turned away and scurried down the street to her own house.

Howard emerged from the front porch, pushing his arms into the jacket sleeves. He descended the steps and opened his car door. Raising his eyes to the now empty street, he adjusted the collar of his jacket. "What are you looking at?"

Florence followed and clambered into the '49 Ford coupe. "Olive. She just came out of the Thomas' house."

"So, what's wrong with that? Doesn't Alice walk to school with the Thomas girls so Olive can get to work early?" The engine stalled. Howard cursed under his breath and turned the key again. The vehicle started with its usual sputtering.

"She does, but when I called out to her, she ignored me." She didn't add that Olive had sprinted away from her last month or that Jane walked to school with the girls too. The Tuesday morning coffee group was only a memory. So much was left unsaid now. Jane wasn't the only one she'd lost.

"She probably didn't hear you."

When they passed the O'Malley's house, Olive was getting into her car. She worked at J.L. Hudson's Department Store. She'd started during the war and had returned to the job when her husband died in a car accident. "I know she saw me. She's avoiding even speaking to me and hasn't called in weeks. When I call no one picks up."

He grunted, his hands never straying from their grip on the steering wheel. "You're overreacting. Olive has to work hard. I'm sure she's just busy."

"Whose side are you on?"

"We should've left earlier." Howard slowed. The traffic inched along. His hand hovered over the horn. Even though it hadn't snowed yet, they were stuck behind a salt truck. Probably getting ready for the upcoming season. On the road, the salt always mixed with the clean snow and made a slushy, dirty slop. After fall, the never-ending chill of winter would settle in for months.

"Why aren't you more concerned?"

"Olive's your friend. She was just trying to get to work. Kind of like what I'm doing." The car in front of them turned, and he sped up. His shoulders relaxed.

"That's not what I'm talking about. Jane. Our daughter. You don't seem to care if she lives or dies."

He sighed and hunched his shoulders again. "How can you say that? We've been over this a million times. I do care. I want her home as much as you do. But you're overreacting. Nothing we can do will bring her home any faster. We can't heal her. We have to wait. Stop trying to control everything."

His reply sounded a lot like his sister, Mildred. *Give your worries to God. He'll heal Jane in his own way and time.* Neither

Mildred nor Howard understood the stakes or her unspoken resolution not to fail again. She would do everything in her power to bring their little girl home. Then, and only then, would their family return to normal. After all, family was everything.

She rolled down the window. A gust of dust made her cough, but she continued to peer out the side window instead of at her husband. On a porch lined with bright mums, a man stepped out of his front door. Small heads appeared in the window, while a woman followed, embraced him, then waved as he left. At another house, a jaunty pumpkin sat on the front stoop. Jane would miss helping her father carve the annual jack-o'-lantern.

After a ride made longer by their shared tension, they arrived at their suburban town's bus station. Howard reached into the space between them and handed her the bags. When their fingers brushed, the familiar spark of electricity surged through Florence. She wanted the tangible comfort of an embrace against his powerful chest. Instead, she gave him a weak smile, picked up her load, and opened the door.

"You're *not* the only one who misses her." His soft voice stopped her with one foot on the ground, the other in the car. Then she exited and shut the door, closing Howard and his gentle protest away.

The depth of his feelings was nothing compared to hers. He had his job, and he was successful. A mother's job was to keep her children safe, and she had failed. She avoided a look at him that might break the barrier she'd raised around her feelings and strode toward the bus. Climbing the steps, she clutched her bags, not wanting to touch the dirt crusted on the outside of the vehicle.

The driver's perky grin greeted her. "Good morning."

She plastered a smile on and, without making eye contact, took her seat. How could the bus driver always be so happy? Passengers boarded the bus, but she didn't see them. She saw Jane running in the garden and swinging from the swing Howard had hung for her. She suddenly shifted her gaze back to their car, but he had pulled away.

The bus started with a jolt. Soon the window view of two-story cookie cutter houses and bare fields gave way to high-rise buildings and stores. People crammed the sidewalks in a hurry to get on with their lives. Horns honked and the streetcar bell clang, clang, clanged. She could disappear into the smog of the city, run away from the pity and her neighbors' perfect families. A new start, a new life.

The half-hour trip always made her drowsy and her eyelids threatened to close. But she forced herself to focus on the familiar city corridors to ward off sleep and another nightmare. Although she didn't even need to close her eyes for the images to return.

A small group huddled at the entrance of the imposing brick building as visiting hours neared. Out of habit, she smiled at the woman next to her, even though she wanted to sit down and have a good cry. At least everyone seemed focused on their shared misery, breathing into their scarves, and keeping their thoughts to themselves.

When a tall nurse opened the door, Florence flowed inside with the crowd that passed the sign identifying the Sister Elizabeth Kenny Polio Center.

A woman in a bright red dress sidled up to her, her clothes vivid against the sterile white surroundings. "I wish they allowed more than two visits a week." Her blonde hair fell in soft waves onto her shoulders. Florence had pinned hers up, too weary to style it.

Grunting in agreement, she lengthened her stride. She didn't want to appear rude, but she intended to make the most of every minute. Surely another mother would understand.

The woman stayed in step with her, eager to talk. "They said my Jenny can go home next week. She'll walk with a slight limp, but in time maybe no one will notice."

Her perkiness and perfume mixed with the bedpan stench. Florence wanted to gag.

"What about your daughter?" She batted her long lashes and leaned close as if they were good friends.

Florence glared, horrified that she might tell a stranger the truth. Mildred was the only person who would safely keep quiet about Jane's diagnosis and Florence's fears. At the end of the corridor, the woman in red headed to the rehabilitation side of the hospital, while she continued toward the isolation side. Lengthening her stride as if pressing toward an invisible finish line that would lead to some sort of victory, she neared the array of iron lungs. She stopped and searched for the dark-haired boy. Had he gotten better, moved into the main room, or …? She pushed the thought down and hurried again toward Jane's room. Right now, she must only think of her daughter.

Peering in the window, she looked for the familiar lump, but a much older woman rested in Jane's spot. Maybe they'd moved the patients around. She fastened on a small shape on the other side, but the girl moved, and her red tresses contrasted with the monotony of the room's white furnishings, bedding, and tiles. Dividers covered a few beds at the back, while other dark shapes remained as indistinguishable as shadows at night. Could Jane be there, or had they moved her? Or had she …

Sweat coated her palms. She rubbed them against her skirt. The air felt heavy and made her head spin. She gripped the door handle, and relief, like a cool breeze in summer, swept through her when it opened. She scanned the hallway. No one. She slipped inside, trying to be silent, inhaling the scents of ammonia and sickness. Where was Jane?

"Hey, what are you doing?" A nurse hustled toward her. "You can't be here."

"Jane. Where is Jane Miller?"

The masked woman pushed her into the hall.

"I'm her mother."

The nurse sighed. "Wait a minute." The door shut, and the lock clicked.

Florence tried to read the lips of the staff through the window as they talked and flipped through papers. Images of Jane's empty bedroom, her vacant dining room chair, and a small gravestone filled her mind. She shouldn't have let her go to school. Should have fixed her meals more carefully.

The nurse opened the door, pointed, and said a word, but there was a ringing in Florence's ears. "What? Where is she?"

Removing her mask, she pointed down the hall again. "She's no longer contagious, so she's in rehab. Go down to the end of the hallway and take a right—there's a sign—and ask at the nurse's station which room is hers."

Florence stared at the closed door while the good news sank in. *Rehab. Rehabilitation.* Jane *was* getting better. Maybe she'd come home soon. Her quick steps carried her past the line of iron lungs that she no longer noticed. In her imagination, Jane ran and laughed.

Out of breath from rising hope and her fast pace, she stood at the nurse's station and pressed her damp hands against the top of the counter.

The young woman at the desk raised her gaze from a pile of file folders. Her starched uniform and prim white cap over tidy hair exuded order and calm. "Can I help you?"

"Jane. Jane Miller, my daughter. They just moved her. Which room is she in?"

She trailed her finger down a list on a clipboard, then stood and pointed. "Down that corridor. Number 307."

In less than a minute, Florence opened the unlocked door and stared at the large room with rows of beds. Sunlight streamed in from the large floor-to-ceiling windows. In the middle of the crowded space with women and girls of all shapes and sizes, Jane slept. Florence trembled with hope and fear, collapsing into a chair beside her and savoring the sight of her thin chest moving up and down. Each inhalation and exhalation seemed to repeat, *asleep, alive, asleep, alive.*

Florence leaned forward and the chair squeaked.

Jane's eyes fluttered open. "Mama?"

"It's me." She kissed her cheek and smoothed her disheveled hair. Jane was a pale shadow of her energetic self, but her words breathed relief into Florence.

"You left. Where have you been?"

"They wouldn't let me stay. I visited you every week, even though I couldn't come near you." Her eyes watered. "I'm here now."

Jane's face scrunched in confusion. The overhead lights buzzed. "It's so bright. How long have I been here?"

"I think you just got to this room, but you've been in the hospital for a little over a month, about six weeks."

"Six weeks? I missed school. But Mrs. Fields… my friends…" Two tears leaked down her face, but she didn't wipe them.

"Shh, it's okay. You were really sick." Could she move her arms and legs? She'd been paralyzed from the neck down. The doctor's somber explanation indicated that following polio, some patients recovered movement, but others didn't.

"I wanna go home."

"Soon, Jane." She resisted the urge to dry her face and was rewarded when Jane wiped her cheeks. Even though her hand fell heavily, the very movement eased Florence's fear. At least one hand could move. "As soon as they let me, I'll take you home."

"I don't like this place. I was so tired and people kept waking me up in the other room. They gave me shots and they hurt. I was hot, and I kept having nightmares, but you wouldn't come see me. I kept asking for you. And …" Her words were a whisper in the cavernous room. "I couldn't move."

The dark guilt and mental accusation of failure washed over Florence. "You can move now. I saw your hand. Do you want to try the other one?"

"No. And I can't move my legs." Jane wailed. The girl in the next bed sobbed too.

A nurse rushed over and rubbed Jane's arm. "You need to be quiet, dear. It's okay."

Jane stared at her. "You have a Santa hat on. Is it already Christmas? Was I sick that long?"

"No, it's not Christmas yet." The cheerful nurse giggled, took the hat off, and held it close to the hospital bed. "It's my magic hat."

Jane reached up and stroked the surface. "Magic? How's it magic?"

"Wearing it stops tears." She plunked the hat onto Jane's head.

Jane touched the hat with both hands. "It doesn't work."

Florence's heart soared. Both arms had moved.

"Of course it does." The nurse grinned, took a sock from a nearby table, and rolled it into a ball. "Are you crying?"

"Well…" Lowering her hands, Jane furrowed her brow. Meanwhile, the nurse rolled up two more socks and juggled all three. Jane giggled, despite the tear tracks on her cheeks. "That's neat."

The girl in the nearby bed hiccupped and watched.

Jane laughed. "Can you teach me?" She tried to sit up, but sank back.

The nurse caught the balls. "Of course, when you get stronger."

"What if I don't?" New tears welled up.

"You will. We have exercises that help. You'll get a wheelchair and you'll be zooming down the halls in no time. I'll see you later." The nurse took the Santa hat, plopped it back on her head, and walked on, doing her juggling routine and visiting the other children in the room.

Florence held Jane's hand, finding comfort from her warm squeeze. She would get better. But when another nurse announced that visiting hours were over, she realized what the first nurse left unsaid. Jane's thin, unmoving legs remained motionless. The nurse said nothing about walking.

Chapter 5

Tired from the hospital visit, Florence had laid down for a quick catnap. At least she'd been able to sleep. She rose, straightened the blanket on her bed, then spied a box peeking out. With her toe, she pushed it back underneath. She'd never been able to throw the letters away or read them. Someday she would find the courage to do something with them, but now she needed to finish her chores.

Downstairs, Florence dusted the living room and straightened the pillows on the couch. The house had to stay clean, so no new polio germs could spread. Yesterday's Sunday supplement lay open on the coffee table. An article on polio had caught her attention with its description of Dr. Jonas Salk of the University of Pittsburgh making great strides in developing a vaccine. Earlier in the year, he had tested the vaccine on himself and his family with no ill effects. She felt nauseous. While the vaccine might help William, it was too late for Jane.

The next article talked about Fannie Farmer, the author of her mother's cookbook. Fannie Farmer had also had polio and had lived a meaningful life, so the possibility that Jane could, too, sparked a flicker of optimism in her.

She tucked a strand of hair behind her ear while she searched the sidewalk for William. He should be home by now. After school he'd come in, then rushed out again with his baseball mitt and a hurried goodbye. Thankful the other boys didn't seem bothered by Jane's polio, Florence wondered why her neighbors lacked the same open-mindedness. No one had dropped a casserole by or asked how she was doing. No one seemed to miss her at the weekly coffee meetup. Olive had continued to avoid her. At least Mildred still corresponded with her. She'd just received a letter and looked forward to reading it.

The spicy aroma in the air reminded her that the soup was almost ready. She'd made it yesterday and had put it on the stove to warm after her hospital visit. She stirred the soup and excitement surged through her. Howard and William would be overjoyed to hear the good news about Jane. Maybe they'd even want to read the articles.

She turned the burner to low as Howard's car pulled into the driveway. Eager to tell him about Jane, she went to the front porch, where the breeze was fresh and cool. Most of the leaves on the trees that lined the street had burst into brilliant yellows, oranges, and reds. Either they were more vibrant than any other year, or she was simply more aware.

"I'm so glad you're home." She grinned at him. "I wanted to tell—" Her words died at the sight of his frown.

"I have to work this weekend. Three men quit." He limped up the porch steps without making eye contact. "They just walked out on the line. I can't believe some people."

"Oh, I'm sorry." Florence avoided his glare. He rarely limped, so he must be feeling bad. "I have some news …" She wanted to add, *to make you feel better,* but she knew he didn't like attention drawn to his limp.

Inside the house, he sniffed the air. "Cabbage soup?"

She swallowed. "I know it's not your favorite, but with the hospital visit, it was easy and we had all the ingredients. We're running low on some things. I need to go to the store."

"I told you I'm working this weekend. I can't take you to the store." He removed his shoes, placing them near the door, then hung his coat in the closet. "And I had leftover soup for lunch."

"Oh, I forgot. I'm sorry." Couldn't she do anything right? If only she drove … Maybe when Jane came home, they could keep saving for another car and Howard would teach her to drive.

Howard started for the stairs when the door opened and William entered. "Where have you been?" he asked.

"Walking around." William's harsh tone matched his father's. For the past week or so, he'd been irritable. Was it his sister's absence or upcoming adolescence? Maybe something had happened at school. She'd read an editorial about juvenile delinquents in the newspaper. At least he wasn't old enough to go cruising.

"Don't talk to me like that." Howard approached his son, who studied the floor. Dirt streaked his clothes. One pant leg had a large hole in the knee. Florence tried to get a better look at his face, but he turned it and adjusted his worn ball cap.

Howard lifted William's chin and his voice softened a bit. "What happened?"

"They wouldn't let me play ball." He shifted from foot to foot, then looked at his parents. His left eye was swollen. A cut ran up his arm.

"Sit down. I'll get some ice." She hurried to the freezer and filled the ice bag.

William lowered himself stiffly to the couch, put the ice on his eye, and moaned.

"Tell us what happened." Howard sat next to him. "Did you start it?"

Florence perched on the couch's armrest, running her hands up and down her skirt. "I'm sure he didn't, Howard. You know William's a good boy. He's even tempered and most of the time he gets along well with—"

Howard frowned her to silence. "Why don't we let him explain?"

William rested his head against the back of the sofa and closed his healthy eye. "Charlie and I went to the ball field. Some guys started teasing me. Calling me names and said I couldn't play. They pushed me around. That's all."

"Why were they teasing you?" Howard's voice was tired. He leaned back as if he didn't need to hear. Florence already knew, and so did Howard.

"They said they didn't want to play with a polio. That I was dirty and needed to stay away." William removed the ice pack, felt his wound, and winced. "I hate polio."

Florence took the ice pack. "Get cleaned up. I'll get some ointment for your cut and more ice." Every day, the disease struck new victims, not content with ruining physical bodies.

When William left the room, Howard stared into space, his brow furrowed. He looked angry, but was he upset about his job, William's friends, polio, or her? Then Florence remembered the good news.

"They moved Jane. She's not in isolation anymore. She's in the rehabilitation wing now. Isn't that great?"

Howard wiped his face with his hands. "So, she's walking around?"

"Well, no, but—"

"The world isn't made for cripples." He sighed and pointed upstairs. "Life's going to be hard for her and for us if she can't get around like everyone else. We can't take care of her for the rest of her life, and we can't expect William to. He deserves to have a life free from all that."

"What are you suggesting?" Anger sharpened her words. She needed Jane in order to keep *this* family together.

He patted her knee, then rose. "Just think about it."

"She has to come home." But even as the words left her mouth, images of Jane filled her mind, of her lying in pain, and moving her arms while her legs remained motionless. "They have exercises that will help her. She'll get stronger. She'll fight this."

"I hope you're right." But his face indicated that the battle had already been lost.

When he trudged upstairs, she went to finish preparing supper. A thin crust covered the top of the soup, reminding her how polio had covered them all with a cloak they couldn't escape. She stirred the soup, restoring the proper texture. If only life could be fixed so easily.

By the time Howard came downstairs, she'd set the dining room table. She recalled the unread letter from Mildred. Maybe that would help cheer everyone up.

"Your sister wrote." She retrieved the letter from the coffee table, then studied his freshened appearance. His sparse brown hair was wet and neat. A clean shirt and dark slacks accented his shy smile. Her mouth felt dry, just as it had all those years ago when they'd first started dating. Was he going to take her out to eat? Maybe after, they could watch a movie. They hadn't gone out to a restaurant since … well, since polio paid its visit.

"You look nice." She moved closer to him, enjoying the scent of his cologne.

He dropped his gaze to his loafers. "Thanks."

William came running down the stairs and stood between them. He'd changed clothes and looked in better spirits, despite the bruised eye that had already begun changing colors.

"What have I told you about barreling down those stairs?" All the lines returned to Howard's forehead and a strand of hair fell into his face.

"Sorry, Dad." William looked from parent to parent and then plastered on his most polite smile. "I finished my homework." He paused and Florence readied the answer for the question she knew was coming. "May I go eat at Charlie's house? Before I came home, his parents asked if I could have dinner with them."

Florence's head spun. He'd just fought with some boys, had a black eye, and now he wanted to eat at a friend's house. She opened her mouth, but Howard patted his son's shoulder. "Sure. Have fun."

"I thought …" The words died on her tongue as Howard grabbed his hat.

"I'll drop you off. Start the car." He tossed the keys to his son, who caught them and left the house with a whoop of delight.

"Howard?" She shot him a confused look.

He slunk into his coat and gave her a quick peck on the cheek, then noticed the bowls on the table. "Sorry, dear. I'm sure the dinner was tasty, but I promised some fellas from work I'd play cards with them. I'll be home late."

Florence stared at the closed door. What had just happened? Empty chairs and dinner plates taunted her, accusing her of failure to even gather her family for a meal. The smell of the soup mixed with Howard's cologne that hung in the air. She pulled out a chair, feeling sick. Her words echoed in the silent house. "I hate polio too."

The next week, when Florence entered Jane's hospital room, the smell of wet wool assailed her. A nurse hovered over Jane's bed. She wasn't the kind one with the Santa hat but a beefy woman with pursed lips and a furrowed brow.

"My legs hurt. Stop touching them." Jane scrunched her face.

Her stomach tightened. Florence longed to do something, anything, to help her.

"This will help." The nurse took cloth strips from a metal tub and transferred them into a wringer washer, squeezing out excess water. The strips resembled cut up army blankets. "All of you complain too much."

Florence clenched her hands and cleared her throat. The nurse gave her a quick glance, unashamed of her insensitivity.

Jane spied her and lit up as the nurse continued working. "Mama, you're here."

She sidestepped the big tubs and kissed her forehead.

The nurse mumbled and, without an acknowledgement of Florence, continued to wrap the cloths around Jane's arms, legs, and middle.

Jane wrinkled her nose. "They stink."

"What are you doing?" Florence noted the nurse's perpetual scowl. Weren't these people supposed to be helpful and caring?

"They're hot packs. It's part of the Sister Kenny treatment. They reduce pain and soreness. They also help with circulation and prevent further muscle degeneration. You both should be thankful that we aren't still using splints and casts. With this process, she might get some movement back."

"It still hurts." Jane tried to shake the cloths free.

The nurse restrained her arm. "Like I told you before, you have to be still." She narrowed her eyes at Florence.

Florence wanted to wind the stinky wraps around the nurse. "How often do you have to do this?"

"Twice a day." She put a rubber sheet on top of the hot packs. "Stay put." With drooping shoulders and a sigh, the nurse pushed her tanks to the next bed.

For a moment, she almost felt sorry for the cranky woman having to attend to a room full of patients. No wonder her wrinkled face matched her wrinkled uniform.

"Did you bring me something?" Jane eyed the bulging bag next to Florence. Her cheeks had more color than last week, and her eyes twinkled mischievously as she attempted to move her arm despite the wraps.

"Be still. Let me brush your hair." She aimed for her smile to infuse Jane with the same seeds of hope that she felt. She picked up a nearby brush and stroked her tangled locks. "Don't they brush your hair?"

"Sometimes." Jane watched the girl next to her, who whimpered while the nurse wrapped the hot packs around her. "They wash it on Fridays, and they always brush it after that."

Emotion clenched Florence while she worked through a big snarl. Jane should be home so that she could care for her and make sure she had clean hair every day.

"What's in that bag, Mama?" She made a small, pointing movement.

"Did you eat the cookies I brought last week?" She put the brush aside and set the bag on the bed. She had wanted to bring barley water, but couldn't figure out how to transport it. Maybe next week, she'd find a spare thermos for the liquid.

"Gracie and I ate them." She grinned at the girl next to her, who lay still under the weight of her hot pack treatment. "Did you bring more?"

Florence took out the brown paper sack. "Peanut butter this time and I brought …" She pulled out a small doll.

"Oh, she's beautiful." Jane studied the doll, rolling her head closer. Her fingers twitched.

"Stay still." Florence moved the doll's arms and legs for her, making the doll dance a jig. "How long do they leave these wraps on?" The nurse was now with a patient two beds away. Another nurse had entered with a similar contraption and was working on the other side of the room.

"I don't know. A long time." Her eyes followed the doll's movements. "Thanks for the doll, Mama. I like her, but I wanted a doll like my picture. You remember? A baby Jesus doll."

Florence burned with anger at herself. How could she forget? William had started raking leaves to earn money to buy one that looked similar to the picture. He'd found the look-alike at Schmidt's, the hardware store, which had an entire aisle full of toys even in the off season.

"The baby Jesus doll would go in my dollhouse Daddy built."

Unwilling to tell her that she'd be needing a replacement even with the smell of the burn barrel fresh in her mind, she tried to think of a way to change the subject. Howard had warned her not to tell Jane about the toys they'd had to destroy. Neither of them wanted to risk a relapse, so she shifted her attention toward the nurse, who had moved down the row of beds and argued with a tall, broad-shouldered woman. "Do you know her name?"

Jane's cheerful expression faded to a poorly masked tension. She whispered, "Nurse Mizie. She's mean, the worst. Nurse Harriet is the only nice one."

As if Mizie had heard the comment, she walked toward them, felt the hot packs, and grunted. Without a word or another glance, she removed them and put a fresh nightgown on Jane, then left for the next patient.

Florence read to Jane from *Little House in the Big Woods*. Nearby, Grace craned her neck to listen. Soon, a staff member announced visiting hours were over. Florence settled all her emotions inside, then like a casserole dish, she put the lid on. In a sugar-coated voice, she said, "We had a good visit today. You're getting stronger and that's so good. I love you, so remember that when I'm gone. I'll see you again as soon as I can."

After planting a kiss on Jane's wet cheek, she left the hospital. Once outside, the lid came off and all her sorrow leaked out.

Chapter 6

You've failed your children. Look what happened to Jane. It's all your fault. You should be ashamed. She'll never walk again.

Her arm was tired, but Florence continued stirring the cookie dough. After today's visit she wanted to make something extra special for Jane. If Howard were home, he'd ask why she didn't use the electric mixer. He didn't understand she enjoyed mixing by hand. The repetitive motion soothed her and quieted the accusing voices in her mind.

Of course, she'd told Howard why she didn't use the electric mixer, but she hadn't told him *all* of the why. She'd endured her father's silent disapproval after her mother's death. She didn't want to give Howard more reasons to see her falling short as well. Today she'd chosen to use Mildred's recipe instead of one from her mother's cookbook. She needed a break from the memories and the guilt.

Once the ingredients were well-blended, she measured, then poured in the chocolate chips. "And a dab more for fun," she said aloud as she added extra chocolate to the bowl. Then she remembered no one was next to her.

The sugary vanilla scent relaxed her but left an empty hole in her heart. Jane's school dismissed before William's junior high, and she had loved coming home to help cook. Without being asked, she'd pull a chair up to the pink Formica counter and lean over the ridged metal edging, eager to learn.

They had rolled the dough into balls and placed them on the cookie sheet two inches apart. They always eyed the treats, adjusted the ones that didn't seem evenly spaced, then popped them in the oven and set the timer. While they waited for the cookies to bake, they sat together and colored or read a storybook.

This afternoon, even though Florence had cleaned as she cooked, she dampened a washcloth, wiped the steel cabinets, then the small round table they kept in the corner. A wedding gift from Mildred, it reminded her of her sister-in-law's strength and friendship. A knock sounded on the door.

Groaning, she set the cloth in the sink, rubbed her back, and rehearsed what she'd say to the salesman. "We don't need one today, thank you," she muttered under her breath.

Opening the door, she parted her lips, then pressed them closed.

"Hello, Florence." Olive O'Malley's perky grin and shining eyes greeted her.

She plastered on a smile as fake as the one her neighbor wore. "Good afternoon, Olive. It's good to see you. Won't you come in?"

"Well …" She scuffed her shoe as if mud was on it, but they both knew it hadn't rained in weeks. "Alice is at the Thomas' house and I have to—"

The timer sounded.

Florence breathed a sigh of relief, inhaling the soothing aroma. "I need to get those before they burn." She left the door ajar and hastened to the kitchen.

The cookies were round and browned to perfection. The front door shut. She hoped Olive had taken the hint and left but turned at the sound of a soft cough.

"I should've come sooner."

Florence kept her voice neutral, but the word came out sharp. "Oh?" Hiding her face, she whirled around and placed the cookies on the cooling rack, even though they weren't ready. Mom had told her they needed to cool for five minutes or they'd fall apart, and Florence hated when anything wasn't just so. The cookies crumbled, remnants of what they should be, what they had been.

"I'm sorry, Flo."

Florence felt Olive behind her, but didn't want to face her. They'd exchanged recipes, parenting advice, marriage tips, and gossip for the past seven years. She'd thought they were best friends.

"Will you forgive me?"

"You never called. You never checked up on me." She clenched her hands. "You ignored me."

"I know. I should have. But you see …" Olive fluffed her stylish blond bob and bit her lip.

"I do see." Rolling the dough into balls, she readied another sheet of cookies. She knew why Olive and all the neighbors had avoided her and their family. She would have done the same. They all gave to the March of Dimes. Supporting former President Roosevelt's organization to end polio was the least they could do. Everyone wanted a cure to be found but, in the meantime, they did whatever they could to avoid the disease. They didn't play in the sprinklers, go to pools, or other crowded places. And when they saw someone with polio, they crossed the street. No one wanted to risk contracting the crippling disease. Mothers did what they had to do to keep their children safe.

She placed the baking sheet in the oven and set the timer. When she turned around, Olive leaned against the wall with tears in her eyes.

"I've missed you, Flo. I really am sorry."

A genuine smile formed on Florence's face. Wouldn't she have done the same? "How about some lemonade?"

Olive fidgeted with her handbag and Florence's heart sank. Her *friend* hadn't come to apologize or visit. She needed a favor. Florence's face grew hot.

"I'm in charge of the bake sale at the elementary school's harvest festival. I was wondering if you would—"

"You want me to help you? Aren't you afraid I'll contaminate the whole sale?" Florence eyed the cookies on the counter and swallowed the urge to throw one at Olive. "No. I'm not available."

Without being invited, Olive sat at the kitchen table. "Your cakes are famous. Everyone loves them. People would pay a lot for your baking. Think about how it could help the school."

Florence considered. Help the school? Bake a cake for the families who had healthy children for a festival she would never attend? In the past, she had volunteered to cook for almost every fundraiser. When a family had a new baby or an unexpected death, she brought a casserole or a cake. Florence straightened and fixed her gaze on Olive. No one had brought her anything when Jane got polio. "I don't think so."

"I can reimburse you for the supplies. It must be tight with Jane in the hospital." Olive rose and moved toward Florence, her hand out as if she meant to comfort her.

With an icy stare, Florence stepped back. "We don't need your help. I'm sorry we were ever friends."

"I didn't mean … I'm sorry … I only meant—"

"You can go now." Florence strode to the door and opened it.

Olive left, her eyes averted. Florence stood on the porch watching Olive walk away with her healthy daughter, who skipped effortlessly out of a neighboring yard. Alice waved to two other girls, then joined her mom. All the girls had been friends with Jane. They'd shared ice cream and spent the night at each other's houses.

She walked to the edge of the porch and called after them. "Jane's coming home soon. She's going to get better. You'll see."

Alice gawked at her, but Olive never turned around. She yanked her daughter's arm and escorted her down the street.

Slamming the front door, Florence went into the house. The only thing that mattered now was her family, the children, and Howard.

They were her job.

Her responsibility.

The timer sounded. This time, she waited before transferring the hot cookies. There were no shortcuts in life.

When they were seated at the kitchen table, Florence described the hot pack treatment to Howard and William.

"They're going to help her get better." She didn't mention the smell, Jane's tears, or the stretching that had followed the hot packs.

Howard grunted and continued eating.

William wrinkled his nose. "That doesn't sound like fun." He spooned up more mashed potatoes. "When can I visit her?"

"Don't talk with your mouth full." Howard narrowed his eyes at his son.

"Sorry, dear. They don't allow kids to visit." She passed him her napkin as his had disappeared. "Howard, you should visit on Sunday. We could all drive into the city and—"

He cleared his throat, while he cut his meat into small pieces. "I think I'm scheduled to work."

"Again?"

"I have to, Flo."

"I know but—"

"Maybe when we hire some more people, the hours might get better." He gave her a knowing look. "You have to admit the extra money helps with our additional expenses."

She nodded. They still weren't sure what to do when the hospital bills came. Before polio, they'd been saving for a new car. Now, they weren't sure if the meager amount would cover the medical costs.

"Charlie said he's going to the harvest festival next Friday, at the elementary school. Can we go? They're supposed to have a bake sale and some other games."

"No, we aren't going." Florence pursed her lips at the memory of Olive's visit.

Howard gave her a curious glance. "We go every year, don't we?"

"We can't go. None of our children attend that school now. Remember?" Distracted, she mixed her corn and mashed potatoes together like Jane did. He never seemed to want to spend time with them anymore. Now, he wanted to go to the festival?

"Does that matter? We need to get back to normal."

She stared at Jane's empty chair. "Jane isn't here. That's not normal."

Howard sighed. "It'll be fun and take your mind off of everything." He nodded at William. "We'll go. Why don't you make a cake, Flo? Your cakes always sell for quite a bit of money. And I know how you love to bake." He winked at her and placed his napkin on his plate before leaving the table.

"Can I call Charlie?" William shoveled in the rest of his meat.

She nodded. When he left the dining room, she stared at the dirty dishes and Jane's clean place. A distraction wasn't what she needed or wanted. The past was repeating itself. First it had been her mother, then her sister, and finally her father. They had all left her. Now Jane was gone. How soon before Howard and William left?

That Friday, on the way to the school festival, Florence's hands shook while she tried to hold the cake steady.

"What's wrong?" Howard placed a warm hand on her knee. "You seem nervous."

Surprised by the unexpected attention, she inhaled calm, trying to quiet her anxious thoughts. "I'm fine."

He massaged her shoulder and spoke in a low voice. "I know lately we haven't been getting along that well, but you can always talk to me. I'm concerned about you."

Her heart warmed. He loved Jane too. She'd been reading too much into his silences and bursts of anger. It must be his way of coping. "Olive came and asked me to bake something, but I didn't…" She glanced at William in the back seat to make sure he wasn't listening, but he stared into the dark night. The wind coming in through the half-open windows usually muted front seat conversations. "I said no, and I wasn't that nice. I was mad at her."

"You should make up with her. She's your best friend. Life's too short to fight." He turned into the school parking lot, which was already full.

After circling the lot, Howard parked at the edge in a grassy spot under a tree. William hopped out. Howard kissed her, then came around to help her out. Her heels sunk into the moist earth and she wobbled a bit. He took the cake and offered her his arm. Latching onto it, she felt like a giddy teenager; butterflies danced in her stomach. Her negativity had been for nothing. They followed William as he trotted across the paved lot filled with vehicles and into the tall brick building. A distraction would be good for them all, and they always enjoyed the festival.

Crowds of cheerful adults and children filled the school gymnasium. Streamers and balloons decorated the space. Children dashed in and out of the adult groupings. Laughter and chatter echoed off the tall ceiling, masking the usual buzzing of the light fixtures. They weaved their way through the crowd to the back, where the bake sale tables stretched from wall to wall. A few ladies whispered and pointed. A married couple stared. Pushing her shoulder blades back and down, Florence hooked her arm through Howard's and smiled at the gaping faces.

"Oh, Flo, I see Dennis. I haven't talked to him for a long time." He shoved the cake at her and strode away.

Gripping the plate, she stammered, "But … Howard …"

"Mom, there's Charlie. See you later." William crossed to the other side of the room and joined a group of boys his age. Hopefully, they had forgotten their polio fear.

Walking toward the bake sale tables, she wished Howard would return soon. Women had much longer memories than children.

"I'm glad you changed your mind." Olive materialized and held her hands out for the cake. She had gotten her hair cut recently and short finger waves framed her dark eyes. Florence wondered how she stayed so slender when she loved sweets so much.

Florence considered pushing Olive's perfectly made-up face into the fluffy, white icing, but grudgingly handed her the platter. She scanned the crowd for Howard. Maybe he was on his way back.

A woman bumped her arm. "Oh, I'm so sorry." Meeting Florence's eyes, fear flashed on her face and she rushed away.

Anger rose, and she parted her lips to yell after her, but Olive hooked her arm through Florence's elbow and tugged her away from nearby listeners. "Her oldest had lice last week. And she brought cookies we had to throw away because they tasted like cigarette smoke."

Florence giggled.

Olive fastened her gaze on Florence. "I was horrible. I won't blame you if you never want to have anything to do with me."

"Well …" She spotted Howard laughing with a group of fathers. She couldn't figure him out. One minute he was distant and angry, the next loving and attentive. Now he was laughing with men he'd never been interested in before. She could use a friend. "It's okay. I forgive you."

"I'm so glad. Life is too short to fight. Plus, I've missed spending time with you." Olive held out her arms.

Florence embraced her halfheartedly. Hadn't Howard said almost the same thing? "Do you need some help with the sale?" She might as well keep busy.

"Yes, please." Olive led her over to the table. "Ladies, you all remember Florence."

The three women stopped talking and flashed polite grins her way, but said nothing.

Florence tugged on Olive's arm. She knew the women from activities at the school, but she'd never been quite chummy with any of them. "I don't think I'm wanted here." The other mothers hovered at the opposite end of the tables.

Olive waved a dismissive hand. "You know them. Don't worry. Next week, those old buzzards will shun someone else. We'll work this end of the table."

Florence turned her attention to the first customer, glad for the restored friendship. The other mothers were busybodies. During her time volunteering with the PTA, she'd seen them shun others. Their opinions were the least of her worries.

Between sales, Olive leaned close to Florence and whispered. "I'm the manager at the new bakery. I still have Tuesdays free for our coffee group. You should come back to it."

Florence handed a package of cookies to some teenage girls. She wasn't sure if she'd be welcome at the coffee group or if she even wanted to return. "I thought you worked at Hudson's?"

"The bakery is closer to home and the hours are so much better. But we need more inventory. We can't keep up with the demand. That's where you come in."

"I can't. I worked before we were married, but Howard doesn't want me to work now."

Olive moved some pastries to the front. "All you have to do is some extra baking at home. I'll pick it up. You don't have to tell him. You already do so much baking. He'll never know. I'm sure he's clueless, like most men."

One mother sold Florence's cake to a white-haired couple. Pride swelled in her when she caught sight of the cash being exchanged. She loved to bake and knew she was good. "I don't know if I can keep a secret from him like that."

"Not telling isn't lying." She winked at her. "Though you could tell him. Just wear some bright lipstick and a low-cut blouse. He won't be able to resist."

Florence giggled. William approached the table, accompanied by a couple of girls and Charlie. Olive handed each one a cupcake. "On the house. We've already made more money than we thought we would."

William licked the icing and whispered something to the girl next to him. He didn't make eye contact with her.

"I know your family doesn't need the extra income, but the money would give you a cushion and something for extra. We all like some extra pocket change, don't we?"

The male physical education teacher passed by and waved at Olive. She grinned at him. Florence wondered why she was still unattached. All the single men and some of the married ones couldn't keep their eyes off her. Florence had always thought it was the stylish discounted clothes Olive bought from Hudson's bargain basement. She wanted Howard to look at her like that again. Maybe if she dressed nicer? The extra money might be useful.

Across the room, the group that surrounded Howard laughed at something he said. Florence rearranged the cakes that were left, then caught Olive's attention. "I'll do it."

Over the next hour, most of the items sold, and the gymnasium emptied. Howard made his way to the bake sale table. "Are you ready?"

Grabbing her coat and handbag, she said through pursed lips, "You seemed to have a good time."

Without sensing her tone, Howard waved toward William. "I did. Though I thought you would join me. I guess you were having too much fun at the bake sale."

Florence shot him a look of confusion. "You thought—"

William ran toward them. "Mrs. O'Malley gave me another cupcake."

Howard grinned and pointed to William's face. "Missed some icing."

Face turning red, William wiped at his chocolate-daubed mouth.

Florence tugged on her husband's arm. "What's wrong with you?"

William gaped at them, his mouth still ringed with frosting.

Howard handed him the car keys. "Start the car. We'll be there in a minute." He glared at her. "Why are you yelling at me? You're the one who wants us to spend time together as a family. I brought you out for a pleasant night and this is the thanks I get."

"But then you ran off without me. You didn't even make eye contact with me all night. You talked to people you've never been interested in before."

He grabbed her hand and led her toward the heavy doors, pushing one open for her. "You could have joined me. I wanted to be with you, but I was talking to Dennis and the others because I've been thinking about switching jobs. Dennis has a construction business, and I wanted to see if he had any openings."

"I didn't realize you were still thinking about that." Outside, the cold air made her eyes sting. She remembered him talking about carpentry when they were younger. He had done projects with William and used to whittle in his free time, but he hadn't talked about leaving the automotive business since Jane was born.

"I never stopped thinking about it. You just weren't listening." He dropped her hand. "You've always been in your own world. Now all you think about is Jane in the hospital. You don't have time for me or your son." He hurried across the emptying parking lot and toward the car.

Was he right? She jogged to keep up. "I'm sorry, Howard. I didn't mean to."

He opened the driver's door as if he'd never heard her apology. They drove home in silence. She missed Jane's chatter.

Chapter 7

Readying herself for what she would face, Florence breathed in calm. She opened the heavy door, entered the hospital, and strode down the long hallway. After months of visiting, she still wasn't used to the smell of bleach accented by a faint whiff of vomit. A boy in a wheelchair sped in front of her while a nurse ran behind him and called out, "Stop."

Jane would be better today. She had to keep progressing. Across from her ward, a familiar figure sat on a bench. She'd said weeks ago that *her* daughter was going home, but today the red dress woman wore somber gray. Florence hesitated at the sight of her bent over her crossed legs, silently weeping.

Florence offered her a tissue and sat next to her. The woman straightened and wiped her face, smudging the trails of mascara tears had drawn. Her loose skirt and blouse were crumpled. Her shoulder-length hair fell in uncombed strands.

"I'm Florence." The words sounded stiff to her, but what else could she say? Comfort was hard to give when she'd already given everything.

"Paula." She whispered, staring straight ahead, crumpling the tissue into a tight ball.

Florence followed her lead and studied the door to Jane's ward. The inset window was smudged with fingerprints. A couple of nurses passed them. One whispered to her colleague, who laughed. Their squeaking shoes echoed in the quiet hallway. A custodian began mopping up the dirt and salt the visitors had tracked in from outside.

"Jenny didn't go home." With a sniff, she uncrossed her legs and planted her feet on the tile floor. "She caught a cold."

Florence knew about the precarious health of polio patients. She still worried. What would happen if Jane caught something in the place that was supposed to heal her?

A scream startled them. Florence gazed at Paula in horror. Was it Jenny? No, it couldn't be. The sound came from across the hall, behind the dirt smudged window. The familiar voice thrust her to her feet. She ran. That was Jane.

In the room, all heads pointed to the bed in the middle. Nurse Mizie stood with hands on her hips. "You need to do your exercises. Don't you want to walk again?"

Jane stuck her tongue out. "They're not exercises. It's torture and my mother—"

Florence clutched her purse tighter, tamping down her fear. Jane appeared unharmed, though her eyes were red and her face puffy. She cleared her throat. "Good morning, Jane."

She sank back into the covers, eyes wide in shame, her voice cowed and timid. "Good morning, Mama."

The nurse flashed an accusing glare and thrust out her meaty arm. Her eyebrows formed one angry line. "We just got back from the therapy room. Your daughter bit me. She has to do the exercises. They prevent permanent limb deformities and help with the muscle contractions. Though she doesn't seem to care."

Florence gaped at the red mark, then forced a smile. "I'll talk to her. I know she wants to get better."

Muttering in stifled anger, the nurse pushed past and left the room.

Jane's head disappeared under the covers and Florence tapped on the metal bedside rail. "Is anyone home?"

"I'm sorry, Mama." She peeked out. "It hurts, and she's mean. And her breath smells like cabbage.

Repressing a giggle, Florence got a brush from the nearby cabinet between the beds and smoothed Jane's hair. That's why it smelled like cabbage when she visited. "I'm sorry." And she was. "But you can't bite her. And you have to do the exercises. You're braver than you know." Florence kissed her cheek. Hadn't her mother told her the same thing all those years ago? Now, she'd be brave for Jane and keep her going.

"I wanna go home."

When Florence straightened her pillow, something fell onto the floor. "What in the world?" She bent and picked up several pills. Placing them in her palm, she held them out. "Jane. What are these and why are they under your pillow?"

Reddening, she pulled the sheet up to her chin. "They're vitamins."

Florence fixed her sternest expression on her. "And?"

"I didn't want to take them. They taste yucky when I swallow them. I feel a lump in my throat and I'm afraid I'll throw up."

"You need to take these. They'll help you get better. Don't you want that?" She understood. The huge pills would tend to choke any child and many adults.

Jane nodded and shot a fearful glance around the room. "Don't tell Nurse Mizie, please."

"I won't, but you have to take them. I bet this isn't the first time you've done this." She dropped the pills into her pocket. How could she get her stubborn daughter to take them?

"I'm still getting stronger." Then Jane sat up and grinned at her.

Florence gasped. "You're sitting up all by yourself." She hugged her. "I'm so proud of you."

Still beaming, Jane said, "Is Daddy going to come next time? He can see how good I'm doing. Maybe they'll let me go home soon."

"I'll be sure to tell him, but you know he has to work. He's very busy." She rubbed Jane's back, marveling that she sat up unassisted. "He'll be so glad to hear how well you're doing." Howard's work schedule always seemed to keep him from visiting Jane or spending time with her or William. She couldn't understand why he wouldn't make time for them.

Jane's frown made her reach for the bag. "You haven't seen what I brought you." When she pulled out the wax paper bundle, an idea occurred to her.

Jane squealed. "Peanut butter and jelly?"

"Yes, and …" She took one of the vitamins and slipped it into the sandwich corner. "It'll be a great way to take your pill."

Jane wrinkled her nose, but ate the corner with the vitamin first and washed it down with a gulp of water. Then she devoured the rest of the sandwich.

When it was time to go, Florence gave her one last long look, needing the sight to sustain her for a week. Glad that Jane's new hospital smell was tinged with peanut butter, she kissed her. "I love you."

"I love you too, Mama." Jane leaned back and yawned.

For the first time, she left Jane smiling, with dry eyes.

Florence cracked the window to let the fall air cool her. She poured a glass of water, sat in a chair, and put her feet up on the coffee table. The sink overflowed with dirty dishes. Flour dusted almost every surface. She'd broken her own rule about cleaning while she cooked, but the boxes of cookies and the two cakes made her smile.

The day had passed with her wrapped in a happy haze of baking. As she sipped the water, she caught sight of the clock. It was so late. Olive should be here soon to pick up the baked goods. Then she'd have just enough time to clean up before William and Howard came home.

Florence rose and ran hot water in the sink. Then she remembered. *Jane.* Jane's slow progress worried her. Even though she could sit up, she easily tired. The sweet smells and repetitive motions of baking had made her forget. Lulled her into a false sense of security. Now the baked goods on the counter reminded her. Fresh-baked cookies signaled coming home from school. It had been what her mother had done and what she did for her children at least once a week. She put her hands into the scalding water and started scrubbing.

The front door opened and slammed shut. "I'm in here," Florence called as she dried her hands. Olive was early. "I baked extra cookies. I know—"

When she turned around, William stood before her. He wore muddied clothes and held his ball cap in one hand. A new bruise was forming around his eye. The other bruise had only faded recently. Was this the same eye as before?

"I hate this family." He threw his cap down, then fled upstairs.

Florence followed him to the bathroom, where he slammed the door. The lock slid into place. "William." She knocked on the door. "Let me in."

"No." Thud. It sounded like he had dropped something.

She went into her room and found a clothes hanger to open the door. The last time he had locked himself in the bathroom was years ago. Jane had snuck into William's room and used his new colored pencils. In an angry fit, he had locked himself in the bathroom. "I'm never coming out. I'll starve to death, then you'll be sorry," he had yelled.

Now, when Florence returned to the bathroom with the clothes hanger, the door was open and William sat next to it, his knees to his chest, his head resting on them. "I'm sick of this."

"Of what?" She lowered herself next to him.

He didn't answer, but hid his face in his knees.

She touched his shoulder. "Let me see your eye. I can—"

"Clean it?" He glared at her. His eyes danced with anger. "That's all you do these days. You clean. Dad works. And Jane …" His shoulders sagged, and he cried.

She held him. He seemed gigantic in her arms. Not the boy who'd cried over broken colored pencils.

"These older boys started teasing me when I was raking the Alexander's lawn. I tried to ignore them, but they wouldn't stop. When Mrs. Alexander saw us fighting, she said that I needed to leave and to not come back. She didn't even pay me. I had almost finished the yard. I'll never have enough for the doll."

She rubbed his back, unsure of what to say. He sniffed. She thought back to the time William had cried about his pencils. "I hate her," he had screamed. She rubbed his back then too and told him one day he'd be glad to have a sister. Now, just when he was okay with Jane, everything was changing. Had polio splintered her family or only deepened the pre-existing cracks?

William leaned against her, and she wrapped her arms around his shoulders once more. Would he outgrow his need for her? Then her eyes grew watery as images of William and Jane sharing new colored pencils flashed in her mind. Suddenly, a sound brought her back to the present. Someone coming up the stairs.

She rose, expecting Olive, but Howard appeared, a scowl on his face. "It's a mess down there. What happened?" Then he spotted William. "Have you been fighting again?"

William returned his father's glare, then went into his room, slamming the door behind him.

Howard stared at the closed door, made as if to walk toward it, but then faced Florence. His eyes blazed, like William's had only seconds before. "This is your fault."

"What?"

"If you didn't insist on visiting Jane, we wouldn't have this problem. You're supposed to be taking care of him. Instead, you're making a mess in the kitchen and letting him get into fights. What will people say?" He shook his head, then disappeared into their room.

Mouth open, she stood in the hallway. No words or thoughts swirled in her head. Her limbs felt frozen. Then heat rose inside her and she stormed into their bedroom.

Howard had taken off his shirt and perused the contents of the closet.

"My fault? William's fighting isn't my fault."

"He didn't start fighting until you started visiting the hospital every week." Howard didn't turn around but chose a striped shirt and changed into it.

His forearms were tan. When had he been out in the sun? She pushed the thought aside and spat the next words at him. "What do you want me to do, leave Jane alone? One of us has to visit her."

His shoulders slumped as he put on a sweater vest. "Haven't we already been over this? She's getting good care there. What can either of us accomplish by visiting? I'm just saying that William never acted this way before. He never back talked me until you started disappearing."

While he brushed his hair over the slight bald patch, she sat on the bed and tried to form the words to contradict him. What else could she say? Jane had gotten polio on her watch. And they'd never had a problem with William before.

He pressed a quick peck on her cheek. "I can't talk about this anymore right now. I'm supposed to join some fellas for a card game."

Stunned by the sudden turn of events, she watched him leave and heard him shuffling down the steps. Thoughts churned in her brain. Visiting her sick child was causing harm to her healthy child? Now he was leaving to go out with his work friends. Nothing made sense.

"Wait," she called after him. She rushed down the stairs.

The front door was open. Olive stood in the doorway talking to Howard. When he turned around, Olive sucked her cheeks in and mouthed, "Sorry."

"You're making things to sell in the bakery?" Howard's leg jiggled. "Is this the first time?"

"No." Despite the frigid air, she started to sweat. Florence stepped closer to Howard and put a hand on his arm. His cologne made her head spin. "I was going to tell you but—"

"But what?" He shook off her hand. "You forgot we already talked about this. We agreed years ago that I would work, and you would take care of the house and kids." He pointed to the kitchen. "You aren't holding up your end of the deal."

Before she could say anything, Howard stormed from the house. The car sped off as she wandered into the dirty kitchen. What had she done? Howard was right. She hadn't kept up her end of the bargain. Jane. William. Now Howard. She had failed them all. History was repeating.

Chapter 8

When Florence arrived at the hospital, a nurse sat on the bench where she had sat with Paula a couple weeks ago. Was Paula's daughter recovering? Or was she ... Florence couldn't afford to think of someone else. Not now.

She took small steps toward Jane's room, then paused to listen. No screaming. The door creaked open. A buzz of quiet chatter filled the room as visitors talked to patients and a nurse made rounds. Cutout turkeys and pumpkins decorated the wall. Her daughter sat up in bed and waved. Relief flooded Florence as she returned the wave.

Jane eyed her bulging bag, a mischievous twinkle in her eye. "What'd you bring?"

The aroma of bleach and antiseptic hung heavy in the air. She missed the grass and earth smells that had always clung to her daughter. Pushing a vacant wheelchair aside, Florence kissed her forehead. "Did you do your exercises today?" She sat on the bed and patted Jane's leg.

With a nod, she reached a hand toward the bag. "Yes, and I didn't scream or bite."

"I'm proud of you." She took the first few items from the bag.

"A table and chairs." Jane laughed. "These will go with the dollhouse Dad built."

Swallowing a bubble of guilt, Florence laid the pieces on the bedspread.

In the next bed, Grace eyed the toys. "Those are nice." The blond girl attempted to sit up but could only raise her head from the pillow.

"Thank you, Gracie." Jane pulled her doll from under the sheet and placed her on the miniature chair. "My brother, Willie, is going to get me a doll too. He's going to look like the baby Jesus. Baby Jesus watched out for me when I got polio."

Florence didn't want to remember that night, but the fear and smell of sweat returned. William's face had shone with love and worry when he promised to get the doll. Now, his face was sullen. After the last fight, he'd stopped talking about the doll and Jane. In fact, he didn't volunteer any information and answered questions with grunts and one-word replies.

Jane held the table up for Grace to inspect, then passed it across to her. "When I first got sick, I had a framed picture of baby Jesus my aunt sent me. He was with his mom and dad. You know, the holy family. His face was beautiful. It looked like he was going to talk to me."

Jane lay her head against the pillow and sighed. "I wanted to hold the picture, but I was so tired."

Now that Jane was healing, why wouldn't she forget about the picture? Florence didn't regret breaking the frame and didn't want to replace the glass. Jesus hadn't spoken to her in any way for years and clearly not during this ordeal. Besides, he didn't seem to want to help Jane either.

"When can Willie come and bring the doll? I want Gracie to see her."

Feeling warm in her sweater, Florence shifted, reluctant to tell Jane that there'd be no doll like Jesus. "They won't let children visit. I'm sorry."

Jane stuck her lower lip out. "But he's almost a teenager. Why can't he come?"

"He wants to, but we can't break the rules." She plastered on a smile.

"What about Daddy? He's not a kid. And he doesn't live that far away. Grace's parents can't come because they live too far away, and they have lots of kids. But we don't. When can Daddy come?"

Florence rubbed the smooth skin of Jane's arm. Howard didn't ask her not to go, and she didn't ask him to accompany her anymore. He drove her to the bus station every week. Their unspoken words filled the distance between them. "You know Daddy has to work." The sound of his words in her mouth tasted like sour milk. "He wants to visit, but he can't." Another lie.

"What about Sunday? Some parents come on Sunday."

Not meeting her daughter's eager eyes, she withdrew another package from the bag. "I made cookies for you. You can share them with Gracie. Guess what kind?" She couldn't tell her she'd given up on Sunday visits. Howard wasn't home then to drive her to the bus station anyhow.

"Molasses?" Grace asked.

"Yes." She gave the girl a cookie and then another one to Jane, who looked like she might cry. She sat back down and fiddled with the bag as Jane chewed, fighting sorrow. How could Howard do this to Jane? He'd always doted on her and had been overjoyed at her birth. They had waited so long for William and thought they couldn't have any more children. Florence had thought the season of childlessness was her punishment. She'd wanted a big family like everyone else in America seemed able to produce.

She fidgeted and searched for something to say. Her gaze rested on the bulky contraption next to the bed. "Is that your wheelchair?"

Jane grinned and wiped at her eyes. "Yes."

"She's good at it," Grace said. "She picks up stuff for me when I drop it."

Jane's lip poked out. "I'm not fast yet. And I need help to transfer from the bed to the chair, then back to the bed."

"I'm sure you're good."

Sinking down into her bed, Jane murmured. "I'm never going home, am I?"

"Of course you will. You're getting stronger every day." Florence stroked her hair.

"But Nurse Mizie said that I'm not going home for Thanksgiving. I won't get to do my handprint turkey or eat pumpkin pie. I've already missed so much school. I'll never catch up." She choked on her words. Even Grace looked weepy. Other patients craned their necks to stare.

Florence withdrew the book from the bag and cuddled next to Jane on the thin bed. She couldn't contradict what the nurse had said. And she couldn't continue to give false platitudes. Instead, she opened *Little House in the Big Woods* and began where she'd left off.

While she read about Laura and her family, Jane snuggled up to her. The reassuring warmth calmed Florence. When she finished the chapter, Jane had fallen asleep. She slipped out of the bed, covered her small body, kissed her cheek, and imagined that Jane was Laura. Florence was her mother, and they lived in the big woods. The hardships they faced strengthened their family. But as the hospital door closed behind her, she knew the story in her heart was fiction, fake. Families don't always stay together.

Florence had lost track of how many cakes she had made over the years. They were her first foray into baking, even though her mother warned her that cake making was one of the hardest things to master. Yet Florence had pressed on, making every conceivable error until she baked the perfect cake. Only Florence and her father tasted the creation.

Now Florence smoothed the last bit of icing on the dessert that would hopefully smooth over her and Howard's argument from last week. Yet the cake seemed to taunt her. A crack marred the surface. She had added too much flour, forgetting that in the winter you needed less. Now the imperfection hid under a double batch of frosting.

You can fix everything with extra frosting, her mother had told her. But was there enough sweetness to fix the crack? So much had gone wrong. Every night since the argument, Howard had gone to bed right after they ate. She hoped this dinner would soften him so they could discuss William, Jane, and the bakery.

Florence paced. Her heels clicked on the floor, the only sound in the house. Her feet ached after cooking and cleaning all day, but she couldn't sit still. While sweat formed on her forehead, the ringing phone startled her.

She ran upstairs and picked up the receiver. "Miller Residence." The table wobbled, and the phonebook slid onto the floor.

"What was that sound? I hope I didn't interrupt dinner?"

Relieved to hear Mildred's voice, Florence leaned against the wall and kicked off her heels. "No, I'm waiting for Howard and William to come home."

"William isn't home? Where is he?"

She needed encouragement, not more questions. "Out playing ball, I think."

"Isn't it late for that?"

Florence ground her teeth together, hoping that no one else was eavesdropping on the party line. "I can't do it all. No, I have no idea where my son is. Ever since the fight, he's been coming home later and later. He doesn't tell me where he goes or what he does." She paused, expecting Mildred to answer. Static crackled in her ear.

Settling onto the soft carpet, Florence exhaled all her stress. "I don't want to stir up more trouble. If I mention it to Howard, he'll just yell at me or William. I don't know what to do anymore. I know I'm a horrible wife and mother. You don't need to remind me."

Mildred said nothing. Like Florence's endless days, silence punctuated with just the scraping of plates and Howard's stiff requests for more potatoes or an extra helping of green beans. It reminded her of what it had been like after her mother's and sister's deaths.

A soft cough broke the silence. "I wasn't implying that you're a bad mother or terrible wife. You're not. We all go through tough times." Mildred cleared her throat. "Have you been praying? I can pray with you if you'd like. I know it's hard."

A soundless scream erupted inside Florence. *Prayer, again?* "I think they're here. I've got to go." She hung up the phone, not sorry for her lie. She didn't know what the answer was, but she knew what it wasn't.

Downstairs, Florence tried to forget the conversation. Not glancing at Jane's empty seat, she straightened a napkin that didn't need to be adjusted. With their wedding china laid out, the table had never looked better. Howard's favorite sides, creamed cauliflower and baked potatoes, lay covered in the middle of the table. Even though they would have turkey for Thanksgiving in a few days, she'd asked Olive to drive her to the store and splurged on a roast, using her money from the bakery. She had second-guessed the decision and hoped Howard wouldn't figure out where the money had come from. A perfect meal would lead to the perfect discussion to put their family back together. That had to be the answer.

In the hallway, she glanced in the mirror. Last night, she had put her hair in pin curlers and now blonde ringlets rested on her blue sweater, Howard's favorite. It was the same shade as her eyes. She had applied light makeup, rouge and mascara, steering away from the red lipstick and dark eyeliner Olive favored.

She opened the front door. Dusk had settled over the neighborhood and the streetlight winked on. The smell of someone's dinner wafted across the brown lawn and up the stairs. Steak? Maybe she should have picked up steaks. Despite the icy wind, sweat ran down her back, and a buzzing started in her head when a police car approached the house, then parked in front. She squinted. Her heart pounded in her ears. A tall, gangly officer got out of the front seat, then opened the back door.

Florence stood frozen on the porch while a familiar figure climbed from the back seat. William. She wanted to run to him, but her legs wouldn't move. What was happening?

He trudged toward the house with his head bent. The police officer followed, a grim expression on his face. Then Howard's car pulled into the drive. The door flew open, and he leaped from the vehicle. All three figures converged onto the porch while Florence remained rooted to the spot.

"What's happened?" Howard asked.

The officer studied Florence, then rested his gaze on Howard. "Is this your son?"

Howard nodded with a sigh.

Movement suddenly returned to Florence. She went to William and lifted his chin to see if there was any damage. Had he gotten into another fight? "Are you okay?"

He flinched and stepped away from her. He had no visible bruises or cuts. His clothes were rumpled but not dirty. His physical appearance seemed healthy.

Howard placed a restraining hand on Florence. "What's he done, Officer?"

"A storekeeper caught him stealing." The tall man fixed a grave eye on William. His mouth set in a straight line. "Mr. Schmidt isn't going to press charges, but he doesn't want him anywhere near his store. He and another boy have been skulking around all week. Mr. Schmidt doesn't want juvenile delinquents nearby. It's bad for business."

"Schmidt?" Florence tried to make sense of what was going on. Stealing? Her son was stealing? William wasn't a juvenile delinquent. "Schmidt's Hardware Store?" What would William steal there? Besides, they'd frequented the store for years. Mr. Schmidt was like an uncle to the kids, giving them lollipops when they came in.

The officer nodded. "If there's another incident, I won't be as lenient." With a stern look at William, the man turned, strode across the lawn, then got into the police car and drove away.

Silence filled the porch. Florence wanted to break it, but she couldn't think of any words to fix the problem.

William studied his tennis shoes. Howard glared at him, his face frozen with rage. In the distance, a dog barked and Howard became reanimated. "Stealing?" He ran his hand through his hair. He stepped closer to William, so they were toe to toe. His voice was cold and quiet. "What were you thinking? Mr. Schmidt is a trusted family friend. How could you?"

William remained silent. He backed up, then ran into the house.

Howard turned his rage on her. "Look what's happening to him." He pointed toward the house. "Our son is turning into a thief."

"I don't know what to do, Howard. Do you think if I stop visiting Jane that will change his behavior?"

He exhaled in a long and low breath, like a growl. "Look at it from my point of view. I work hard all day. I've been picking up extra shifts to make ends meet. You go behind my back and work, forgetting all your responsibilities at home. Then William starts fighting and stealing."

Her head buzzed. First Jane, then William. She thought she was doing the right thing by visiting. How could she forget her daughter? She couldn't toss her aside. She'd already lost so much.

"Florence." His hands were on her arms. His breath caressed her cheek. In his dark eyes, she saw not rage, but pain. "I love her too. But all of this started when she got polio. What if we have to let go? We have to think of what's best for our family."

What's best for the family? The words echoed inside her head. She'd heard those words years ago.

Her mother's breathing was shallow and her voice a hoarse whisper. "Florence?"

Florence put her anxious face next to her mother's. "I'm here."

"Take care of them. Your sister and your father." Her mother closed her eyes, and Florence feared it was the end, but her chest rose and fell slowly. "Do what's best for them. You'll know."

"I can't. Don't go, Mama." She stroked her mother's face and cried. "Please," she begged.

"Your name means blossoming. Remember."

The hand that dried her tears now wasn't her mother's, but Howard's. Her mother was gone.

When he spoke, his voice softened to that of the Howard she knew all those years ago. "Stop visiting her so often. We'll see if she gets better. Visiting doesn't change anything."

She let Howard embrace her and rested her head against him. Her shoulders relaxed. It had been so long since she had felt close to him. But how could she choose between him and Jane?

William coughed. He stood in the doorway. His jaw set in the same line as his fathers. "I was doing it for Jane."

Howard pushed himself away from her. "What? You were stealing for your sister?" He turned at the sound of crunching gravel. A neighbor strolled by and waved at them. Howard returned the wave, then said to his son in a low voice, "Let's go inside. We shouldn't be discussing this out here." He stepped toward William and muttered, "It's bad enough the police were here."

But instead of obeying, William stepped onto the porch. His voice rose. "That's all you care about, isn't it? You don't want Jane around because you don't want people to see a polio at your house."

Florence froze again. Her heart thudded in her ears. William had never spoken to his father like this. She feared the red color rising in Howard's face.

"It's not my fault I couldn't finish raking the lawns. I have to get the doll for Jane. That's what I was stealing." He crossed his thin arms over his chest and glared at his father. "I'll take care of Jane. If I need to, I can carry her around. I won't cut Jane out of my life like you."

Howard's face darkened. "She can't come home if she can't walk. We have to do what's best for our family. There are places for polios …" His next words came out quiet, like a snake's hiss. "And there are places for thieves." He stalked into the house.

William avoided Florence's wounded look and followed his father inside. From the porch, Florence heard two slams. She slumped onto the swing. The porch light illuminated the dead grass and bare tree limbs. She shivered and pulled her sweater tight around her. She'd forgotten to put her shoes back on after the phone call. Now the bottoms of her nylons were torn. Her feet felt like blocks of ice. She exhaled and watched her breath form little cloud-like puffs, then disappear. If only it were so easy for her problems to vanish.

Florence's mother said her name meant blossoming, but everyone that she ever took care of died. Her mother. Her sister. Now her family.

Chapter 9

Florence welcomed the cold as she hurried across her frost-covered lawn and down the sidewalk. The breeze whipped her hair and stung her eyes, but she walked upright, each step sharp and quick.

Days had passed since the police officer's visit. Her sadness had morphed into anger and confusion. How could Howard have given her such an ultimatum? Choose between Jane and him? And William? Her wonderful boy was stealing.

Cars whizzed by. One honked its horn. The business man in the front seat leered at her. She clutched the cloth bag and her handbag tighter, then squinted into the distance. A little further to the end of the street. A right turn, then after a couple of blocks, another left. She'd never walked to the bus station, but guessed it was a mile or two. Checking her watch, she lengthened her stride, stepping over a crack in the sidewalk. She'd need to hurry to make the next bus.

A blue sedan passed her, then stopped. Slowly, it backed up.

Florence froze. Was it another leering businessman? She surveyed the area for somewhere to run. She didn't know any of the neighbors in this section.

The car stopped next to her. Florence braced herself. Should she make a break for that house? She balanced on the balls of her feet, wondering how fast she could run in kitten heels. Why hadn't she worn loafers?

The driver got out. "What are you doing?"

It was Olive.

Florence exhaled, her breath making a large puff in the cold air. "I'm glad it's—"

"Get in." Olive clambered back inside before Florence could say anything.

Opening the passenger side door, she leaned in. "I can't. My bus will be at the station soon. I'm already late."

"It's freezing." Olive patted the bench seat. "I'll take you. It's on my way."

Florence pushed Olive's large handbag aside, climbed in, and balanced her items on her lap. "Don't you go into work earlier than this?"

"I start work later now. Since you stopped baking for us, the owner hired someone new. Though people still ask for your cookies and cakes." Olive gave her a pointed look and accelerated through a curve.

Florence clutched the door with her free hand. "You know why I can't. You were there. Remember?"

"Hmm. I remember. Howard. And why isn't he taking you to the bus station?"

"You wouldn't understand." She loosened her grip on the door. Olive sped through a stop sign. Resuming her death grip, Florence pushed her feet against the floor. "What are you doing?"

Olive gave her an annoyed look. "No one was coming. I don't want you to be late." She grinned in the rearview mirror, showing her teeth. Probably checking for lipstick. "So, what wouldn't I understand? That your husband doesn't want you visiting your daughter. That he wants you home, cooking his meals and making sure your juvenile delinquent son doesn't get in any more trouble."

Surprised, Florence raised her eyebrows.

Olive shrugged. "People talk."

They pulled into the bus station and Florence gave her a weary look. Howard had changed. He showed no remorse for how he had spoken to William. True, William *had* stolen, but Howard had done the one thing he accused her of doing: over-reacting. He had always been so gentle. She'd first fallen in love with him when she saw the way he handled the animals on the farm and the way he held her. Her cheeks grew warm.

Florence put her hand on the door and prepared to get out, but Olive said, "Flo, I'll drive you whenever you want to go. I can pick you up after Howard leaves for work."

She nodded. "Thanks, Olive. And I can bake a few things for you. Not as much as last time, though."

"You know, your life's not that bad."

Florence looked at her in confusion. "What do you mean?"

"You're lucky. At least you have a husband. He provides for you."

With a nod, she said, "You're right. Thanks for driving me."

Olive left with screeching tires and waved at Florence. Or was she waving to the group of men by the station?

Florence boarded the bus with more questions than answers. Complaining about Howard had been insensitive since Olive no longer had a husband. Though if the rumors were true, it wasn't because she hadn't been trying to snag one.

She chose a seat in the middle of the bus, ashamed of her thoughts. Olive was a loyal friend. Florence should be grateful for all Howard did for their family. Maybe she shouldn't work behind his back. But she couldn't stop visiting Jane and she needed the extra money for the bills and another car. Could Olive teach her to drive? But she remembered her fright when Olive drove. She shut her eyes while she waited for the bus to depart. Would it be worth asking her friend to teach her anyway?

When Florence arrived at the hospital, she made time to find nurse Harriet, the nice one who doted on the patients. She was in the area with the filing cabinets, seated at a desk that overflowed with files, books, and stacks of paper.

Upon seeing Florence, Harriet set her sandwich on a piece of waxed paper. "Mrs. Miller, what can I do for you?"

"Well …" She straightened. "I need to help Jane get better. What can I …" Her voice caught with emotion. Howard's angry face flashed in her mind. He wouldn't approve of anything she was doing.

Harriet came closer and placed a hand on her shoulder. "I understand, but you know recovery is up to the patient. You're doing the best thing by coming and visiting as often as you can. Jane looks forward to your visits. That's one reason she keeps improving. And every day her muscles are stronger."

She sniffed, not trusting herself to speak.

"There are a couple of things you can try. She hides her salt tablet in her oatmeal, then won't eat it. You could bring her some salty snacks, like pickles or crackers. She needs the extra sodium right now and the extra calories. So, any snacks would help. She's thin and a picky eater." The nurse winked. "I'm sure we can fatten her up."

Making a mental list of the items she could bring, Florence nodded. "Anything else?"

"Let me get back to you. I need to check in with some other patients right now. But there are some exercises I can show you." She moved some books, picked up a clipboard, then smiled warmly at Florence. "You're doing a good job, Mrs. Miller, and so is Jane. She's a spunky young lady. I think I know where she gets that from." Harriet took the last bite of her sandwich, patted her shoulder, then strode down the hall.

Feeling encouraged, Florence headed to Jane's room. Her hand was on the door when a sob caught her attention.

Harriet had her arms wrapped around a well-dressed woman who looked familiar. The woman's sobs grew louder and less controlled. Even without the red dress, Florence recognized her. Paula. Then she knew. Jenny was gone. That was the only reason a mother would break down like that. For a moment, she wanted to comfort her. Instead, she opened the door to Jane's ward. A mother is nothing without her children.

Florence peeked out the window. She'd arrived home a few minutes ago and was tired, but determined. Her plan to help Jane had been implemented. Now she needed to carry out her idea for William. Howard had ordered him to come home right after school. No more baseball games. Pushing back the floral curtain, she hoped she wouldn't need to track him down.

To her relief, he trudged toward the house, kicking a stone. When he ascended the porch steps, his shoulders slumped.

She opened the door. He groaned. Fighting back a grimace, she steeled herself for what needed to happen next. He would most likely oppose her idea. "Do you have homework?"

"No." He clutched his books to his chest, frowning. "So, now you're going to give me a bigger punishment?"

Pushing away the thought that he might be lying, she studied her son. Instead of the moody, almost teenager, she saw the active little boy he had been. "You're going to help me with dinner. Put your books away and go wash your hands."

His brow furrowed, but before he could say anything, she went to the kitchen. "Hurry," she called over her shoulder. "We need to have the meal ready by the time your dad gets home." Howard had been right about one thing. She needed to spend more time with William.

A few minutes later, he joined her in the kitchen, his frown still in place. "Girls cook, not men."

"Everyone should learn. My dad had to take over the kitchen duties when a horse injured his mother." The mention of her father startled her. She didn't remember the last time she had spoken of him.

"Your dad? Grandpa? Was he the one who taught you?" Open-eyed curiosity replaced his frown as he leaned against the counter. "His mom got kicked by a horse? That would hurt. What happened?"

"One question at a time." Florence laughed. "No, he didn't cook all the time, just every once in a while. My mother did the baking and most of the food preparation. She taught me." Not wanting to talk more about her family, she took the worn book from the shelf. But cooking was so tied up with her family, how could she avoid mentioning them?

He studied the volume. His eyes were the same shade of blue as hers and his grandmother's. "That cookbook's old. Was it your mom's?"

With a nod, she ran her hand over the cover and the memories returned. "She would have loved you, William. You have her laugh, you know. And the same sense of adventure."

"What happened to her? You never talk about her."

"Spanish flu."

Suddenly fearful, he asked, "Is Jane going to die too?"

"No, she's getting stronger. You should see her in her wheelchair. She loves speeding down the halls."

"Really?"

"She loves to get things for patients who aren't as mobile as her." Pride filled Florence. Jane was a fighter and a helper like her brother. William cared for his sister just as much as Jane cared for those around her in the hospital.

William ran his hand over the fraying cover. "*The Boston Cooking-School Cookbook* by Fannie Merritt Farmer," he read, scanning the page. "1896? That's old."

"You're right. Your grandma loved this cookbook. She told me it was the first one that taught people to prepare food, just like the culinary schools my mother dreamed of going to. It used exact standard measurements instead of saying a handful of this or a pinch of that."

He flipped through the pages. "That's neat. So, everyone could learn, even men, right?"

She grinned. "Exactly. Your grandmother always wanted to start a restaurant using these recipes, though adding in her special touch. Dad said we should call it Annabelle's after her. My sister…" She swallowed the lump of emotion. The lost dreams had evaporated like the steam from soup.

"I didn't know you had a sister. What happened to her?" William leaned closer.

Florence faced away and blinked back the memories. "Let's get started. We're going to have roast chicken, stuffing, mashed potatoes, gravy, and a salad."

William melted the butter on the stove. She looked over his shoulder as he poured the hot liquid into the bowl she had prepared with crumbled crackers and spices. "Be careful. Don't burn yourself." The fragrant smell of the powdered sage and summer savory took her back to the times she had made the same recipe with Mom. After her mother died, she had avoided making chicken, because she hated butchering the bird by herself. Her mouth watered at the thought of her mother's fried chicken.

"What do we do now?" William wiggled the legs of the chicken and grinned.

An unexpected giggle escaped from Florence as William peeked into the chicken's cavity. He scrunched up his nose. "Is there something in there?"

"Not anymore. I already prepared the chicken before you came home." She'd gotten rid of her squeamishness after she and Howard had married. Though she was relieved she didn't have to butcher live chickens anymore. "Now, you just have to stuff it."

His eyebrows raised in question, but then lowered as he followed her instructions and pressed the bread mixture inside. When the bowl was empty, he trussed the chicken and put it into the hot oven.

Even though it was his first time, William peeled the potatoes quickly. "I bet Charlie's never done this before." He laid a potato on the cutting board and started on the next one. "Charlie's a good friend. He stood up for me when the other guys were teasing me."

Florence wanted to say something, but he was still peeling and not looking at her. So, she chopped the potato into cubes and added it to the pan.

"He didn't think I should steal the doll. He even tried to make me stop. I'm sorry I did it." The peelings fell into the trash can as he worked the knife around the vegetable. "I'm worried about Jane."

When the potatoes filled the bottom of the pan, she ran water over them, then set them on the stove to boil. "You're a good brother."

He sniffed and placed the knife in the sink.

"Maybe Mr. Schmidt would give you a job or at least let you help a little around the store. You could—"

"I'd work for nothing." William turned around, his face lit with a wide smile. "I could make it up to him. Show him I didn't mean to make trouble."

Words her mother had spoken to her returned. *Men and women are different. Women nurture. Men need jobs to do.* Though maybe men and women weren't that different. William and Jane both seemed to thrive when helping others.

"That sounds like a good idea." She patted his arm. While the potatoes boiled, they made gravy. When the side dishes were finished and warming on the stovetop, she slipped the last prep pans into the soapy water for a quick soak and sat at the kitchen table while the chicken finished.

William poured them each a glass of lemonade and handed her one. "You're different when you're cooking."

She'd never thought about it, but being in the kitchen had always stirred something in her. Contentment. Joy. A sense of happy usefulness. It reminded her of being next to her mother, watching her knead dough and hearing her hum "Amazing Grace." Not all her old memories were painful.

"What song is that?" William looked puzzled.

She hadn't realized she'd been humming. "It's a hymn we used to sing at church."

William drained the glass. "How come we don't go to church?"

Life had changed after her mother and sister had died. After God had let them die. She'd never go back to church.

"I think the chicken is finished." She ignored his curious look and showed him how to cut and serve the meat.

After they plated the food and set it on the table, William studied the meal, a broad grin on his face. The grin was reward enough. The moody boy had disappeared when they were cooking, and she had enjoyed getting to know the young man he was becoming. Hope lifted her heart. The front door opened.

"What smells so good?" With his coat over his arm, Howard pinched off a piece of chicken and chewed appreciatively.

"I helped." William's eyes twinkled.

As silence descended on the room, her hope leaked away. As if they were problems to be solved, Howard assessed the table, then his son and wife. His brow furrowed. He jiggled his leg. "Cooking? You were *both* cooking?"

"Grandpa did." William straightened and jutted out his chest, a scowl on his face.

Heat filled Florence. "You can't possibly be mad now. You wanted me to spend time with William. And I am."

"Boys don't—"

"Stop it," she stomped her foot.

Howard and William looked stunned. Florence had never yelled or talked back to her husband.

"I'm spending time with my children. Maybe the problem is that you don't. I'm not giving up on either of them, even if you do." She put her hands on her hips.

Howard said nothing. After a few seconds, he turned and left the house. Tires squealed in the driveway. Florence and William ate a quiet dinner. While she cleaned up the kitchen, she didn't think she would lose her children, but what about her husband? Their growing rift was worse than ever.

Chapter 10

Jane was coloring a picture of a Christmas tree when Florence arrived at the hospital. She hugged Jane, then draped her snow-dappled coat over the back of her wheelchair. Florence settled herself on the bed, then withdrew crackers and a jar of pickles from her bag. Jane's eyes sparkled as she watched. Placing the snacks on the bedside, Florence took out the next item with exaggerated slowness.

At the sight of the chocolate bar, Jane grinned and put aside her crayons. "Yummy." She opened the candy and chewed the first square. "I thought Daddy would visit today. You keep telling me he'll visit soon."

"You know he has to work." Florence hated how Jane asked about him every week. Howard had no clue she still went to the hospital. Besides a few essential words, they hadn't talked since the dinner fiasco weeks ago. Now, with William cooking more, she'd kept up with the household chores and baked a few dozen cookies for Olive's bakery. Cookies that Howard knew nothing about. Her relationship with William had improved, but her relationship with her husband was nonexistent.

"I wish he didn't have to work so much." She wrapped up the remaining candy and yawned.

"Eat the rest. Aren't you hungry?" Jane had become so thin.

She shook her head and yawned again. "Can I go home soon?"

Thinking about Paula and the homecoming her daughter wouldn't have, she wondered if Jane would ever go home. No matter the cost, Florence would help her heal. She couldn't lose her.

"I want you at home. You're getting so much better in the wheelchair. They'll have you up and walking in no time. Aren't you looking forward to that?"

With a grin, she said, "I'm fast in my chair. A boy from the men's ward can do wheelies in his chair and he's going to teach me."

Horrified, Florence's mouth fell open, but she quickly clenched her jaw and narrowed her eyes. "No, he isn't. No wheelies. We can't have you getting hurt."

Jane stuck out her lower lip.

Florence ignored the pouting and pulled back the sheet. Nurse Harriet had told her that massage might help. Trying not to think of the round, sturdy legs that once ran everywhere, she rubbed the thin, withered leg. Jane called it her skinny leg and the other one her fat leg. The nurses reassured her the difference was typical for polio patients.

"I can't wait to get the baby Jesus doll." Jane pulled out her doll and cradled it.

Florence set the first leg down and massaged the other one. The thought of the doll still made her sick. After William apologized, she'd worked out a deal with Mr. Schmidt so that her son would work at the store on Fridays for a few hours. He'd ride his bike over after school. Mr. Schmidt had agreed to have him work a couple of weeks for free, and if he proved to be reliable, he would start paying him. Florence hoped William and Jane would forget about the doll, but they hadn't. She kneaded the limp leg, wondering what would have happened if polio had never ravaged her daughter and her family.

The leg wiggled, and Jane grimaced. "Ow, Mama. You're rubbing too hard."

Florence stopped. "I'm sor—" Jane's leg had moved. "Move it again."

Jane looked at her thin limb in question, but then rolled it an inch and giggled.

Grace, who was propped up in bed, laughed. "Do it again."

With a grin of concentration, Jane moved her leg more than the previous time. A few other patients followed the movement and cheered. A woman in a wheelchair rolled closer, stretching her neck to see better. Florence hurried from the room.

In the hallway, a nurse studied a chart. Her mouth moved as she mumbled. Florence tapped on her shoulder. "My daughter. Come." She gripped the white sleeve and tugged the woman toward the open doorway.

The nurse yanked her arm away and followed Florence into the room, where a crowd had gathered around Jane's bed.

"What's wrong? Are you in pain? Did you have an accident?" It was Nurse Mizie, the one Jane had bitten.

Florence wedged between a couple of patients. "She moved her leg." Grasping her daughter's hand, they exchanged excited grins.

"Hmm." The nurse pulled back the cover and studied the scrawny limb. She bent and manipulated the leg.

Jane wrinkled her nose at the nurse. Florence understood her dislike. She wanted to bite the nurse, too, or at least stomp on her toe. A few weeks ago, Florence overheard her hissing at her daughter, "You should be thankful. You aren't dead and you didn't have to be in an iron lung. You're one of the lucky ones."

Florence shivered at the memory of the rooms with rows of machines. The mechanized breathing and the pitiful heads protruding from them always made her want to throw up. She was thankful the polio had spared Jane's lungs.

While the nurse continued her examination, a girl with a dour expression wheeled next to Florence and eyed Jane. "You only moved it a little. That means nothing."

Jane stuck her tongue out and said, "Shut—"

The nurse stared daggers at both girls, but then flashed a slight smile. "I think it's time for braces."

The sour-faced girl wheeled away with a huff. The crowd leaned in closer, and Jane's smile grew wider. Florence hadn't seen such delight since … She rolled back through her memories and an image filled her mind.

They all sat at the table. Howard cut the roast while William entertained them with a story. Jane laughed at the tale, then held out her plate for the meat her father offered. Florence and her family were the lucky ones.

The memory vanished. The nurse crooked a finger at her, motioning to the hallway,

Florence followed the grim-faced woman.

The nurse closed the door and tentatively patted Florence's shoulder. "Braces don't mean she'll walk again. She's getting stronger, and the movement is a good sign, but sometimes the progress doesn't continue."

While the woman talked, her words faded into the buzz of chatter from Jane's room. Across the corridor, a child whimpered. Then, from down the hallway, an alarm echoed. Florence knew from previous visits that an iron lung had stopped working and would need to be operated manually.

The nurse stopped talking and exchanged looks with another nurse. Both women dashed toward the sound.

Back in the room, Florence's joy returned at the sight of her daughter's bright face. Jane giggled with Grace while they munched on chocolate squares. "Does this mean I can go home for Christmas?"

Christmas. Though Florence had been baking Christmas cookies for Olive, the reality of the holiday hadn't settled on her yet. Jane was the driving force behind every celebration. She cajoled her parents into decorating early and baking fudge. Every year, she convinced William that he hadn't outgrown decorating gingerbread boys and girls. Without her, how could there be Christmas?

Nurse Harriet approached and told Jane, "We'll have our own celebration here. And your mom can visit."

All the joy drained from Jane's face. The hand that held the chocolate drooped, and she whispered, "It won't be the same."

Florence perched on the bed next to her and withdrew the book from her bag. They had finished *Little House in the Big Woods* and were reading *Farmer Boy*. Jane snuggled close, and as Florence read, she knew Jane spoke the truth. Christmas wouldn't be the same. Nothing would ever be the same. But then a sliver of hope snuck in. Jane had moved her leg.

On the lookout for patches of ice, Florence pulled out of the grocery store parking lot, glad that the trip for baking ingredients hadn't taken too long. She slowed, then braked. Stopping at the intersection, she checked Olive's expression from the corner of her eye. Olive reapplied her lipstick using the side-view mirror. Looking both ways, Florence accelerated, then coughed to get her friend's attention. "How am I doing?"

"You drive like my grandmother, if my grandmother had ever driven."

A car behind them honked. She pulled over to the shoulder and let it pass. "I'm doing good with the clutch. I haven't stalled the car today. Not once."

Olive scowled. "You give women drivers a bad name, you know."

"I just want to be careful." Disregarding her hesitations, she'd been taking lessons with Olive for the past few weeks. Surprisingly, Olive was a wonderful teacher.

"You're doing fine. Have you told Howard?"

Keeping her eyes focused on the road, she shook her head. Christmas had passed just as Thanksgiving had. They'd made a half-hearted attempt at exchanging gifts and hadn't even put up a tree. The days were silent and long. The tension in the house resembled the Michigan winter—cold, dreary, and never-ending. She and Howard had established an uneasy truce, speaking only when necessary. He didn't know about the lessons, her baking, or her visits to Jane. A confession would only heighten their tension. Mildred had told her that honesty was always the best, but Florence disagreed. Some things were just too big to say.

"Are you going to tell him you can drive? Or just wait until you have enough for a car? I'm sure he'll be glad to not have to pay for another vehicle."

Florence thought of the growing nest egg in her dresser drawer. She hadn't counted it in a while.

"The bakery owner is selling a car that would be good for you. I can loan you the difference and you can pay me back when you're able to."

"I don't know. I'm getting better at driving, but I don't think I'm ready to drive by myself. And Howard would be upset that I owe you money. It'd take a long time to pay it back." Florence didn't want Olive to know that her marriage was falling apart. She had made gains with William, and Howard came home for dinner almost every night. But his frequent card games concerned her, and he'd taken up bowling. Any conversation between them was brief and one-sided. He crawled into bed late every night. She had to figure out a way to thaw their relationship, not make it worse.

Olive waved a dismissive hand. "You worry too much. Besides, what are friends for?"

Florence sighed. Howard would echo her friend's sentiment. "What time is it? I don't want to be late to pick up William." Her son now worked two days a week and Mr. Schmidt had begun paying him around Christmas.

Olive studied her sparkly wristwatch, a Christmas gift to herself. "Turn around in that parking lot and we can cut through on Fifth."

Florence followed Olive's directions. By now, she knew her way around the streets of the suburb, even though she still hadn't braved the city. Driving was more fun than she had thought, but not as calming as cooking. She pulled into a parking spot in front of the hardware store, pleased with her new skills. The car was slightly crooked, but between the lines.

"I'll wait here," Olive called when Florence stepped onto the curb. "Don't take too long. Remember, we have groceries."

Florence buttoned her coat and tightened her wool scarf. Their groceries would be fine. The car was as cold as a refrigerator. In the hardware store's window, a red and silver Lionel Santa Fe train sped around a loop of track. The diesel locomotives with four gleaming passenger cars mesmerized her. She knew William had wanted the set for Christmas, but with the tight finances, he'd only asked for a new ball mitt.

Mr. Schmidt turned off the transformer and waved at her. She returned the wave, then stepped inside. The bell over the door jangled. With a grin, Florence said, "You know Christmas is over, right?"

The white-haired storekeeper pushed his glasses up on his nose and laughed. "That's a marketing strategy. I'm not the only one who enjoys watching it. That's the last set and I'm hoping someone will buy it, but I know it's out of most people's price range. The $18 Scout sets sell out first."

"I hope so, too." She scanned the store for William. The toy aisle was off to the right. Dolls, games, and puzzles crowded the shelf. The Howdy Doody game she'd bought for Jane stood out from the stack of boxes. The other shelves were just as crowded. Howard, like many of their neighbors, enjoyed coming into the store rather than driving into the city. *If they don't have it at Schmidt's, they don't have it*, was a popular refrain on their street.

"William's been busy today. He finished stocking for me. I sent him to get his coat when I saw you outside." Mr. Schmidt looked at his watch. It was almost closing time.

William walked out between the center aisles, putting on his coat. "I'm ready and hungry. What are we having for dinner?"

Florence shook her head. "Let's let Mr. Schmidt close up."

The bell rang when she turned around and almost ran into the tall man in the doorway. "Oh. Sorry." When she put a hand up to steady herself, her breath caught in her throat.

It was Howard. "Flo. What are you …" He peered around her where William tried to hide. "Willie? What are you guys doing here?"

Trying to hide her confusion, she asked, rather too sharply, "What are you doing here? It isn't time for you to be finished with work."

His brow still furrowed, he held up a bent key. "I got off early and I needed to get a new key made. This one bent during the last hard freeze."

Mr. Schmidt, who stood next to the train set looking uncomfortable, took the key from Howard. "Let me fix this for you."

While the shopkeeper retreated to the back, Howard stepped closer to her. "What's going on here?"

Florence grabbed William's hand, pushed past Howard, and exited the store.

Howard grabbed her elbow. Frowning, he glanced from her to the Studebaker, where Olive sat, waving at them as if she enjoyed the whole scene. Howard's eyebrows knitted together as if solving a puzzle. "Flo, tell me what's happening."

William stood with his head bent. A pile of old snow had accumulated next to the store wall. He pushed his foot into it, packing it down further and further. She'd hidden nothing from William, and she'd never told him not to tell. But she'd never discussed her deception. *Deception.* That's what it was. She was deceiving her husband. She knew she should be ashamed, but she wasn't.

"William got a job here to make up for his past mistake. And I was driving. Olive has been teaching me."

"Driving?"

"Yes. And that's not all." Her brain screamed, *stop talking,* but her mouth kept moving. It was as if the spring thaw had arrived early. "I've been baking for the bakery, and I've been visiting Jane."

Howard continued to stare. Then a red flush crept from his neck to his forehead.

She considered apologizing, but Mr. Schmidt poked his head out the store door. "Howard, your key's ready when you are."

Florence and Howard both smiled plastic grins and waved. "Just a minute," Howard said.

Florence grabbed William's hand and led him to the car. Over her shoulder, she called, "I'll see you at home."

William got into the backseat without a word. Florence slammed the door shut and backed out.

"What was that all about? What did he say?" Olive asked.

Florence said nothing. Confidence filled her as she navigated the streets with ease. No one honked at her for going too slow. When she pulled in front of Olive's house, she felt different—light and free. Without a word to Olive or William, she grabbed her groceries from the backseat and strode toward her house. The frigid air rejuvenated her as William jogged to keep up.

In the house, he gave her a sheepish grin. "I'm going to do my homework," he said and disappeared upstairs.

In a daze, Florence put the groceries away, then started preparing supper. Her mind suddenly whirred to life. Her confidence dripped away, and she second guessed her actions. It felt good to have the truth out there, but how could she have talked to her husband like that? She'd been the ideal house-wife, but now she was turning into a different person. Being in a family meant that all the members worked together in harmony. Hadn't that always been her goal?

But she was doing the opposite. She was bringing chaos into their world. Teaching her son to cook? Working outside the home when her husband had forbidden her? Hoping that her daughter, her sick, crippled daughter, could come home?

Yet, since she'd begun William's cooking lessons, baking for Olive, and encouraging Jane, a peace and hope had settled on her, one that she'd never experienced before. The only problem was…

"What are you doing?"

"Howard?"

He stood behind her, his face contorted into a questioning look. The water was running in the sink for no apparent reason. She turned off the tap and stared as it drained, trying to prepare herself for his tirade.

"I'm sorry," he said.

She whirled around, surprised. "What?" Maybe she'd misheard.

"I'm sorry." He sat at the table. "I overreacted to the driving and you working at Olive's bakery. Women do drive and work outside the home now. I know things are changing. But I didn't want you to have to get a job. I wanted to provide for you and now I've failed."

Sitting next to him, she tried to digest what he was saying. "You've failed? But I enjoy driving and the part time work. I'm still—"

He held up his hand and smiled. "I know. Life has been great around here these past few weeks. On the way back from the hardware store, I realized that you've been doing everything around here. Besides that, you've taken on extra baking, learning to drive, and visiting Jane." He laughed. "I wish I was as productive as you. And that you felt comfortable enough to share with me about William's work and everything else. It's not good for us not to talk to each other."

She grinned and tentatively reached toward his hand. Maybe her confession would help to bridge the gap between them. He grasped her hand, and their eyes met. For the first time in a long time, she felt connected to him. The ice was melting. "I hate when we fight."

He nodded. "Me too, but, about Jane …"

She released his hand.

"I miss her too." His eyes misted. "But think about it, Florence. Life is going to be hard. Are you sure you can take care of her?"

Something inside her dropped. "She's getting stronger, Howard. She moved her leg. They're going to teach her to walk. Don't you want her to come home?"

"Of course, I do." He rose and ran a hand through his hair. "But think what life would be like for her. A fella from work told me about a place. I made an appointment for us in a couple of weeks. You could visit her there. It would be better for all of us, especially Jane. She could be with others who struggle like her. Professionals would care for her and give her what she needs. What we can't provide."

"If you go to the hospital, you'll see. She can get around." She grasped his arm. He smelled like pine, and she remembered how he used to whittle out on the porch while telling stories to William and Jane. The last time she'd seen him whittle had been that day at the hospital. Had he finished that piece?

He kissed her forehead, and for a moment, she thought he might relent. But then he looked into her eyes. "Let's visit the place."

When he went upstairs, she didn't watch him leave. He'd apologized and for a moment they'd connected, but now he was a stranger again. Something had shifted between them, and she wasn't sure what it was or how to put it right.

Florence pushed the chairs under the kitchen table. After Mildred had gifted them with the table, Howard had found the chairs at yard sales. He'd taken great care with the mismatched chairs, repairing them, then staining them so they would match. If only their relationship could be fixed so easily.

98

Chapter 11

Florence entered Jane's ward. A sour-faced girl she remembered from previous visits sat in a wheelchair and gazed out the window. Outside, a boy ran ahead of his mother who clutched her packages tighter and caught up to him, grabbing his arm. The trees in the park swayed in the breeze. Snow glistened on the branches. Florence took off her coat and placed a hand on the girl's shoulder. "It's beautiful out, isn't it?"

The girl flashed a withering look at her, then patted the blanket that covered her thin legs. "Does it matter? It's not like I can walk."

"Oh … I'm sorry. I didn't mean …"

"Jane doesn't know how lucky she is. She has a family who will take care of her. My family doesn't want me." The girl pushed herself away.

She stared at the retreating wheelchair and wondered if Jane would ever lose her positive outlook. Howard's questioning returned to her. *Are you going to carry her around for the rest of her life? What about when you're gone? What then? Think about me. Think about your son. You have to put your family first.* Maybe her daughter wasn't that lucky.

"Hi, Mrs. Miller." Across the room, Grace waved to her.

Glad for the distraction, Florence crossed to the small girl, noting with a twinge of concern that Jane's bed was empty. "Good morning, dear. How are you?"

"Good." Grace wiggled in bed.

"Where's Janie?"

"A nurse took her somewhere. I think they went to therapy." She continued to wiggle. Her forehead creased with effort.

"Are you okay?"

"Well, I wanted to sit up … but …" Her eyes watered and she slumped back in bed.

"Let me help you." Turning the crank at the end of the bed, Florence elevated the head. Then, taking an extra pillow from Jane's bed, she slipped it behind the fragile girl, placed her hands under Grace's armpits and helped her into a more comfortable sitting position. Grace had been in the ward when Jane came, but wasn't progressing as well as her daughter.

"Thanks." Grace sniffed, then took a small toy from under the covers. It was one that Florence had brought weeks ago for Jane. "I'm happy that Janie gave me this. She's nice." She leaned her head closer to Florence and whispered, "Not like Linda." She motioned toward the sour-faced girl who had again taken up her spot near the window.

Florence cleared her throat, unsure of what to say. Howard might not like to know that Jane gave her toys away. She had so few now, and they hadn't even discussed what they were going to do about the hospital bills or the price of housing Jane somewhere else. Worry twisted Florence's stomach.

"My mom can't visit, so I like it when you come. Are you going to read to us today?"

She patted the bag and nodded. They had just started *Little House on the Prairie*. "When Jane's finished with therapy." She slid her hand into the bag, took out a wax paper bundle of cookies, and handed them to Grace. "I'll go check on her and be right back."

On the way out of the room, Florence deposited a similar package on Linda's lap.

She walked down the hall, passing the ward for the smaller children whose cribs lined the room. For a second, she peeked in. Many of the patients had balloons taped to their crib's headboard. A rosy-cheeked girl, with casts on her legs, swatted at her balloon. Florence didn't know whether to be encouraged by the sweet girl playing or upset by the sickness that had hurt her. When she reached the stairwell, she climbed slowly. Someone had opened a window, and crisp air replaced the stale odor of bed pans that permeated the hospital.

In the therapy room's corner, Jane sat in her wheelchair, watching a boy walk with crutches. Her daughter's face lit with wonder and excitement as her eyes followed the boy's slow, stiff-legged steps.

Florence crept up to Jane and tapped her shoulder.

Jane startled, then seeing her mother's face, she wrapped her arms around her. "I'm next. I hope I do as well as him."

"You will." She pushed a chair next to her and sat.

"Are you sure?" Jane fiddled with a buckle on her leg braces. "Linda says that everyone falls a lot when they learn to walk. She says I might never learn and I'll have to stay in a wheelchair for the rest of my life like her."

Florence smoothed her hair. "Linda doesn't know what she's talking about. You'll do great."

Jane gave her a weak smile and continued watching the boy. "If I don't learn to walk again …" She swallowed, then studied the floor.

"You'll learn." She held her hand and squeezed the thin palm.

"But if I don't," Jane raised her head. "Can I still come home?"

"Of course."

"Linda said that if you don't walk, you can't go home. She said she's going to live somewhere else."

Florence pushed the hair out of her daughter's face. "You'll come home, no matter what." But even as she said the words, she thought of the appointment at *the place*. She swallowed and tried to form words of reassurance for both of them, but a nurse settled the boy into the wheelchair, and the physiotherapist motioned to Jane.

Jane wheeled over to the parallel bars and waited while the physiotherapist made notes on a clipboard.

Florence approached them, but kept replaying Howard's words. Every conversation they had seemed to go in circles, both of them convinced they were right.

The physiotherapist helped Jane stand and showed her how to push the button on the side of the braces to lock them. "You need to sit back there if you want to watch," she said and gave

Florence a look that seemed to say, sorry, but rules are rules. She was another of Jane's favorites, who always thought of funny things to keep the patients entertained. Right now, her hair was in pigtails and dyed bright red. She'd overheard her telling another patient she used the same henna rinse actress Lucille Ball used, just more of it.

Florence returned to the chair. When the therapist leaned close and whispered to Jane, she laughed, and Florence relaxed.

The therapist handed Jane the Canadian crutches that had been measured and fitted for her. The walking sticks came to her elbows. She slipped her arms through the leather loops and grasped the wooden handles.

Her first steps were small, and Florence's insides tensed with excitement and worry. She leaned forward, eager to catch each stiff step. Her daughter's legs were thin and weak, but after all her work in the wheelchair, new muscles had formed in her arms and shoulders.

A sound of breaking glass startled Florence, and she whirled around to see a red-faced custodian cleaning up a mess of broken bottles. She was out of her seat to help when a cry made her turn around. The therapist held Jane.

Florence ran to her daughter.

The therapist helped Jane reposition the crutches. "Mrs. Miller, she's okay. You need to step outside while we finish."

"Janie?" Florence bent over them.

Jane's tears and labored breathing made Florence's heart ache. "I'm here, dear."

"Mrs. Miller, I need you to go into the hall." The therapist's voice was firm while she patted Jane's shoulder. With the other hand, she guided the nearby wheelchair over and let Jane sit down.

Another nurse came and escorted Florence from the room. Her head pounded with Jane's cries and Howard's words. When the door shut, the nurse's curt voice reached her. "You don't have the training to help with this kind of situation."

Florence slunk to the floor and leaned against the cool tile of the wall. Howard was right, she couldn't help her daughter. Maybe they would all be better if Jane went somewhere else.

Maybe Howard would change back to his old self. But what would she do with the hole in her heart, the one where her daughter lived?

The lifeless tree line and the highway seemed to stretch on forever. For the past hour, neither of them had spoken. Howard passed a salt truck, then cleared his throat and said, "It's pretty out here, isn't it? It'll be a pleasant drive when we visit."

Florence scowled and crossed her arms. Nothing looked nice this morning. Dirty snow lay in clumps on the side of the road. Even though they had driven out of the smog of the city and into the country, the gray sky and barren trees did nothing to lift her mood. A small brown sign read *Lakeside State Home, 5 miles.* Even the name made her stomach do somersaults and her head ache. A name didn't fool her. It wasn't a home, and the nearby lake meant nothing.

Howard glanced her way, but she pretended not to notice. He seemed softer today, and she wanted to beg him to change his mind, but she didn't want another argument. The words of Mildred's last letter burned in Florence's head. *I'll be praying, you'll reach a solution that will work for you all.* She'd grown sick of Mildred's letters. Her sister-in-law didn't seem to understand what she was going through.

"I think this is it." Turning at the next sign, Howard slowed and drove down a gravel drive, avoiding the large potholes. Someone had recently plowed the road. A tall mound of snow bordered an imposing three-story building.

As they neared the monstrosity, Florence gasped. "Howard, they have bars on the windows."

Howard cleared his throat and parked under the visitor sign. "I'm sure they're there for the safety of the patients."

She frowned at him.

"Let's just try it, Flo." He picked up his hat from the bench seat. He looked haggard and sad.

She sighed and opened the door, but then stopped to scrutinize movement from an upstairs window. For a moment, haunted eyes peeked from behind a curtain, then a large hand appeared and the curtain closed as quickly as it had opened. Her legs felt rubbery, and she feared they might fail her.

"What's wrong?" Howard followed her gaze.

She pointed to the window, but her mouth wouldn't work. Howard took her outstretched arm and led her toward the building. Above the wide front porch, *Lakeside State Home* was etched in stone. So far, she had spotted no lake.

The building reminded her of a medieval castle, with turrets on either side and round columns that flanked a tall door. Howard pushed it open with a grunt. The lobby was as dreary as the day outside. From the vaulted ceiling hung a light fixture with burned out bulbs. A musty odor wrapped around her. Once, this building had been grand.

"Someone should be here to greet us," he mumbled. "We have an appointment."

A cracked wooden sign hung above them, pointing toward the director's office. The hardwood floors creaked when they walked down the corridor. The sterile white walls reminded Florence of the hospital. When they rounded the corner, the office door stood ajar, and a well-groomed man greeted them.

"You must be the Millers." Dressed in a tailored suit, he offered a thin smile. He glanced at his watch. "You're not scheduled for another fifteen minutes."

Howard studied his bare wrist. He had forgotten his watch in the rush to make their appointment. "I'm sorry. I didn't realize. We didn't have any traffic."

The man pointed across the hall to a room filled with neat rows of chairs. "Why don't you wait here while I get everything ready?"

Florence and Howard had just stepped into the room when a burly man in a white uniform ran past them and toward two tall wooden doors. He withdrew a large ring of keys, unlocked the door, then opened it. A short scream punctuated the corridor's stillness. The door closed, and the sound stopped. The sign on the doors glared—*Do Not Enter*.

The director held up his hand. Florence wasn't sure if he meant to calm or stop them. She backed away and turned toward the doors.

"Ma'am, you can't go in there."

Florence pushed through the door. The hallway was identical to the one they'd walked through, except strange stains spotted the peeling paint. The scream repeated, followed by low murmurings that grew in intensity. She started toward the sound, driven to know exactly what kind of place would shelter Jane. Howard followed close behind. The musty smell grew, filling her mouth with the taste of something rotten.

"Mrs. Miller … Mr. Miller …"

The man called after them, but Florence heard nothing except for the unspoken scream that formed in her throat. In the hallway stood a line of young men, all dressed in white shirts and pants. Without making a sound, their shaved heads rocked back and forth. The murmurings came from further down the hall, where the screams had restarted.

"It'll quiet down soon. You're early." The man navigated in front of them while he pulled out a set of keys from his pocket. He put a hand on her shoulder.

Before Florence could shrug it off, Howard glared at him. "Don't touch my wife."

The screams increased as they fled the building.

Back in the car, Florence shut her eyes, trying to block out the sights and sounds, but the haunted eyes of the residents remained. She yearned to bathe and wash her mouth out. Anything to erase the experience. They drove for a while, the scenery passing in a blur. At the first diner they came to, Howard stopped. It wasn't until the waitress had left two steaming cups in front of them that Florence spoke. "She can't go there."

"You're right. She can't." His eyes filled with tears. He sniffed, held a paper napkin to his eyes, and sipped his coffee. "I don't want her to have the life I had."

Florence stared at him, puzzled.

"I can't stand the thought of her being teased and made to feel less than everyone else. I wanted her to have a good life. Then, when the teasing started with William, I thought if she went somewhere else …" He rotated his coffee cup, avoiding her eyes. "I've always tried to provide for the family, but I realize I've failed all of you."

She wanted to encourage him and ask him questions, but she'd learned from her time with William that sometimes just listening worked best. She sipped her coffee.

"Remember how they teased me at school?"

"No." She'd thought he was the star of their school and assumed everyone else thought the same. Her childhood infatuation had always colored her view of him.

"After my accident."

The memories cascaded back. He had fallen from the barn loft and had missed some school toward the end of his senior year. "You were what, eighteen? A senior?"

"Twelfth grade. Seventeen, almost eighteen. The months I was out, I couldn't do farm work. Nothing except having my sister wait on me. Mom was sick too. And Dad grumbled all day about how he had to run the household."

She recalled the dark circles under Mildred's eyes, but she'd been so busy with schoolwork, helping her dad in the grocery store, and keeping up with the household chores that she had little energy for her best friend. She'd also tried to forget her crush on Howard and dated a lanky boy in her own grade. By the time Howard returned to classes, his mother had died. At school he limped, remained quiet, avoided his usual crowd, and never engaged in pranks or sports. But that made no difference to her. Limp or no limp, she'd always been drawn to him.

Howard picked up the spoon next to his coffee cup and stirred the black liquid. "Life was different after that. I couldn't play sports for the rest of the year, and I had to wear a back brace for a while. The fellas called it my corset. Though that wasn't the worst part. Dad had always been strict and demanding, but when Mom died, and I injured myself, he became mean."

He didn't need to say anything else. Florence remembered the frosty night a couple of years after his accident when they began dating. She'd spent the night with Mildred, like she often did. She'd slipped downstairs for a glass of water when she caught sight of Howard outside. Putting on Mildred's heavy coat and her boots, she trudged out into the winter night.

Howard threw a snowball against the barn with a satisfying whack. Not seeing her, he reached down and made another one. Stepping closer to him, the snow crunched. He whirled around, the snowball aimed at her.

"Don't shoot. It's just me," Florence said in a teasing tone.

"Sorry." He hurled the ball, hitting the same place as before.

In the light from the barn, she could tell he was mad. His jaw clenched and his shoulders tensed. "What's wrong?"

"Nothing." Again, he lobbed another snowball at the barn. This one off by a few inches.

"I don't believe you." She scooped some snow and threw it. It missed the mark.

"You need to wind up. Let me show you." He made another snowball. Winding up, he threw it, hitting the same spot as before. He grinned at her. "You try."

She mimicked his actions and hit the barn with a loud thud. She jumped up and down, clapping. He laughed, but then, catching sight of her red hands, he clasped them in his gloved fingers. "Where are your mittens?"

Despite the snow, warmth traveled up her spine. Their eyes met. His shoulders relaxed. A smile replaced his former scowl. For the first time, he had seen her as more than Mildred's friend.

Dropping her hands quickly, he coughed. "I know where my sister keeps the cocoa."

They went inside, his limp hardly noticeable. She scalded the milk while he found the cocoa and sugar. Mildred had hidden them in the back of the cupboard.

"Why did she hide them?" Florence asked as she measured the ingredients.

Howard shrugged, his face red from either embarrassment or the cold. "I don't know. I guess she thinks Dad or I'll eat them up. But neither of us knows how to cook."

Florence poured the hot liquid into the mugs. "I could teach you."

He carried the drinks into the living room, where they settled on the couch next to the fireplace. He handed her a mug and sipped his. "I'm not sure anything would taste as good as your cooking."

"What were you doing outside? You seemed so mad." As soon as she spoke, she regretted prying. "I'm sorry, Howard. You don't have to answer if you don't want to."

He gave her a sad smile. "It's okay. I don't mind telling you. I hate him."

She knew who he was talking about. She'd heard the way his father ordered him around and called him names. Every time he called Howard crippled, she cringed. But since Mr. Miller ignored her, she preferred that to her silent father and the family pictures that reminded them of what they'd lost hanging everywhere. Besides, Howard and his father spent most of their time outside tending to the farm's business, not bothering her and Mildred.

"Nothing I do is ever right. He thinks that because I had one injury, I'm not good enough." His eyes blazed with fire. He set his mug on an end table, then rubbed his palms up and down his pant legs.

She leaned closer, not wanting to miss anything he said. The warm fire and his hands so close to hers made her head spin.

"I'm going to show him. I'm getting away from this town. I'll have more money than he's ever dreamed of." He set his cup on the side table and grabbed her free hand. "I'm going to the city to make something of myself." He took her hand and squeezed.

When he looked into her eyes, she wanted to kiss him and for a moment she thought he might kiss her, but he dropped her hand and looked down at the shadows the fire made on the floor. "It'd be nice … if I … had someone to … take to the city with me." When he raised his head, his eyes looked different. Still full of fire, but a different one.

Uncertain what to say, she sipped her hot cocoa.

He reached out and grabbed her hand once more. "Do you think you'd like the city?"

She nodded, very aware of his large hand covering hers and his face inches away from hers.

Outside, an owl hooted. He squeezed her hand again before letting go. "I better take care of this fire before I go to bed. I'm still a farmer and farmers have to get up early."

She slipped back into the bed she shared with Mildred, still thinking of his serious face shining by the firelight. Now the diner light illuminated his face. The hopeful, defiant youth had dissolved into a man who seemed adrift, robbed of all his dreams.

This time, she grabbed his hands. "Your dad was wrong. Your injury didn't define you. You've always been hardworking and determined. You're a wonderful person. The man I fell in love with." She stroked his long fingers. "Jane's sickness doesn't define her either. We can stick up for her and fight for her, just like your father should have fought for you."

He nodded, and a hesitant smile filled his face. When their lips met over the cups of cold coffee, Florence wondered if her Howard had returned to her.

Chapter 12

Burrowing deep under the warm covers, Florence slowly opened her eyes to her floral wallpaper, a pattern she'd chosen because it reminded her of her mother's love of flowers. Contented, she imagined she was sleeping in a garden oasis.

For the last month and a half, her routine had returned to normal. Or at least as normal as life could be with a child in the hospital. Jane had grown stronger and was walking fairly well with braces and crutches. The physiotherapists had even taught her how to fall without hurting herself. William had continued his cooking lessons and working at Schmidt's hardware store. And she felt as close to Howard as she had during their first days of marriage.

She rolled over, eager to snuggle into her husband's warmth, but his side of the bed was empty. Strange, when Howard didn't work on Saturdays, they usually slept in. The sound of hammering startled her.

She rose, wrapping her robe around her. They'd cracked the window last night, and the room was frosty. Parting the curtains, she looked down at the yard below. William and Howard talked in low tones and pointed. Tools littered the surrounding space. A large hammer lay at William's feet. Howard stretched out a tape measure and gestured to the porch. What were they doing?

Shutting the window, then quickly dressing, Florence tried to remember when the two had last spent time together without yelling and shouting. Before Jane's sickness, they were always doing a woodworking project or playing catch. She buttoned a cardigan sweater over her dress, picturing Jane's tiny figure tagging along with her two favorite guys, helping and chatting. The glue that held the family together.

On her way downstairs, William flashed by, his cheeks red and chapped from the cold. "Good morning, Mom. Dad wants me to get my hat and gloves."

"Wait, Willie—" His bedroom door slammed.

Florence stared in confusion, then descended to the open front door.

Outside, Howard stored the last tool and placed the toolbox on the porch. He dug a piece of paper from his pocket and studied it, his eyebrows knit together in concentration.

She left the house's warmth for the Michigan chill and joined him on the porch. "What's wrong?" She shivered, poorly clad for the temperature. Spring would come soon, but mornings were still frigid. Gray piles of snow littered the sidewalk.

"Where's your coat?" Folding the paper, he rubbed her arms, then embraced her. "Let's get you inside where there's heat."

He closed the front door, kissed her again, then led the way into the kitchen.

"Why are you up so early?"

He poured them each a cup of coffee from the percolator and got the milk from the refrigerator. After adding some to her cup, he handed it to her, then joined her at the table. "I saw Jane yesterday."

"Jane?"

"Yes." He smiled into his cup, then took her hand.

His touch warmed her more than the coffee. How could she have doubted him? He'd been a doting father from the beginning. Jane was his princess. Why had she feared he'd abandon her or their daughter? Then a strange thought occurred to her. "But Friday isn't a visitation day."

"I charmed my way in." He winked and released her hand.

Something inside her shifted. *He charmed his way in.* What did that mean? He'd never used that phrase before.

"I should have gone sooner. She's so strong, just like you." He sipped his coffee. "She's stubborn too. I wonder who she gets that from."

Pushing aside her doubts, she drank her creamy coffee and enjoyed studying him. He was so relaxed, and she hadn't seen him like this since, well, since before.

"Are you ready, Dad?" William smashed his hat on, zipped his coat, and grinned at them.

"Where are you going?"

"Didn't Dad tell you?" His eyes sparkled. "We're—"

Howard put his finger to his lips and pointed at the door. "Get the keys, Willie. Warm the car up and I'll be out once I've finished my coffee."

When the door banged shut, he took a long sip from his mug. She tapped her foot, wondering what he could be doing.

He grinned like he had when he first asked her to dance all those years ago. "We're building a ramp. I have to get the wood." He drank the rest of his coffee and set the mug in the sink.

Speechless, she stared.

He kissed her forehead. "How else can our daughter get into the house?"

"What?"

The grin stayed plastered on his face. "I saw the doctor when I visited Jane. She's coming home right before Easter. We have to be ready."

She remained speechless, full of happy uncertainty and disbelief.

He leaned down and whispered. "Our girl is coming home. Our strong, stubborn girl is going to be okay, and so are we."

After Howard left, Florence studied her leftover coffee. Could it be true? She let the good news repeat in her head. A bubble of excitement and happiness started inside her and grew. Jane was coming home. The family wasn't falling apart. Everything would be okay.

She searched the pantry and got the ingredients for cupcakes. It was time to celebrate. Jane would be home in … she checked the calendar on the pantry wall. Easter would be in a couple of weeks. Maybe they'd go to church. When they were first married, they'd gone because Mildred had guilted them into it. But they never attended regularly, and they'd stopped when Jane was small. After all, church attendance never seemed to make a difference in their lives. But now, maybe she'd give it another try. Her mother had always made her go as a child. Taking a piece of paper from the drawer, she began her shopping list. Flour. They didn't have enough for the cupcakes. What else should she buy for Jane's Easter homecoming celebration?

The doorbell sounded. She put the pen and paper down, still considering what she'd need. Menu ideas filled her mind as she opened the door.

"Good morning." Olive wore a hesitant smile and clutched a large paper sack. A handbag rested in the crook of her other arm.

The wind blew into the entryway and Florence shivered. "Come in. It's cold. Let me get that for you." She took the bag, which was stuffed with clothes, and placed it on the kitchen table.

Olive set her handbag next to it.

Florence noted with a twinge of jealousy that the handbag was new, as were Olive's shoes. But she pushed the thought away. That didn't matter. Jane would be home soon, and life would fall into place. Once they paid the hospital bills, there would be money for new things.

"How about coffee?" Florence asked. "I think there's some left."

Olive situated herself at the table. "Yes, please. I looked at the calendar and thought spring was coming, but it's still freezing."

Florence added milk and sugar, just the way Olive liked it. Then she refilled her mug and joined her at the table.

Olive sipped her coffee and motioned to the bag. "Alice has a lot of winter clothes she's grown out of. I thought Jane might…" She stopped talking and glanced down at the floor. "I'm sorry. I know she's not—"

"It's okay. She's coming home."

"That's wonderful. When?"

"In a couple of weeks."

"Oh, I'm so glad." She pulled the first garment out of the bag, a light blue dress edged with lace.

"It's beautiful! Thank you so much. That will be perfect for Easter."

Olive continued to pull dresses, tops, and skirts from the bag. Many of them appeared new. "Her grandparents always buy her clothes and she can't wear them all. I hope they fit."

"They look like they will." A tear glinted in her eye when she envisioned her petite daughter in the clothes. Jane never minded wearing Alice's hand-me-downs and with all the bills, they would be a big help.

Olive refolded the clothes and put them back in the bag. When she reached for the last garment, she sniffed and shifted in her seat.

Florence looked at her with concern. "Are you okay? If you don't want to give Alice's clothes away, that's all right. I still have a few of the kids' baby clothes tucked away and I couldn't bear to part with William's blue suit from his—"

Olive placed her hand on Florence's and shook her head. "It's not about the clothes." She pushed the sack to the back of the table, meeting her friend's gaze. "I … I wanted to tell you …"

Florence looked at her in confusion. Her heart thudded, and dread settled over her. "What is it?"

"There've been rumors." She drank from her mug, then cleared her throat. "I was sure they were rumors, but I saw..." She bent down and brushed a nonexistent speck from her nylon.

"Yes?"

"Well, I heard people saying and then I saw …" Olive crossed and uncrossed her legs.

Florence shot her a confused glance. This woman was maddening. "Just say it."

Olive stared at the floor and blurted out the words. "I saw Howard kissing another woman."

Everything in the room stopped. The clock stopped ticking. The wind outside stopped howling and her heart stopped beating. "No."

"I'm sorry, Flo. I thought they were just rumors. That's why I didn't say anything before. But when the delivery boy was out sick, I had to take some bread to a restaurant. That's when I saw him."

Time started once again. The clock ticking. The wind howling and her heart beating a rhythm in her ears. "Who was it?"

"I don't know." Olive chewed her lip, then she ran her hand over the paper sack, reminding her of how Howard used to caress her hand absentmindedly. When had he stopped doing that, and why hadn't she noticed?

"No." Olive had shunned her. She hadn't returned her calls. She ignored Florence when she greeted her at the grocery store. "It can't be true." Things had been so much better.

"It is."

She met her friend's eyes, and hated what she saw—pity. If anyone dared to make eye contact after the polio, it was the same look and she couldn't stand it. "You're jealous. Jealous, I have a loving husband and you don't. You're trying to break up my marriage so you can grab my leftovers. But you can't have him." She picked up the bag and shoved it into Olive's arms. "Get out of my house."

She opened the door without meeting Olive's eyes. "Go." Her voice was as icy as the wind outside. A light drizzle started as Olive descended the steps and walked down the street.

The house was warm and cozy. Florence poured the last of the coffee. It was hot in her hands, but inside she felt cold. She remembered Howard's comment about charming his way into the hospital ward, then the nights out with the fellas, the strange outing at the hardware store. Then she thought about Olive's familiar ways with men. What if Olive wasn't lying? What if he really was having an affair with Olive or someone else?

Chapter 13

Florence rested her cheek on the cold window and watched the snowflakes coat the outside. Before, the snow would have discouraged her. It was early April, after all. But now, the clean whiteness excited her. Nothing could ruin today.

Jane sat in her wheelchair talking to Grace. Florence crossed the room to them and asked Howard. "Do you have everything?"

He pulled back the cover on Jane's bed and scanned the floor. He handed the overflowing bag of Jane's possessions to Florence. "Yep, I think we do."

"I wish I could go with you," Grace sobbed as she squeezed Jane's hand.

Florence wished she could take Grace home, but it wasn't feasible. "Howard, check the bedside table."

While he opened the cupboard and peered behind it, Florence took a coloring book from her purse, handed it to Grace, and kissed the top of the girl's head. "Jane will write to you."

The two friends hugged.

"Are you ready, princess?" While Jane nodded, Howard pushed her across the room.

Jane waved to Grace, then to the other patients, who waved and cheered. Even Linda, who held her coloring book, managed a quiet, "Goodbye." With her crutches tucked next to her, Jane sat straight in her wheelchair, dressed in a new winter coat. Florence had combed her hair and put it into a ponytail, accenting it with a bright red hair ribbon. When they entered the hall, a group of nurses gathered.

Harriet stepped forward and draped a crocheted blanket over Jane's lap, then kissed her head and sniffled. "Just a little parting gift from all of us."

"Thank you. I like all the colors," Jane said. Then she stood.

"You don't have to get up, dear. Daddy's going to push you outside." Florence remembered that Howard had salted the walk and retested the new ramp this morning. With the fresh snowfall, everything would be slippery.

Jane handed the blanket to her father, locked her braces, and positioned her crutches. "I'm going to walk."

Mizie wedged herself between Florence and Jane. "Mr. Miller, why don't you pull your car up front? Mrs. Miller and I will be here if Jane needs any extra help. But I don't think she will."

In amazement, Florence watched Howard snap to attention and obey the nurse, striding with purpose to the exit. Mizie walked next to Jane, her arms extended in case of a fall. Then the gruff nurse called back to Florence, "Are you coming?"

Harriet had wheeled the wheelchair away, and the other nurses had resumed their duties. Florence followed Mizie and Jane, who were already halfway down the hall. When they reached the exit, Mizie opened the door so Jane could step through.

Jane lifted her face to the gray sky.

Mizie, still smelling of cabbage, whispered to Florence. "I know I can be stern. But …" She coughed and readjusted her glasses. "So many don't get to walk out."

Florence had never been this close to the woman before. Lines crisscrossed the face, tracing the years she'd lived, the hardships she'd witnessed. How much of this woman's story had Florence never even guessed at?

"Mama, taste the snowflakes." Jane stood in the middle of the sidewalk. Her tongue stretched out. Her face gleamed with melted snow and joy.

Florence smiled at her, then turned to say goodbye to the nurse, but Mizie was gone.

"You ladies are going to freeze." Their car was parked at the curb. The front door opened. Howard smashed his hat on, then moved to carry Jane, but she swatted him away.

"I'm almost there." Once she got to the car, she handed him the sticks, then scooted onto the bench seat.

Florence joined her and they huddled close, rubbing their hands together, glad for the car's heater.

When Howard scooted back into the car and they drove away, Florence stifled a yawn. They'd awoken early, and she'd instructed William to warm the soup and finish preparing the simple meal for Jane's homecoming.

Jane snuggled into her side and pointed. "It's a winter wonderland, Mama. That tree is covered in white. She looks like a dainty lady."

Howard grinned at his princess and patted her thin leg. "You'd think you'd never seen snow before."

"It's just so pretty." Jane yawned and fought to keep her eyes open.

Howard winked at Florence and his hand intertwined with hers.

Jane giggled at the joined hands on her lap. "Daddy, you have a gigantic hand, just like Pa's in the *Little House in the Big Woods*. Do you think any of these trees have maple syrup, like the ones in that book?" Without looking at them for an answer, she closed her eyes. Within minutes, she snored softly.

Howard put both hands on the wheel, but Florence could still feel the warmth as she shifted her arm to encircle Jane's shoulder. She had pushed Olive's accusations to the back of her mind, not even mentioning them to Mildred when she'd placed the brief call to tell her about Jane's homecoming. Howard was more attentive now. There were no signs he was seeing another woman behind her back. Olive was trying to stir up trouble. Hadn't she heard other mothers at the PTA complain about Olive being a troublemaker?

She tried to banish her worries. "There's been so much excitement this morning. I'm sure she's worn out. Hopefully, she won't be too tired for her surprises or lunch. Maybe you could carry her into the house. I don't like this snow."

Howard winked at her. "It's beautiful out here, just like you."

She marveled at the change in him over the last few weeks. Mostly, he'd stopped the card games and bowling. When he came home, he didn't seem as on edge. Now, with Jane's return, everything would be all right.

"Do you remember our first snow?"

Puzzled, she studied him and the sly smile plastered on his face. "When I made you hot cocoa, and you held my hand?"

"That was memorable. But that's not what I'm talking about. It was the first time I noticed you and noticed how beautiful you were."

Jane wiggled and Florence whispered, "What are you talking about?"

"Surely, you remember." He stopped at an intersection and waited for his turn to go. "I was about fourteen, so you would have been around twelve."

She shook her head. She didn't know what he was talking about but remembered what had happened that year.

"It was January and so cold. I'd had a fight with Dad, and I had gone on a walk to get away from him. You were in your front yard."

Then she remembered. In the moonlight, new snow sparkled on the barren fields. But she'd seen nothing and felt nothing. Numbness seeped into her toes. Kicking the snow, she paced the lawn. Walking, but going nowhere.

"Are you okay?"

She had startled at the words and poised herself to flee, but as he leaned against the fence his familiar voice and form registered. "What are you doing out here?"

"Just out for a walk. Wanna join me?"

Without responding, she continued pacing and kicking the snow.

"Why don't we build a snowman instead?"

Again, she said nothing. He bent and began forming the base. Soon, she started on the middle section. By the time they had finished the small, lopsided snowman, the cold seeped into her extremities. It felt good to feel something.

They made their way to the barn and sat down on a hay bale. The heat from the cows and horses warmed her cold insides.

"Mom died yesterday," she said.

He nodded. "I heard. I'm sorry."

"She made me promise …"

Howard scooted closer and put his arm around her.

"She said to me, Flo, it's your job to keep our family together. Promise me you'll do it?" Florence sniffed. "I said yes, then she was gone." She cried into his chest and whispered, "I can't do it."

In the warm barn, a horse snorted and Howard held her closer. "I'll do what I can to help you. I promise."

Jane shifted in her sleep and mumbled. Glad that she was no longer a twelve-year-old girl, Florence pushed a stray hair from Jane's forehead, relishing the sound of the even breathing that reminded her of the animal's breathing in the barn. "I always thought you considered me like a little sister," she said. They'd been in school together since she entered first grade, and she had been friends with his sister since they were toddlers.

Howard laughed. He smiled warmly. "I did. At first. You were like a pesky little sister. But after that night, I realized what a strong woman you were turning into. And still are." He turned onto their street.

"You didn't make a move. You didn't say anything." For years, she waited and hoped for a date with him.

He drove slowly in the slushy snow, passing Olive's house. "I was foolish. I should have, but it was weird with you and Mildred being friends, and I convinced myself you didn't feel the same way. And, you know, my life was complicated."

Complicated. She knew about complicated. "I didn't keep my word to my mother." A month after her mother's death, her sister Hattie passed away. Florence had been unable to save her, unable to keep her family together.

"You tried. It isn't your fault that Hattie died." He caressed the hand that was draped over Jane's shoulder. "You were a child, and you did the job of a woman after your mom died. You've proved that you can do anything you set your mind to."

He pulled into their driveway and put the car into park, then he reached across their sleeping daughter and kissed her. "You're strong and stubborn, just like our girl."

Florence wanted to lean in for another kiss, but there was a tapping on the car window and the door flew open.

"Janie," William leaned into the car.

Jane sat up and yawned, then saw her brother. "Willie. You have to see me walk."

Florence got out of the car while Howard retrieved the crutches from the trunk. She lovingly dusted off William's coat where he'd rubbed up against the dirty car.

Jane scooted to the edge of the car seat. Pulling her skirt up a bit, she said, "I have to lock my braces first." She showed her brother the shiny braces she had put on over thick white knee socks.

"I'll carry you in this time." Howard handed William the crutches. "You don't want to overexert yourself."

Scrunching up her nose, Jane scowled at her father. "No, Daddy. I can do it. Plus, Willie wants to see. Don't you?" She held her hand out to her brother and looked up at him hopefully.

Shuffling his feet, he handed her the crutches. "Uh… well… I guess so."

Before Howard could argue, Jane had risen on her crutches and was walking toward the door. William rushed ahead. "Wow, that's great. You're fast."

Even though William had shoveled the walk again, Florence hovered nearby, hoping that there wasn't any black ice.

At the ramp, Jane stopped. "Where did this come from?"

Howard beamed. "Your brother and I made it."

"It's nice. I practiced going up curbs and on stairs at the hospital, but I can do this too."

Florence studied her daughter, who seemed so skinny and frail despite all the layers of clothes she wore. "Dad can carry you if you need him to. Are you sure you're okay, honey?"

Jane sighed. "Yes, Mama."

"Wait until you see your surprise." William held the door open. "You won't believe it."

Chewing on her lower lip, Jane navigated the ramp. Crutch, crutch, step. Crutch, crutch step. Concerned, Florence opened her mouth, but Howard nudged her and shook his head.

When she stepped through the doorway into the living room, Jane gasped. In the corner stood a tall Christmas tree. The bubble lights illuminated the tinsel and brightly colored glass ornaments. The tree had been Howard's idea. He and William had driven out to the country to find the perfect one.

"But Christmas was a long time ago, and it's not time for next Christmas yet." Jane seemed to sway in her excitement. William led her to the couch. She released the button on her braces and sat down with a grunt. "I can't believe it."

"You weren't home in December. We didn't want you to miss anything." Her brother engulfed her in a hug, then jumped up from the couch. "But there's one more surprise. Wait and see."

When William left, Howard put a record on and the soft strains of Bing Crosby singing "White Christmas" serenaded them. He sat next to his daughter. "How do you like the tree?"

"It's just perfect, Daddy. The best one we've ever had." She hugged him.

Florence studied the happy, content pair.

"Look at this." William held the doll out to his sister and beamed.

At first, she said nothing. She stared at the doll. Then William placed it in her lap and she sobbed. He sat down next to her. "You're not supposed to cry."

She sniffed and squeezed the doll. "It's just like baby Jesus. Thank you, Willie. Jesus kept me safe when I had polio and now, he's brought me home. I'm so happy."

Florence let her daughter's belief sink into her and soften her heart. Jesus had kept Jane safe and now her family was together. To hide her tears of joy, she gathered up Howard and Jane's coats and took off hers. Wreathed in the pine scent of the tree, she opened the coat closet and hung them up. Then a splash of color caught her eye. On the lapel of Howard's dark gray overcoat was a stain. A red stain. Blood? Had Howard cut himself shaving?

Using her fingernail, she tried to remove the blemish from the scratchy wool. It wasn't blood. From all of William's cuts and scrapes, she knew it wasn't blood. The texture and color were different. What could it be? Paint? Had he been painting in his nice coat? Then, a lead weight inside. She shut the door, with the truth ringing in her ears.

The stain was red lipstick. She only wore pink.

Chapter 14

Florence finished Jane's exercises, then began massaging her leg. Jane crossed her arms and frowned. "Why can't I have my old room back?"

"We've had this conversation every day since you've been home. I don't understand why you don't like the den. Willie and I fixed it up just for you."

Before she'd had her latest falling out with Olive, they had found secondhand bedding and some new toys for the room. William had helped her cart out Howard's desk and framed awards. They'd painted the walls pink, just like her old room. She'd bought a new frame for the picture of Jesus, even though she hadn't wanted to. He'd never helped her.

Florence continued massaging the withered leg while Jane glared at her. "It's not the same. I want to be upstairs."

"I know you can do the stairs, dear. But this way, you only need to go up to use the bathroom." Even though Jane managed the stairs well, refusing to let anyone help, Florence could tell that the exertion wore her out.

Jane narrowed her eyes. "You're being mean to me."

She took a deep breath and exhaled all the words she wanted to speak in reply. "Hold still, dear. I need to finish this massage. It'll help you." She tried not to take Jane's harsh words personally. The nurse had assured her the excitement of her homecoming and Easter would give way to moodiness, pain, and fatigue until Jane's endurance returned to normal. The negative emotions should subside, eventually. Florence hoped it would be soon.

"Why did you have to burn my toys? They didn't do anything bad." From the bedside table, Jane took the doll that William had gotten her.

"We told you before. Dad had to burn them to get rid of the polio germs. We didn't want anyone else to get sick." Florence winced, remembering the ashes and the acrid smell.

Jane squeezed the doll tighter. "I hate polio. And I hate this room. I want my old room." Tears cascaded down her face.

Florence climbed into the bed and held her while she sobbed. She smoothed her hair. She'd hoped life would return to normal, but polio proved to be a beast that still held them in its clutches. "Why don't we put on your braces and enjoy the fresh air? The snow's melted and the sun is shining."

Gripping her doll tighter, she shook her head. "Can't I practice my walking later? I'm too tired. I want to take a nap."

"Okay, but just for a little while. I need you to help me with the cookies after lunch."

Jane wiped her eyes and smiled. "Chocolate chip?"

Glad her daughter still loved to help her bake, Florence nodded. She tucked her in, then turned out the light. Blowing her a kiss, she left the room feeling tears in her own eyes. Every morning, Jane helped her mom fix breakfast for Howard and William. After they left for work and school, she made her bed and dressed for the day before massage and exercise time. The morning routine wore Jane out, but she usually took her nap after lunch and always looked forward to her outside walk.

This morning Jane had been extra irritable. Since it was Saturday, William kept chattering on about playing ball with Charlie. The more he talked, the more she scowled.

On the way to the pantry to check for chocolate chips, Florence spotted the table full of dirty dishes. She'd been too tired to clear it. William had left the mail on the edge of the table. She'd already hidden the letter from Iowa. Later, she'd put in her box upstairs. An envelope from the March of Dimes caught her attention. She slit it open and read the letter. Giddy excitement filled her. The organization had agreed to pay for most of Jane's hospital expenses. Florence couldn't believe it. Pulling out a chair, she sat and let the good news fill her. On the clean tablecloth, a glob of strawberry jelly caught her eye. The dark feeling that had settled on her since finding the lipstick returned. Bills were the least of her worries.

From the stack of mail, she picked up an already opened envelope. Florence had tried to read an excerpt from Mildred's letter to lighten the breakfast mood, but William had dropped his plate. Jane had hobbled from the room, crying. Then, Howard had slammed the door shut without a goodbye to anyone.

Mildred had sent a family photograph with the letter. Now the snapshot lay in the middle of the table, surrounded by the dirty dishes. Instead of cleaning, Florence collapsed into the chair and picked up the picture. A photographer had taken it during last fall's Iowa state fair, with everyone in their Sunday best. Her niece, Peggy, clad in a floral dress, stood between her parents on long, straight legs. All three wore bright smiles. What was their secret? She scanned the letter. The humorous anecdotes and news made her frown. Why was their life so easy, so happy? Jane had been home for almost a month, and it seemed as if everyone in her family was falling further and further apart. Hopefully, the news of the paid hospital bills would lift everyone's spirit.

The doorbell rang.

Florence smoothed her hair and opened the door.

Olive stood behind three girls on the front porch. The tallest one, her daughter, Alice, asked, "Mrs. Miller, we were wondering if Jane can play?"

Olive patted her daughter's shoulder. "We can come back another time if Jane's not up to it."

She wanted to send them away. Jane needed her rest, and Florence didn't want to talk to anyone, especially not Olive, but Jane had been so lonely. This visit might be what her daughter needed, and maybe what she needed too. "Come in." She motioned to the couch. "Sit down and I'll get her."

When she switched on the bedroom light, Jane sat up and opened her mouth to complain, but Florence put a finger to her lips. "Shh! You have company."

"Company?" Her eyebrows rose, and a frown formed. "The doctor?"

"No. Alice and the Thomas girls."

Jane's eyes sparkled, and she reached for her braces. "I'm going to show them my doll. Can we have some of the Kool-Aid you just made?"

"Of course. Are you sure you're not too tired?" Florence got a fresh pair of long wool socks from the dresser.

"No, Mama." In record time, she slid on the socks and braces.

Florence gathered her matted hair into a ponytail. "I'll get your doll."

"I've got it." Holding on to the bed for support, she lifted a bag from the floor and stuffed her doll and other toys in it. Standing, she grinned with fresh energy and put her arms through the loops of the crutches. "I'm ready."

When she entered the living room, the three girls stared. Olive nudged Alice, who said, "We can play paper dolls on the couch, if that's okay with your mother." She held out a box.

Without a trace of her former moodiness, Jane held up the bag. "I wanted to show you my new doll, and we can swing."

"You can do that?" The smaller Thomas girl said. Her older sister squeezed her elbow, and she yelped.

Jane giggled. "Yes, but I can't jump off."

Florence helped Jane into her coat while the other girls got theirs.

Alice whispered to Jane. "You must be strong to walk with those crutches."

Florence overheard Jane's low reply. "I almost beat Willie in arm wrestling."

Olive, seated on the couch, asked, "Can I fix us some tea?"

Florence turned from watching the girls in the side yard. She'd forgotten Olive was still there.

"I wanted to apologize, Flo. Somehow I keep messing up and I'm sorry. I'm sure I was mistaken about Howard."

A breeze through the open door blew a stray leaf that had come in on the bottom of someone's shoe. Florence picked up the dead leaf, tossed it out, and shut the door.

"I'll get the tea," she said, but when they entered the kitchen, she saw the mess. "I'm sorry. I haven't had time to clean yet."

"Don't worry about it. Let me help you." Olive ran hot, soapy water.

Florence moved dishes from the table to the sink. At the sight of her mother's chipped bowl, she swallowed a lump in her throat. "You can't do that. It's my job."

Olive fixed her with a firm grin. "You've got a lot to worry about. You're taking care of that little girl and the rest of your family. It's the least I can do. Now bring those dishes over, and we'll finish them in no time."

Florence stared at the woman in her kitchen, washing her dishes, doing her work, and she sobbed. Her family was falling apart, and it was all her fault.

Dropping the dishrag into the sink, Olive embraced her. "Oh, honey. It's okay. You're tired. Let's go sit down."

Florence let her lead her to the couch, embarrassed that she couldn't stop crying. "I'm so sorry for the mean things I said to you. You were right. There is another woman. I found her lipstick on his coat."

"Don't apologize. You did nothing wrong, and I know this must be hard for you. Did he tell you?"

She shook her head. "He didn't have to."

"Have you confronted him?"

"I wanted to, but he seemed so happy and content after Jane came home. I thought that had fixed everything. He was so attentive and came home after work every day. Then yesterday, he stumbled home late. This morning he didn't even lie about having to work. He just left. I don't know what to do."

Olive patted her hand and leaned back on the couch. "Chester had a girlfriend once."

"What did you do?"

"I gave him some extra attention, and he eventually dropped her."

"What do you mean?"

"Fix him his favorite meal. Doll yourself up. Rouge, mascara, the works. Be available." She gave her a knowing wink.

Florence sighed. "I wish I could, but I'm so tired after helping Jane and doing the usual chores. I don't have time or energy for anything else."

"Let me help." Olive beamed. "Tomorrow, we'll fix this problem, and he won't have eyes for another woman. Trust me."

Florence gazed into the hallway mirror. The red lips and made-up eyes startled her. Her face seemed to belong to another woman, someone younger and less tired. She smiled at her reflection and patted her blond curls. Olive said she looked just like Elizabeth Taylor and Howard wouldn't be able to resist. She wasn't sure she looked like a movie star, but her appearance had definitely improved. This night *had* to fix their marriage.

The front door opened and a hesitant voice called out, "Hello?"

With his coat in his hand, Howard stared at the spotless living room. While the children played that morning, Olive had helped her clean and cook dinner.

"The house looks great." Then he caught sight of her. "Wow, you look …"

She wore a long black pencil skirt, a white blouse, and her wedding pearls. Per Olive's instruction, she'd left the top three buttons undone, showing off more than normal.

Howard moved closer. For an instant, a grin spread on his face, but then it was gone, replaced with a frown. "Why are you dressed like that?"

She stared at him, speechless. Heat rose in her cheeks.

"And where did you get that makeup? You know we don't have money to spend on frivolous stuff like that." He took his coat off and hung it in the closet.

"I did it for you. I was trying to look pretty. For you." Tamping down her anger and confusion, she grabbed his hand, but he shook her off.

"You are beautiful. You don't need makeup." His eyes darted around the living room, but didn't seem to focus on anything. "Even though the March of Dimes is covering most of Jane's hospital stay, we still have more expenses. Then there's the surgery that the doctors want to do next year. We can't afford new clothes and cosmetics."

"They're Olive's. The makeup and clothes are hers." She fiddled with the collar, suddenly feeling exposed.

He grunted. "Well, it figures that she would have an outfit like that." He glanced down the hallway. "Is Jane in her room?"

"She's at the O'Malley's. So is William."

He raised his eyebrows. "They're both there. Why?"

"Olive's babysitting them, so we could have some time together, just the two of us. They wanted to watch *I Love Lucy*."

"I guess our house isn't good enough for them, since we can't afford a television." He paced, then returned to the couch.

She sat next to him. The evening wasn't turning out how it was supposed to. Olive told her it would be easy once he found the clean, empty house, and she greeted him with a passionate kiss. But she hadn't been able to get near enough to give him any kind of kiss.

"Our house is fine. She's doing us a favor." Running her hand down his leg, she leaned in close. When her red lips were inches from his face, he took her hand away.

"Flo, I can't." He got the throw pillow from behind him and held it on his lap, a buffer between them.

"What's wrong with me, Howard? Am I that repulsive?" She studied her outfit. The skirt was tighter than it had been on Olive. She had put on a few pounds since they'd married, but so had he. Where was the attraction, the friendship that had once fueled their relationship?

"I'm not sure I can do this. I think it'd be better if we spent some time apart. I need time to think. Maybe this marriage was a mistake." Arching his back as if in pain, he studied the pillow, his long fingers raking through the fringe.

Florence gently took the pillow, wanting to make eye contact, wanting to fix whatever had broken. They used to talk about everything. Then, anger pulsed up from her stomach and filled her head, making it throb. "It's the other woman, isn't it?"

He shook his lowered head.

Her fingers dug into the couch cushions as anger dug into her stomach. Bile rose in her throat. "Don't deny it. I know about her. Olive saw you kissing."

When he raised his head and finally looked at her, tears pooled in his eyes. "It was just that one time, I promise. After that I knew I'd made a mistake, but I didn't know what to do about it."

She looked down at her white knuckles. Taking her hands from the couch cushions, she rubbed them together. This had to be a dream, but her heartache felt real and the tears falling in her mouth tasted salty. He had been unfaithful. When she spoke, her voice came out, part hiss, part sob. "It wasn't just that one time, was it? I saw the lipstick on the coat. And what about all those late nights and the hardware store? It was all her. Wasn't it?"

He ran his hands through his hair, then smoothed it back over his bald patch. "You have to believe me. It was just that one time. I told the truth about the hardware store. You saw the key. And the late nights with the fellas were late nights. You can ask Don or any of the others, but I bumped into her one of those nights. And—"

A low growl escaped from the back of her throat. "You forgot you had a wife and children?"

Howard sighed, picking up the pillow that had fallen to the floor. "It's not like that. The other guys had gone home. She worked at the bowling alley. We got to talking. She listened. Then when she asked me out for lunch, I accepted. It was just talking until she kissed me. After that, I knew I'd made a mistake. I told her we couldn't see each other anymore. I had to put you and the kids first."

Florence shook her head, as if the act would make the snippets of information form a cohesive whole, as if she could put the pieces of their life back together. "But now you don't want to? You just said you don't want to be married anymore. Do you still love me?"

He placed the pillow on the coffee table, then grabbed her hand and held it between his two larger ones. "I don't know what to think anymore. I've made so many mistakes. Wanting Jane to live somewhere else. Kissing another woman. All I wanted to do was to provide and protect you and the children, but I haven't done that. I don't deserve to be married to you."

Even though his old fear of not measuring up had never left, she was the victim, not him. She withdrew her hand. Taking the pillow from the table, she squeezed it. Then with a glare at Howard, she spoke in an even voice that didn't sound like hers. "Why? I was here. You could have talked to me. You could have kissed me. Why her?"

"Could I really? All you did was clean and worry. If every-thing isn't perfect, you can't leave it be. I can't measure up to what you need. I'm flawed and I've made too many mistakes to be of any use to you and the kids. Our kids deserve to grow up in a house full of love. You deserve someone better, someone who isn't broken. A marriage that works. And I'm not sure ours does." He shook his head.

Florence wanted to shake him, to make him understand, but she didn't know how to fix a broken marriage, especially if he didn't love her anymore. Did he still love her? All his words whirled into confusion. *Another woman. Just one time. Marriage. Broken.*

"I think we should spend some time apart. Don said I can stay with him and Francine. Since they don't have kids, he has plenty of room."

Numbness settled over her. He had already planned to leave. All her efforts were too late. She closed her eyes, trying to shut out his words, but she heard him leave the room, climb the stairs, and close the bedroom door. She couldn't hear what he was doing in the quiet, but knew he was packing up his life to go and try a new one. A life she hadn't messed up.

Florence didn't move from the couch until Howard left with his suitcases. When he shut the door, she went into the dining room. On the table where they had shared so many family dinners, she blew out the candle he'd never seen. Then she put away the two clean place settings. In the kitchen, the Salisbury steak, mashed potatoes, and vegetables were ready to be eaten. She'd used his mother's recipe for the meat. It was his favorite. She wanted to throw the food away, but she put it into containers to be reheated for tomorrow's dinner. She couldn't waste food now.

The dark bananas on the counter caught her attention. She peeled them, put them in a bowl, and smashed them into a yellow pulp. Then she set them aside and gathered the rest of the ingredients.

A few hours later, a soft knock sounded. With a sigh, Florence opened the door, nodded at Olive, and went back into the kitchen.

Her friend followed her. "What's wrong? Howard didn't come home?"

"He came home." She scrubbed the cookie sheet, rinsed it, and then dried it.

"What happened?" Olive rubbed her arm.

Florence silently put the cookie sheet away, looked around the kitchen, and sighed. Two loaves of banana bread sat on the table. A batch of oatmeal cookies cooled on the counter. The washed dishes dripped dry. Now, all that was left was to face the truth. "He left."

Gathering the plates and a knife, she sat at the table and sliced the warm banana bread. The sweet smells of baking strengthened her. She put a slice on each plate and handed one across to Olive.

"The bananas were almost rotten, but I rescued them."

Chapter 15

The sun peeked over the horizon. Florence shivered in the early morning air, glad no one appeared in her neighbors' darkened windows. If they escaped before anyone woke, there'd be less gossip.

She tapped her foot and peered down the silent road in the pre-light before dawn. They had to catch the early train to make the trip in one day. "Where's that taxi? It should be here."

"What?" William ran a hand along the dew-covered fence, then wiped his palm on his pants.

She hadn't meant to speak out loud. "Nothing. Are you excited about the trip? I think you'll have a lot of fun."

Jane walked toward the hopscotch board Alice had drawn on the sidewalk the day before.

William groaned. "I'm going to miss a lot in my classes. Why do we have to go now? The school year's almost over."

"Don't you want to visit your cousin?"

"No." William picked up a stick, then cracked it in two. "She's nine. We have nothing in common."

Jane put her crutches in the first square of the board, then hopped into it. Moving the sticks forward, she balanced on her good leg and crouched as if to jump.

Florence ran to her, bracing for the worst. "What are you doing?"

Jane hopped into the next space, wobbled upon impact, and began to fall. William lunged forward and steadied her.

"I almost did it that time." With a grin, Jane lifted her withered leg and prepared to hop again.

"What do you mean *that time*?" Florence stood in front of Jane, blocking any more movement. "You can't play hopscotch. You need to save your strength for the trip."

With scrunched up eyebrows, Jane scowled. "The girls and I play. Besides, I'm getting stronger every day. Isn't that what you told Aunt Mildred?"

William held up his ball. "I need to practice my pitching. Jane, can you play catcher from the porch?"

With a sigh, Jane nodded and sat down on the stoop with her sticks balanced next to her.

Glad that one disaster had been averted, at least this time, Florence leaned against the fence, trying to calm her racing heart.

"Why can't Daddy come? When is he going to be back from his work trip?" Jane easily caught her brother's underhanded throw, then lobbed it back to him.

William caught it and coughed, giving Florence a knowing look. She knew he didn't believe her feeble excuse. The daily life of automotive foremen revolved around the plant. They didn't go on work trips. Lying to her children made her nauseous, but the truth was a tricky beast.

"I don't know when he'll be home, Jane." At least that wasn't a lie.

"You can tell us. We're old enough." William gave his mother a stern look that reminded her of his father.

When he tossed the ball back to his sister, images of the children and Howard flashed through her mind. After Jane's birth, he'd kissed her soft cheek, then leaned down to tell young Willie. "Now our family's complete."

Childhood always ended, but the inevitable shouldn't be rushed. She'd tell them the truth when they needed it. Down the road, a puff of dust preceded the approaching taxi. Even from the distance, she could tell it was the old Model A2. Howard always liked to point out the different cab models.

"I told you. With your dad away, we can all use a break. We haven't taken a trip together for several years. And don't you remember your aunt invites us in every letter she writes. It'll be a wonderful opportunity. Peggy can't wait to play with you,

Jane. It'll be like having a sister." She almost believed her words, but remembering her past, she dreaded the trip as much as her empty bedroom.

Jane's eyes sparkled with excitement, but William scoffed in disbelief. He gathered his and his sister's suitcases as the taxi pulled in front of their house. When Jane started toward the car, William whispered to Florence. "What's going on? Some kids at school were saying things about Dad."

Her heart dropped. So much for pretending everything was okay, but maybe she could quiet his fears. "Please, don't say anything to your sister. It's just gossip. You can't believe every-thing you hear. It's best for us to get away."

William shook his head and followed Jane.

The cab driver took Florence's suitcase. Then he gaped at Jane, who balanced on one crutch and reached for the door handle with the other.

Jane straightened, as Florence had told her to do when people stared, and flashed him a grin. "Nice to meet you, sir."

"Oh …" The man gazed at the ground and adjusted his cap. "You're one of them—"

"She's a young lady and you're late." William shoved one of the suitcases at the man, nearly causing him to lose his balance.

Florence stifled a giggle. She couldn't reprimand William for defending his sister.

Jane handed Florence her crutches, then slid onto the seat. After making sure they stowed the suitcases in the trunk, Flor-ence sat next to her, settling the sticks between them. William got in on the other side.

The car started with a shudder and rumbled down their street. Florence twisted to catch one last look at the darkened house. Her heart felt as empty as the driveway where Howard parked his car. Was this the right decision, or was she fleeing one mistake for another?

Pushing down her doubts, she faced forward. "Michigan Central Station."

"Yes, ma'am." He lit a cigarette, then turned sharply onto the main road, trying to dodge the potholes. When they hit a large one, Florence and the children raised off the backseat, then dropped. Howard's voice floated into Florence's mind. *If you keep bouncing along in a car, it's the suspension. You have to watch those shocks and struts.*

Jane clutched her mother's skirt as they bumped down the road. Florence held onto the seat with one hand. Howard didn't think seatbelts were very safe. *In an accident, it's better to be thrown from the car*, he always said. But as they bounced along, Florence wished she had something to keep her in place.

When the driver's cigarette smoke wafted into the backseat, William and Jane covered their noses. Florence coughed, then leaned forward. "Can you crack the window? Smoke isn't good for my daughter's lungs."

The driver sighed and crushed the cigarette in the ashtray.

Jane snuggled next to her. "I'm hungry. Can we get breakfast at the train station?"

She withdrew two wax paper bundles from her purse and gave one each to William and Jane. While the kids ate the ham biscuits, she rechecked the cash wedged in her purse. The bakery money and the emergency stash from the dresser seemed like a sizable sum, but much of it would be needed for the taxi and the train.

The neat, evenly spaced houses of their suburban town turned into industrial buildings. As they neared the city, tall downtown buildings loomed over them. They sped through streets where buses and streetcars were beginning their morning routes.

William glared at the cab driver, who twirled an unlit cigarette. "I'm thirsty."

"Can we get a Coca-Cola?" Jane asked as she licked her lips.

Florence spotted the station's tower in the distance. "No, Coca-Cola's just for special occasions. They'll have a water fountain at the station."

The traffic flow grew heavy when they neared Roosevelt Park. William pressed his face against the window and Jane leaned over Florence. They stared at the massive station while the driver slowly navigated the circular drive. William's former annoyance turned to excitement. Florence realized she'd never taken the kids on the train.

Muttering, the driver slowed in the congestion and then stopped, unable to go farther. The line of cars at the front of the station blocked the entrance. She exhaled loudly, fearful they'd miss the train.

"Sorry, lady. It's always busy in the morning. Most people walk from here." The driver put the unlit cigarette on the dashboard. Then he opened the door and peered at the line of automobiles.

"I'll get the luggage." William got out of the car.

The driver already had the trunk open. By the time Florence climbed out and called after William, he held his suitcase at his side. "Put that down. Your sister can't walk that far. We'll have to wait for the cars to move on."

Jane huffed. "I can walk from here." Taking her crutches, she moved next to her.

"No, it's too far." Florence studied the crowd. Others had gotten out of their vehicles and walked toward the entrance. What if they missed the next train? She didn't want to wait all day in a congested station. She wanted as much distance between her and Howard as possible. "I don't want you to get too tired. What if you fall?"

The driver fiddled with his cigarette package. "It'll take a while to clear."

William took Jane's suitcase with his free hand. "Mom, if you carry the luggage, I can carry Jane when she gets tired."

Heavy puffs of exhaust made Florence cough. The smog seemed thicker than normal. Car horns blared in the distance. She turned at the sound of crunching metal. Behind them, one car had rear-ended another. Smoke poured out of an engine. The man whose car had been hit got out and yelled at the other driver. When she turned back, Jane was striding toward the station.

"It's okay. I like walking." She threw a glare back at her brother. "And I won't get tired."

Florence groaned. William caught up with Jane, swinging their suitcases. Taking hers from the driver, she paid him, then paused to pull her coat closed and ducked her head from the sting of the cold air. She jogged, reaching the two of them when they were halfway to the building. "Slow down. Walking so fast isn't good for you."

"The doctor said I need to exercise." Jane grinned, and William chuckled.

Florence pursed her lips. How would she keep them safe in this gigantic space?

A gentleman gawked at Jane. Florence pushed her shoulders down, smiled a smile she didn't feel, and herded the kids toward the station entrance.

"Is that a polio, Mama?" a little boy asked.

Jane stuck her tongue out at him.

Florence glared at the boy's mother, who pulled her son away. "Ignore them. Remember, stand tall and—"

"Smile. I know. I'm sorry." Jane's face stretched into a wan smile and she continued on, keeping pace with William's long steps.

Florence hated the stares and comments. She wanted to stick her tongue out and scream at the people like Jane did the first time someone pointed at her.

Both children froze when they reached the station. Massive marquees that covered the main entrance captured their attention. Their eyes traveled the length of the place and continued up to the top of the fifteen-story building. Jane's mouth formed a wide O, while William's eyes took in the whole scene.

"It doesn't look like a train station. It looks like a hotel. Are we in the right place?" he asked.

Florence nodded. The building didn't resemble the simple stone and brick structures of her Iowa childhood. Three arched windows above the door and to each side showed a busy world of rushing passengers. The tall columns and sturdy brickwork even made her eager for the trip and the promise of excitement.

"Keep walking." Florence nudged them. When a man exited the station, she grabbed the heavy wooden door and held it open for them.

Inside, a long arcade led to the ticket booth. They slowed their pace, staring at the arches and ornate light fixtures. Echoes of footsteps, chatter, and announcements bounced off the tall ceiling. She tapped William on the arm and pointed to a nearby bench. "You and Jane sit over there while I buy the tickets."

The pair weaved through the crowd while Florence headed to the ticket window. From her position in line, she tried to spot them, but one of the stately columns blocked her view. Never mind, she'd have to trust that they'd found a seat.

"Next."

The white-haired ticket agent at the window reminded her of her father. Although he looked older, he had the same piercing eyes.

"Can I help you, ma'am? We're quite busy this morning." He coughed.

Definitely not her father. Why was she even thinking about him? Hopefully, she'd be able to avoid him. The hands on the clock above his head moved. She had a short time until the train departed, but her reason for fleeing beat inside, distracting her. "Yes. I'm sorry. I need to … uh … I need to …"

He drummed his fingers.

Florence felt unreasonably certain he knew what a mess her life had become, yet she needed to keep going, just as she'd urged the kids to do. "Three coach tickets to Newton, Iowa, please."

He pulled out a thick dog-eared manual that resembled a telephone book. The cover read *Official Guide of the Railways*. He riffled through the pages muttering, "Newton, Iowa. Rock Island Rocket out of LaSalle Station." For a few more minutes, he continued calculating, then took out three tickets, stamped them, and put them in an envelope.

"That'll be $24.75."

She handed him the bills in exchange for the tickets.

"Ma'am, your train, the Wolverine, will be on track three and will take you to LaSalle Street Station. You'll then take an afternoon Rock Island Train, number seven, to Newton, Iowa. Listen for the announcements. The train stops for ten minutes, so you'll need to be ready to board as soon as they make the announcement."

While she slipped the envelope and change into her purse, he held up his hand and called, "Next."

Scooting away from the counter, she scanned the room for William and Jane. They huddled close together, still fascinated by the open lobby's high ceiling and multiple arches. Satisfied that they were safe, she found a pay phone. She should have called Mildred that morning. Farm families always woke early, but she hadn't wanted to say the truth out loud.

Ever since Howard left, she'd moved out of habit. She'd packed clothes for her and the kids and hadn't let herself think about Howard or what would greet them in Iowa. At first, she thought they'd just show up at Mildred and Henry's farmhouse, but their home was miles from the station and there were no taxis at the rural Newton Station.

With another quick look at her kids, who stared at a mom and dad surrounded by a brood of children, she found the closest pay phone and inserted a dime. Her sister-in-law answered on the second ring.

"Hello."

"It's me, Mildred." Florence fought her sudden rush of emotions.

"Flo? What's wrong?"

The suppressed tears from the night before erupted, and she sobbed.

"What did my brother do?"

"He left … another …woman."

"You'll come here. You and the kids."

"We're at the Michigan Central Station." Florence wiped her face, steadied her voice, and read their train's arrival time.

Hanging up, she calmed her breathing, strengthened by Mildred's voice, which had offered her much needed serenity on many occasions. From school bullies to planning weddings and baby showers, Mildred was her rock, but she doubted even Mildred could help her through this. No one could force a man to be a husband and a father if he'd given up.

She ran her finger over her town's name on the ticket. She was going home. For the first time in a long time, she thought about the farmhouse where she'd been born. Then the grocery store where she and her father had moved after her sister's death. Would she see him again?

Chapter 16

"Be quiet." William's sharp tone carried across the large room. He stood between Jane and two tall teenage boys who towered over him.

Florence rushed through the crowd. One teen said something, and the other one laughed. William held up his fists. Florence's heart thudded. She didn't want to have to stop a fight. When she was a couple of feet away, they sauntered off, still laughing.

"What happened?" Florence said, out of breath. How could she make this trip and take care of them all alone?

"Nothing." William picked up the suitcases. "Are we ready to go?"

"He saved me, Mama." Jane took her crutches and stood. "They were making fun of me and he stood up to them." She patted his arm.

William appeared not to notice and scanned the station. "Looks like the platforms are this way."

Florence checked the tickets, then returned them to her handbag. "Our train is on track three, but we have a few minutes before boarding. Let's get some Coca-Cola."

Surprise brightened their faces. She winked at them. Today was a special day. They all needed a treat, something sweet to balance their long season of bitterness. She'd savor this time with them because once they got to Iowa, she'd need to get a job.

William wanted to stop at the newsstand and look at a baseball magazine, but Florence hurried him toward the concession booth. While they waited in line, Jane traced her finger over a postcard of the Grand Circus Park in downtown Detroit. The place looked more modern than it did in real life. Florence patted her shoulder and whispered, "Look with your eyes, not your hands, dear."

Jane returned her hand to her crutch handle and stepped up to the counter. Florence was about to pull the nickels from her handbag when William pushed in front and handed the clerk some coins. "I'd like three Coca-Colas."

After the woman handed him the glass bottles, he winked at his mother. "I had some left over from my job. Mr. Schmidt gave me a good deal on the doll."

Taking her and Jane's cold bottles from him, a warmth grew in her heart. How could she have ever doubted William's intentions? As they made their way across the crowded lobby to the platforms, Jane stopped, pointed, and squealed.

Florence said, "We need to go, Jane." With Jane's crutches, they might need extra time to get on the train.

"Mama, this way." Jane took off toward the lunch counter.

When she and William hurried after her, Florence saw the wheelchair and the familiar grin.

"Grace." Jane bent down and hugged her friend.

Propped up with white pillows, Grace wore a white coat and hat. Her smile looked almost translucent on her pale face.

A woman with white gloves and perfectly coiffed hair leaned over the wheelchair and greeted them. "Jane. It's so good to meet you. I've heard so much about you. And you must be Jane's mother and brother. I'm Grace's mom, Carol."

Carol flung her arms around her. Florence patted the woman's shoulder, feeling warm and uncomfortable, not used to hugs from strangers.

Sniffing and wiping her eyes, Carol said, "Thank you so much for looking out for Grace. I wanted to be there. I wanted to visit, to sleep in the bed next to her, but I couldn't. We live in Toledo, and I have six other kids at home. I'm glad we could get in the Sister Kenny Polio Center. It has such a good reputation, but…" She sniffed again and wiped her eyes.

Up close, Florence could see the tired lines on Carol's face and the faded coat and hat.

"Mom." William tugged at her coat sleeve, then pointed to the clock.

She nodded to William, knowing they needed to be on the train soon. But these few minutes gave her a deep kinship to this woman. Another person who knew what it was like to juggle the needs of a sick child, a marriage, and a family. There were so many questions she wanted to ask her and things she'd love to discuss with her. But she only thought of Linda, the sour-faced girl at the hospital who would probably spend the rest of her life in an institution. "I'm so glad Grace is going home. I'm glad they let you come get her."

Carol glanced at Grace, who talked animatedly with Jane. "Well, they didn't want to release her, but I had to have her home with me, so I came and got her. A neighbor is watching my other kids. My husband and I have been saving up for the train fares. The doctor wanted her to have more therapy, but I promised to do the exercises at home. We hope we can find a good physiotherapist. But I wanted to thank you. I love how God places people in our lives to help us when we need it the most." Again, Carol hugged Florence.

This time Florence sunk into her arms.

An announcement echoed over the loudspeaker, "New York Central announces the arrival of train number seventeen, the west bound Wolverine with stops at Ann Arbor, Jackson, Battle Creek, Albion, Englewood, Chicago LaSalle. Now boarding on track three."

William nudged her. "Mom." A horde of people streamed toward platform three.

She gave Carol one last squeeze. "I'm sorry. We need to go or we'll miss our train."

After they all waved goodbye, they hurried toward their platform while Florence considered what Carol had just said. Ever since Jane's polio diagnosis, she'd felt alone. But had she really been alone? Mildred had called her and sent letters. Olive had been distant at first, but eventually proved to be a good listening ear, even if her advice wasn't always the best. The nurses at the hospital, even Mizie, had encouraged her and Jane. And Howard, in an off and on way had been there for her part of the time. Could it be possible that God had placed people in her life to help her? Maybe she wasn't all alone.

"Mama, hurry," Jane called.

Engrossed in her thoughts, Florence had fallen behind her children. She hurried to catch up and followed them outside into the cool air. When they arrived trackside, the train had pulled in. William strained to see the engine, but the steam between the cars obscured the view. Jane coughed as a steam engine pulled out on a nearby track. A shower of coal smoke and cinders fell over them.

William read the words on the passing engine. "Nickel Plate Road."

Florence took out their tickets and rechecked them. "We need to go down here."

At the entrance to the car, a young boy, maybe five or six, jumped up on the step box, then sprinted inside. His parents followed. A uniformed conductor checked his pocket watch and sighed.

"I can do it." Jane stumbled onto the step box, wiggled for a minute, then regained her balance. Looking up, her eyes widened.

Florence gulped at the four-foot-high stairway leading into the coach car, steeper than Jane had encountered.

A Red Cap station porter appeared. "Want me to help you, young lady?"

Before Florence could respond, the man picked up Jane and nimbly climbed the stairs. She and William followed behind. Gently, he set Jane down. "There you go, little miss. Now where's your seat, ma'am?"

With cheeks turning red, Jane used the seat to help steady herself. "Thank you."

Florence pointed to the seats next to them. "We're right here."

He grabbed the suitcase from her and hoisted it into the rack above their seats. Then he took the ones William held and placed them next to the other one.

Florence dug into her purse for a dollar, but when she looked up, the man had already disappeared. Strange, Red

Caps usually waited for a tip. Florence sat across from William, still thinking about Grace's mother, Carol. Had the man just appeared out of nowhere when they needed him, or could it be something else? Receiving help wasn't always a bad thing, especially when assistance came at your time of greatest need.

When the train lurched out of the station, Jane shifted the canvas tote she carried to her lap. Florence had assumed she'd only put her doll in it, but Jane pulled out a thick volume, *Little House in the Big Woods*, her favorite book. Howard had gotten the whole set last Christmas and somehow, every volume had survived the polio madness. Jane clutched the book to her chest as if clinging to her absent father. She and William stared out the window.

Within minutes, the city skyline turned into Michigan farm fields that stretched as far as the eye could see. By the time the conductor came to check their tickets, Jane was snuggled against her mother fast asleep. Opposite them, William leaned against the window, snoring softly. Even though her eyes grew heavy, she tried to stay awake to experience the trip. They hadn't had a vacation in years and the few times they'd taken the kids to the lake seemed long ago.

As Florence drifted off to sleep, a sliver of a memory drifted across her mind. She and Howard sitting on a blanket in the sun, while William and Jane splashed in the lake. They had been happy once upon a time.

Near to Newton, Florence hesitated to wake her children, who'd slept for a second time on the long ride from Michigan. After their brief morning nap, they watched the changing scenery of woods and fields, reading the name of each town they passed. The Michigan plains and small towns turned into the Lake Michigan steel mills, which then turned into the blue-collar townhouses built almost on top of each other. Jane made up stories about the people who lived in the houses, while William looked for ball fields. Using the bathroom proved to be a singular challenge because other children stared, and Jane needed help to open the heavy door.

When they'd arrived in downtown Chicago, they'd had to switch trains. Jane grew tired of climbing the stairs and William carried her on his back while Florence struggled with all three suitcases. A Red Cap finally helped her with the luggage. Once they'd resettled on the train, she thought they might grow bored, but they continued staring out the window, mesmerized by the scenery.

The nearer to Iowa, the more her emotions overwhelmed her. The landscape grew familiar. Memories of her childhood returned. Roasting marshmallows, jumping in leaves, swimming in the pond. Recalling her forgotten joy failed to dispel the dread that cloaked her. The conductor came through and announced, "Next stop, Newton, Iowa."

She roused Jane and William. "Wake up. We have to collect our luggage."

When the train entered the yard and began slowing, she reminded herself that she was no longer a hurt child but an adult responsible for her own children. Her job was to make sure they were safe and happy, not let herself live in the past.

The kids moved with heavy steps. Suddenly awake and on guard, Florence urged them off the train. After the two large stations, they seemed disappointed at the small brick building.

A sturdy lady in a shapeless floral dress standing apart from the crowd waved at them. Florence dropped the suitcases and rushed into Mildred's arms, comforted by the remembered scent of dough and earth.

"I can't believe my brother—"

Florence pushed away, held a finger up to her lips, and pointed to William and Jane, who stood behind her, confused.

Mildred enveloped Jane in a hug. "You are as beautiful as your mother."

Jane gasped. "Are you and Dad twins?"

Mildred chuckled. "Thank goodness, no." She had the same twinkling eyes and the same wrinkles on her wide forehead as her brother. A major difference between the two was her thick, dark hair pulled back in a bun.

Jane wasn't the only one who had forgotten the similarities between her aunt and dad. Noting them anew, Florence pushed down a sick feeling. Only letters and phone calls had passed between Florence and Mildred in the past few years. Had she made a mistake in coming here? Perhaps Mildred would take Howard's side.

"And who is this handsome young man?" When Mildred crushed William into a hug, he blushed.

A thin girl leaned against the building.

"You remember your cousin, Peggy?" Mildred pointed to her daughter, who had Mildred and Howard's twinkly eyes, but her tanned face had soft angles.

Peggy laughed in greeting, then stepped up to Jane. "I like your crutches. Can you teach me how to use them? Are they hard?"

Jane giggled back. "They're easy for me." She hurried across the platform to the parking lot.

Peggy jogged to keep up. "You're fast."

Florence ignored Mildred and William, who were discussing baseball, and hustled after the girls, squinting because of the setting sun. How could Jane move so quickly after such a long train ride? "Be careful, you—" Her feet slid across the gravel. A powerful arm stopped her sudden fall.

Mildred took the suitcase from her. "You're the one who needs to be careful. Let them be."

William sprinted past and walked alongside the girls, who had slowed.

"You don't..." Florence dusted off her skirt. "You don't understand what it's like. She gets more tired now, and she's not as strong as she used to be. I have to—"

"Everything will be okay. You'll see." Mildred hooked her arm through Florence's. "Farm life is a good life. And Jane's a child. Let her be a little girl."

Florence cocked a skeptical eyebrow at her sister-in-law. What she just remembered about farm life made her think this was a mistake. Neither the farm nor Mildred could fix the mess that was her life.

When they came to a rusty pickup, Peggy jumped up onto the running board, then leaped into the bed. She held her hand out for Jane. Florence stopped and braced herself to yell, but before Jane's name could form on her lips, Peggy had hoisted her in with a little boost from William.

"I told you." Mildred giggled and shoved the suitcases next to the children.

"Won't they be cold?" Florence shivered. The spring air felt warmer than the city, but a slight breeze raised chill bumps under her light cardigan. Gray clouds threatened rain.

"Not a chance." Peggy held up a couple of blankets and spread them over her and her cousins. "Like Pa says, we'll be as snug as a bug in a rug."

Florence swallowed hard. Howard used to say that to Jane every night when he tucked her in.

William looked a little annoyed at the girls' closeness, but managed a reluctant grin.

"This is fun, Mom. I've never ridden in the back of a truck before." Jane snuggled down between her cousin and brother, then wrinkled her nose. "What's that smell?"

Peggy laughed. "Papa says that's the smell of money. It's manure."

As she launched into an explanation to her city cousins, Mildred steered Florence to the door. "Stop worrying so much. This'll be a wonderful vacation for you all."

Vacation? In the beginning, she'd thought it could be, but she was reflecting more and more that nothing about a farm could be called a vacation. Getting into the front, she tried not to gape at the hole in the floorboard. The Chevy truck had been built before the war. She clutched her handbag to her chest and hoped that the vehicle worked. Much to her astonishment, the engine started smoothly and sounded better than the newer one in their car.

Mildred winked at her. "This old truck might not be much for looks, but Henry always keeps it running in tip-top shape."

The town had changed so much since her last visit. New houses and businesses lined the main street. She swallowed a lump when they passed the grocery store, but saw no sign of her father. On the outskirts of town, the depression era shanty neighborhood was gone, replaced by a neat row of apartment buildings. A group of children played out front.

They left the town behind and entered the countryside where farmhouses, many new, dotted the fields. Mildred drove slowly on the hard-packed country road. Florence listened to the girls' excited chatter through the open window.

Jane asked, "What kind of animals do you have at your farm? Do you have any dogs or cats?"

"We have lots of barn cats, but no dogs. We also have chickens, cows, horses …" Peggy continued chatting about the farm. Then, she named the families who lived in each house.

Soothed by the girlish chatter and the cool breeze, Florence's eyelids drooped, and she imagined she was a girl again, running across the fields.

As the truck picked up speed and the girls' voices stopped, Mildred leaned toward Florence. "Did you tell him you were coming?"

She'd considered calling Don's house and asking Howard to come home. But then had second-guessed herself. "No, I'm not going to beg him to come back."

"I didn't mean Howard."

Florence gave Mildred a sharp look. "That isn't any of your business."

Mildred coughed and kept her eyes on the road. "Do your kids know about him?"

Not wanting the kids to hear, she fiddled with the window crank and tried to roll it up. "How do you—"

"That's broken. I forgot to tell Henry. He'll fix it."

"Where's the Neils' place? Did we pass it?" She looked behind them. Most of the people they had grown up with hadn't lasted through the Depression. When banks foreclosed on their farms, they had moved to cities or moved in with other relatives, if they were lucky. Some just disappeared. Most never returned. The Neil family and Howard's family were some of the few that had stayed and eked out a living through the lean years.

"You're changing the subject. You always were a master of avoiding."

Florence rolled her eyes.

"I forget who they sold it to. I guess the parents moved to Florida. They're tired of the winter and their kids didn't want the farm."

"I thought Junior—"

Mildred patted her leg. "Your kids deserve to know their grandfather. And he deserves to know them. He might be more help than you think at a time like this."

"He's never helped before."

"People change, Florence."

She pressed her lips together and studied the fields. A farmer bent over a fence pole and waved to them. Mildred honked the horn and waved back. Florence kept her arms tightly crossed. She'd never speak to her father again. People didn't change and the past couldn't be undone.

Chapter 17

Florence woke in the middle of the night, shivering. The blanket had slid off the bed. Leaving Jane's warm sleeping figure, she groped in the guest room's inky darkness. No streetlights in the country. The cold wooden floor raised goosebumps all over her. When her toe collided with the bed frame, she bit back a scream. Finding the thick quilts, she spread them over her and Jane. Snuggling against Jane, she shut her eyes, hoping for more sleep. The crickets and frogs had kept them both awake for quite a while.

William's snores floated from the living room couch where he slept. Jane mumbled and stirred. Florence rubbed her arm and shushed her. Jane's breathing evened and slowed, while Florence peered into the darkness, having forgotten how noisy the country could be.

A creak sounded. Just the house settling. Or maybe someone upstairs going to the bathroom. But when one fear left, another replaced it. Whose house was Howard really sleeping in? Did he think about her and the kids? Why had he chosen another woman in the first place? What should she have done differently to make him stay, to make him love her again?

Jane moaned in her sleep, then rolled over. Florence closed her eyes and tried to think about something else, anything else. The only images in her mind were of her husband kissing a red-lipped, dark-haired woman. Then someone screaming. Except it wasn't Howard or his girlfriend. Florence must have fallen asleep. The screaming was close to her. Jane.

"Shh." She rubbed her daughter's arm.

Jane moaned and yelled again. "Help me." She was still asleep.

Florence shook her. "Wake up. You're dreaming."

Jane sat up. "Mama?"

"You're okay. It was a nightmare. You're safe."

"It was so real." Jane huddled next to her and sobbed.

"I know, but it wasn't. Do you want to tell me about it?"

"I was on the floor." Jane shivered. "It was hard and cold. I couldn't move. When I called out, no one heard me. Then I peed on myself." She cried.

Florence stroked her hair and pulled the blankets tight around them. "That didn't happen. You didn't fall out of bed. It was only a nightmare."

Jane stopped crying and hiccupped. She burrowed into her mother. "It did happen."

"What?" She stared at her daughter in the darkness, wishing she could see her face. "No, it didn't. You're here at Aunt Mildred's. I'm here. Willie and Peggy are here. We're all safe. You didn't fall on the floor."

"I did, Mama. In the hospital. I fell one night. I don't remember when. But I woke up on the floor and I was so weak, I couldn't cry out very loud. When the nurse found me, I'd wet myself."

Florence's heart grew cold. She'd let that happen to her daughter. "Oh, Jane. I'm so sorry. I—"

Jane wrapped her arms around her. "It's okay. I know I'm safe."

For a while, they lay close together. Florence tried not to imagine her daughter on the cold floor, but pictured her running as she once had. She had almost drifted off to sleep when Jane's voice woke her.

"Did Daddy leave on his work trip because of me? Because I got polio."

"No. He didn't leave because of you. It wasn't your fault you got polio, or that you fell out of bed, or that you had an accident. None of that was your fault. You're such a good girl."

Jane sniffed. "Then why did Daddy leave?"

What could Florence say? Could she tell her daughter the truth? "He's working. I already told you that." But she knew her daughter didn't believe her lie. The time in the hospital had matured Jane beyond her years.

"Aunt Mildred says that farm air can fix anything. I know it'll bring Daddy back. It's already made me stronger."

She held her daughter close, not wanting to tell her that Mildred was wrong. Nothing could fix all the things Florence had broken.

Florence rolled out the last ball of dough. She placed the cookie cutter in flour, then stamped out stars. With practiced skill, she transferred the shapes to the baking sheet. At least she was good at one thing. When only scraps of dough remained, she rolled them into three small dough balls. Those were always William and Jane's favorites.

The front door shut. Henry and Peggy passed by the kitchen with a wave. Mildred stopped in the doorway and pointed to the heaping plate of cookies. "When I saw you in the kitchen this morning, I thought you were getting water and going back to bed."

Florence placed the cookie sheet in the oven. "I told you I wasn't going back to bed. I'm more than capable of helping with chores."

Mildred squeezed her shoulder. "And I told you to rest. You don't have to start working the minute you get here. There'll be time for that later." She grabbed a fresh cookie from the counter. "I smelled these out in the barn. Your mom's sugar cookies." She bit into it. "Tastes just like hers. Amazing."

Florence nibbled on one. The buttery goodness transported her back in time. She was a small girl standing on a chair next to her mother. She could almost hear her voice. *First you sift together the dry ingredients. Turn the handle…*

Florence reached for the sifter's handle when Mildred coughed. "Why were you up so early?" She continued coughing and went to the refrigerator, taking out the milk.

Florence took a glass from the cupboard and handed it to Mildred. It hadn't taken her long to remember where Mildred kept everything, though the kitchen was larger than hers. She missed the cozy comfort of her own home. "Jane had another nightmare."

"You mentioned something about that before. Does she have many?"

Nodding, Florence wiped the counter.

Mildred took her hand. "Stop, Flo. Let's talk about it. You don't have to keep everything tidy inside."

Florence threw the wet rag down. Anger surged through her. "You don't know what it's like. I've ruined everything."

Mildred pulled out a kitchen chair and patted it. "Tell me."

"Sugar cookies for breakfast?" William stood in the doorway, yawning. His mussed hair touched the collar of his pajama shirt. Definitely time for a haircut. He stretched, then picked up a cookie. "These look like Christmas cookies. I like Iowa."

Florence glanced from her gangly son to the look of concern on Mildred's face to the remaining traces of flour on the counter. Too early for her to answer questions. "I'm going on a walk." She hurried out of the kitchen, slipped on her shoes, and took her coat from the hook. The wind caught the door, slamming it on Mildred's protests.

The chilly spring air offered a welcome relief to the warm kitchen. For the first mile or so, she walked with her coat over her arm, dodging mud puddles. A truck approached. The driver honked and hung his head out the window. She stepped off the road into the field, barely missing the mud spray. Why had the man been staring? A glance down at one of Mildred's large aprons over her nightgown answered her question. Not wanting to wake Jane, she hadn't gotten dressed. The wind blew across the fields. Shivering, she put her coat on and buttoned it.

At the top of the rise, her childhood home came into view. Weeds had overtaken the yard. The shutters hung askew beside every broken window. After Mom and Hattie had died, Dad sold the house, and they'd moved into town. The new owner had sold it soon afterwards. Then the bank foreclosed on it, like many other farms.

The tilting gate still marked the front drive. When she was five, her mom told her they were going to have another baby. Swinging on that same gate, Florence announced to the entire world, "I'm gonna have a baby!"

Dad came in from the fields and found her there, still screaming. He bent down, held her face in his and looked into her eyes. His voice was serious, but his eyes laughed. "You know what that means, don't you?"

"What, Daddy?" She wiped at a dirt smudge on his cheek. It felt like sandpaper.

"You'll have to take good care of that baby. Can you do that?"

She nodded. "Yes. I'll take good care of her."

He swung her up onto his shoulders.

Now, as the wind blew the trees in the overgrown yard. She could almost hear his voice. *I hope it's a girl, just like you.*

Florence pushed the rusty gate open with her loafer, no longer the foot of a child. The squeak sounded like her childish laughter. She started toward the house when a voice stopped her. Was that her father? He was—

When she looked back, Mildred leaned out of the truck window. "You can't go in. The city's condemned it."

Florence ignored her and continued.

When she reached the sagging porch, Mildred caught up and pointed to the upstairs window. "That was your room. Remember when we climbed out?"

"We were using Rapunzel's hair." Florence had held the rolled-up bedsheet, while Mildred inched her way down. When it was Florence's turn, no one was there to hold the sheet. "What did I tie the sheet to?"

Mildred laughed and steered Florence toward the truck. "I don't know, but whatever it was, you didn't tie it tight enough."

She joined in the laughter, remembering that she and the sheet had tumbled to the ground. "Dad wasn't happy that I broke my arm. He threatened to nail the window shut."

"Did he?" Mildred held the passenger door open.

A shutter hung crookedly over the window, now without glass. This time Florence didn't see her childhood self, but her teenage self climbing nimbly down the trellis, then landing in Howard's brawny arms.

"No, he never did."

Mildred started the truck, then pulled onto the road.

"Why'd you come get me? I haven't been the ideal house guest."

"That's what friends do." She eyed Florence. "I can't believe you left in your nightgown."

Florence unfastened the top coat buttons, warmed up from her walk and too tired to be embarrassed about her nightclothes. "Where are you going? This isn't the way home."

"I thought you could use a drive."

They passed the site of their one-room schoolhouse. An elementary school had replaced the building, with a junior high and high school next door. When they turned left, the steeple of the small country church appeared in the distance. She and Howard had walked here many evenings when they snuck out. His hand held hers the entire way while they talked late into the night.

At the church, they parked and walked behind the building to the cemetery. They passed through the creaking, rusty gate of the wrought-iron fence, and went to the far-right corner. Florence kneeled by the graves and brushed dirt from her sister's marker.

Mildred leaned against the fence. "Remember walking out here? In the spring, we'd bring wildflowers—"

"And in the fall, we'd arrange leaves on their graves." She rubbed her hand over her mother's name. "When Howard and I first started dating, after he'd graduated from high school, we'd come here. Did you know?"

"I used to get so sick of hearing him talk about you. He'd go on and on about how pretty, how smart, how perfect you were." Mildred rolled her eyes. "He loved you so much."

"Loved." She stood and brushed off her coat. "He loved me, past tense."

"That's not what I meant, and you know it. He still loves you. You can't stop loving someone. After all you've been through."

She walked toward the tree in the center of the graveyard. "But he did."

"Do you have any idea what happened? That doesn't sound like him."

"He said he doesn't love me anymore." She leaned against the sturdy trunk, trying not to think of how many times she and Howard had kissed under the tree. "I've messed up."

Mildred put her hands on her hips. "*He's* the one who messed up. Don't go having a pity party for yourself. I'm sure he'll come to his senses soon. He loves you and the kids. Let's go so you can put some real clothes on. That'll make you feel better."

Florence followed her to the truck, convinced that sometimes love wasn't enough.

When they returned to the farmhouse, a car pulled out of the dirt driveway. The driver, a well-dressed man with round spectacles, honked and waved. Florence waved back. Out here, you were either a resident, a visitor, or lost. "A friend of yours?"

Mildred didn't wave, only turned into the drive, and drove faster than normal. As they bumped along, she flashed Florence a look of concern. "He's the doctor."

When Mildred parked, both women rushed out of the car and onto the porch. Florence pushed in front of Mildred and flung the door open. Horrible images filled her mind. Why had she thought the farm would be a safe place for her children? She'd forgotten about the dangers of her childhood. The animals, the machinery, the barn. Over the years, there'd been so many horror stories. "Jane? William?"

Mildred rubbed her side and shut the front door. "Skinny women have sharp elbows. Calm down, Flo."

"Everyone's fine." Henry came out of the kitchen, wiping his forehead with his blue kerchief. Dressed in standard farmer's attire of dark blue denim pants and a chambray shirt, he was wiry and two inches shorter than his wife. "Doctor said it's just a twisted ankle. It'll heal soon."

In the kitchen, Peggy stood at the sink, washing dishes. William dried the sifter with a worn towel. Jane sat at the table, both legs propped up on a chair. A bandage wrapped around one of her ankles.

"I'm okay, Mama." Jane rooted in the paper doll box.

"What happened?" Florence leaned over her, trying to calm the heartbeat still pounding in her ears. How would Jane get around now?

Peggy dried her hands on her dress. "She accidentally fell off my bed." She leaned over the table and peeked into the box Jane held.

"How did you fall off her bed?" Anger rose inside Florence as she pictured the two girls roughhousing. Then she realized where Peggy's room was. "You went upstairs without an adult?"

Both girls stopped searching. William put a plate away and left the kitchen.

Henry moved toward Florence and put his hand out in a calming gesture. "It's okay, Flo. They're just kids. They were—"

She swatted his hand away. "Where were you?"

He stepped back. His normally calm face reddened. "Well, I was feeding the stock when William came out. It's really not a big deal. The doctor said—"

Not a big deal? Florence stalked out of the kitchen. "William."

Her son huddled in the hallway.

"Why weren't you taking care of your sister?"

"I stood next to her when she went up the stairs, just like I do at home." His eyes watered. "I was tossing my ball in the hallway when I heard her fall. I got Uncle Henry as quick as I could."

"It's not his fault." Jane balanced on her crutches in the doorway. "I wanted to see Peggy's room."

Peggy peeked over at Jane. "William was next to her the whole time. I held the crutches at the top. She scooted all the way up on her bottom. I thought you'd be proud of how fast she went, Auntie."

Florence gave her niece a bewildered look, then studied the stairs. Jane went up their steps at home by herself, but they were carpeted and not as steep. With the bathroom on the ground floor, Jane shouldn't have to go upstairs.

"Accidents happen." Mildred placed a hand on her shoulder and then whispered in her ear. "Remember all our accidents."

Florence rubbed her arm, recalling the time she'd broken it. Sometimes rainy weather still made it ache. "Well …" Everyone stared at her, seeming to see inside her and judge her wanting. The heavy air felt like it might choke her. Fleeing the concerned looks, she went into the guest room and slammed the door.

Laying on the bed, she pulled the cover over herself. Why was every day so hard? She hadn't kept her promises to her mother, and she'd driven her husband into the arms of another woman. Now, she'd failed to protect her daughter. She considered closing her eyes and napping when the trunk caught her attention.

Chapter 18

Why hadn't she noticed the trunk before? This one had been her mother's, but they hadn't had room to take it in the car when they moved. They'd stored it here and always meant to come back for it. Rising from the bed, she faced her mother's hope chest, which was wedged between the dresser and the back wall. Florence ran her hand over the simple wooden surface. In some places, the plain wood was rotting away. Howard had offered to make her a better one, more ornate and sturdier, but she'd refused. This box of hope was her mother's.

Young Florence and her mother had crouched on the floor near the trunk. Sleeping Hattie lay under the bedcovers, fast asleep. Her mother had whispered to her, "This will be yours one day."

Florence had stared in wonder. After a peek at Hattie's sleeping face, she stroked the cold metal bands around the treasure. Having a sister had been harder than Florence had imagined. She had to share everything, including her parents. "Mine? What about Hattie?"

Her mother opened the lid. "This trunk is just for you. My father made it for me. I carried it on all my adventures, when I left my parents' house, when I moved into this house ... all my adventures."

Her mother's face had taken on a faraway look that young Florence had never thought to question. She'd been too enraptured with the contents of the prized trunk. She and her mother had dug through the treasures—candlesticks, a sparkly gown, sheets, and towels. Now, adult Florence wished she'd asked her mother more about her adventures—still unsure when her mother was born or who her parents were. They'd died before Florence was born. If only she could have one more conversation, she'd ask her how she had managed to go on without a mother.

Florence looked at the bed, but Hattie wasn't there. She wasn't a child, and she wasn't in her childhood home but in Mildred and Henry's farmhouse. When she unlatched the chest and opened the lid, the faint aroma of her mother's perfume returned her to the past.

A faded quilt lay on top. She pressed it to her nose and lilacs mixed with a whiff of mothballs floated on the surface. The few holes could be patched, and she could use the blanket to keep her and Jane warm.

Removing the blanket showed that most of the former contents were long gone. The sheets and towels had been used. The candles had been burned. Her mother had been buried in the gown. She recognized Howard's handwriting on the yellowed envelopes that lay on the bottom in ribbon-tied bundles. The return address and posted date told her that they were from when he had first worked at the Dodge plant in Hamtramck.

The door opened slowly. "Are you okay?"

Replacing the letters but not shutting the trunk, she returned to the bed. Clutching the quilt to her nightgown, which she still hadn't changed, Florence shrugged.

"Jane can still get around pretty good on that ankle. I don't know how she does it. She's just as stubborn as you."

Pushing her knees to her chest and drawing strength from the quilt, Florence fought the urge to scream at her. Why did she seem to have all the answers?

Mildred joined her on the unmade bed, then pointed to the papers in the trunk. "What are those?"

"Letters from Howard, when he first started working at the Detroit-Hamtramck plant. I thought I had them all at home, but I guess I left a few."

"He was so mad that he needed to send almost half of his earnings back home. Remember?"

She nodded. "That's probably what's in the letters." His familiar scrawl had made her heart ache. She missed him so much.

"The money helped us make ends meet. I don't know what we would have done without it. Even though Henry did the same thing when he graduated from high school, his dad still had to foreclose. I don't think Howard ever realized how much he helped. Your dad was lucky he left farming before the bottom fell out."

Florence rested her head on her knees. When Dad told her he had sold the farm and used the money to buy the grocery store, she'd been wary, but he'd looked at her with such a hopeful expression. "It'll be a new beginning for both of us."

At first, she believed him. For a couple of days, his melancholy lifted. They worked together, making the apartment above the store their new home. He showed her how to use the cash register, and she thought she'd regained his approval. But by the end of the second week, he had reverted to not looking into her eyes and going through the motions of life. What she had done was unforgivable.

By the time she reached high school, she stayed most nights with Howard and Mildred. She still helped in the store and did some light housekeeping for him, but when Howard went to work in Detroit and she turned seventeen, she'd moved into the guest room at Mildred's house. Unlike her dad, Mildred and her father were glad to have the extra help.

"Florence." Mildred tapped her leg. "What are you thinking about?"

She shook her head. "I need to get dressed."

"You can't sweep away your pain. You need to talk about it," Mildred said and left the room.

Florence dressed and combed her hair. Mildred had been with her through it all. What else was there to say? How could she ever understand the guilt, shame, and anger that whirled inside her? Like oil and vinegar, the mixture of emotions never seemed to become anything.

Her father had said nothing when she'd announced she was moving out. She'd pretended she was part of Mildred and

Howard's family and had counted the days until Howard would marry her and she would be part of his family for real. She believed it would be a new beginning, another chance to have a family that she hadn't ruined. The letters on the bed caught her attention. Picking up one of the faded envelopes, she withdrew the letter.

My Florence,

I'm sitting in the hallway and it's late. The city has finally gone to sleep. You know our boarding house is by a nightclub and it doesn't close until late. I've gotten used to going to sleep with the noise. I'm usually so wore out that I fall asleep almost as soon as my head hits the pillow. It's a different tired than farmwork tired.

Tonight, I couldn't go to sleep because I kept thinking about you. I wish I could marry you now. But we need to wait. This boardinghouse isn't a place to raise a family, and I don't make enough to support you and our kids yet, especially since I have to send so much back to my dad and sister. I know they're struggling, but I want to keep all the money for us. I wish they could see how easy it is here. The work isn't as strenuous as farm labor. Plus, Dad isn't here yelling down my throat.

You'll love the city, Flo. There are so many opportunities. I want to build us a life here. We can get a place a little way from the city, and I'll make a nice home for us. We can have a big yard like in the country but still be close to my job and all that's going on. It'll be perfect. I can't wait to bring you here, so we can spend our lives together.

My eyes are tired and I want to go to sleep, but

first I have to tell you about a dream I had last night. We were on a porch swing and watching two children play, a girl and a boy. I think they were playing tag. They both had your smile and the little girl came up and gave me a big hug. Her eyes twinkled, just like yours.

I love you.

Yours always,

Howard

She sniffed and returned the letter to the envelope. They'd had it all, but she'd ruined it.

The house was quiet when Florence left the guest room. She listened at the stairwell. Nothing. The bathroom door was open. Where was everyone? In the empty kitchen, clean dishes dripped dry on the counter. William's bedding lay folded next to the couch. The front door was open. Loud banging and laughter wafted in from the porch.

She opened the screen door and it shut with a bang.

"Look what they're building." Jane sat on a chair with her ankle propped up. She pointed to her uncle, who leaned over a pile of wood. The smell of lumber reminded her of Howard. Henry held the structure steady while William pounded a nail into place.

"He says I'm a natural carpenter." William dusted off his pants.

Henry beamed at his nephew. "Your dad taught you well."

At the mention of Howard, the familiar ache returned. She wished she could forget him. He'd surely forgotten them. She moved closer to the group. "What are you building?"

"He's finally finishing that dollhouse he started a while back." Mildred leaned against the porch railing and sipped from a mug.

"My other one is small. But this one's big enough for Jane and me to play with." Peggy danced around the structure. "William can play with it too."

William shot his cousin a look of contempt and handed his uncle a nail. "I don't think so." He wiped a bead of sweat from his forehead. The day was heating up.

Florence leaned over Jane and studied the building. It was three stories high and made of scrap wood. "You've done a great job, Henry. Howard built Jane a dollhouse, but it…" The words died on her lips when she met Jane's darkened eyes and crossed arms.

"They burned my dollhouse."

Peggy stopped dancing. "Why?"

"Stupid polio." Tears welled in Jane's eyes.

Henry stopped pounding. "Whose dolls are those on the porch? Do you think they're big enough for this grand dollhouse?"

Jane sniffed. Peggy ran and picked up the toys. Then she and Jane bent to see if the dolls would fit. Glad for the distraction, Florence turned. There was probably something that needed to be cleaned inside.

Mildred cleared her throat. "Flo, let's go into town. I need some groceries. Someone used up all my flour making cookies." She shot a knowing look at Florence.

Florence shifted. She couldn't go to the store. She wasn't ready to meet him. "I was going to—"

"Let me get my list, then we can go." Mildred went into the house.

Henry and Peggy glanced at Florence. They knew Mildred's no-nonsense tone when they heard it. Florence sighed and went inside. If they were going to be in the same town, she couldn't avoid him. Maybe if she pulled her hat down low enough, he wouldn't notice her. Her appearance had changed over the years and his probably had too.

They rode in uneasy silence until they reached the outskirts of town. Mildred said, "He doesn't own the store anymore. He moved on."

With wide eyes, Florence stared at her. "Why didn't you tell me that before?"

"You're the one who didn't want to talk about him. Do you blame me?"

"No." Her insides relaxed and her stomach growled. "You know, I've only had a couple of cookies today. I'm starving. Do you want to eat lunch out?" With a quick glance at her handbag, she tried to remember how much she had left. Maybe she could pick up a part-time job at the restaurant. There'd been a family-owned diner a few doors down from the grocery store. "My treat." Surely, she had enough.

"That sounds like a great idea. I know just the place."

They passed the grocery store her father had owned and other businesses she didn't recognize. For the first time since she had arrived, Florence let herself feel happy. The children were safe and fairly healthy. Her dad had moved. She didn't need to worry about him anymore. After a pleasant lunch with her friend, everything would be different.

When they pulled into the restaurant's parking lot, tension bubbled up inside her. The diner had changed.

In large letters, the sign over the door read Annabelle's.

Suddenly, she and her sister sat at the kitchen table. Dad danced Mom around them. "That was the best meal yet. You should start a restaurant." He twirled her in a circle and kissed her on the mouth. He patted each of his daughters on the head. "What do you girls think? We could call it Annabelle's."

Florence shot Mildred an icy stare. "What is this?"

Without making eye contact, Mildred got out of the truck and shut the door. Florence continued to stare at the sign, not believing what she was seeing. How many times had Hattie and she played restaurant? When her mother taught them to cook, they'd pretend they worked at a restaurant. Florence was the cook and Hattie the waitress. She could still hear her sister's small voice. "Welcome to Annabelle's. May I take your order?"

Now Florence stared at the sign's black letters.

The truck door opened and Mildred helped her out.

"You said he moved."

"No, I said he moved *on*. It's time, Flo."

Her legs felt rubbery, and she leaned on her friend, not sure how to feel. "Why didn't you tell me?"

"Would it have mattered?" Mildred linked her arm through Florence's and walked her toward the restaurant.

She opened the door, half expecting to see her mother, but when the bell jingled, it wasn't her mother's face.

"Good morning, welcome to…" The man's hand, raised in greeting, froze.

He couldn't be her father. The long face was right, but not the white hair or the wrinkles. Who was this old man? Before she had time to process the familiar face, he scrambled forward and embraced her.

He hadn't hugged her since before her mother died. Her arms hung limp and her heart thudded. He smelled different. A mixture of spices she couldn't quite make out. A strange sound came from him. Feeling warm and uncomfortable, she pushed away. He was crying.

He wiped his eyes. "Florence, I've dreamed about … I can't believe…" Turning to Mildred, he pumped her arm. "Thank you." He led them to a booth and plopped down a couple of menus. "Sit here." He caressed Florence's cheek. "I can't believe it's you. You're so beautiful. Sit, sit." He motioned to the seat.

Florence, like Mildred, sat. Not wanting to look again at the old man who was her father, she studied the menu and gasped. Every item was something her mother had made. "What is this?"

"It's for your mother. They're her recipes. It's her restaurant."

She looked at her smiling dad. He'd done it. He'd created the family fantasy that they had talked about. Her mouth felt dry. She stared at him, unable to speak or think.

He patted her shoulder. "I'll show you." He turned on his heel and left. On his way across the restaurant, he greeted a couple of patrons and gave an order to a waitress.

Pointing at her father, she gave Mildred a confused look. "I don't understand." Her dad seemed happy, but more than that, he moved with purpose and the steps of a much younger man. His face had aged, but his spirit seemed fresh and new. "He's like a different person. What happened?"

A waitress put glasses and place settings on the table. Mildred shrugged and sipped her water. "I told you. People change."

The sparkling restaurant was just how they had dreamed it. White tablecloths covered the tables. Pictures of Iowa scenery hung on the walls. People filled the space, quietly chatting and eating. It was a restaurant that felt like a home. Florence looked back toward the kitchen, expecting to see her mom again. Then a thought occurred to her.

"Dad said 'thank you' to you. Why? What did you do?"

Mildred pursed her lips and continued studying the menu. "I only did what you know I did. I brought you here so you could see him."

Florence raised her eyebrows in disbelief.

"You think I can make *you* do anything? I had nothing to do with Howard or with you coming here. I've asked you to come home for the past fifteen years. And it was your idea to eat lunch."

"But what did you say to my dad? Why is he thanking you? You've been talking to him, haven't you?"

Mildred groaned. "Florence, don't act like a teenager. Your leaving devastated him. Then you never answered his letters. He asked me about you and the children. What was I supposed to do? Lie? I only told him little things."

Florence glared at her. "You shouldn't have talked to him." She gulped her water, then coughed when it went down the wrong way. She didn't want to talk to him, and she didn't want to be in this place that reminded her of what she'd done.

"I'm not mad at him, Florence. This is a small town, and he has the best restaurant in the area. I can't avoid him. What would you do if something separated you from your children?"

A young waitress set a basket of bread and two cups of coffee on the table. "Compliments of the owner."

Florence wrapped her hand around the hot cup. She would do anything to be with her children. She couldn't live without them. Wasn't that what Howard had accused her of? Putting her children above him. It wasn't the same with her father. She loved her children, but her dad didn't love her anymore. Maybe he never had.

"All parents are the same. They want to do the best they can for their children." Mildred poured cream into her coffee, then passed the pitcher to Florence.

Even though she wanted to leave, she stirred in cream and held the warm cup in both hands. Her father crossed the crowded dining room with a large tray. He nodded to a man and smiled at a child who chewed a grilled cheese sandwich. He seemed so at ease that she looked around for the camera. Was this some kind of movie? Nothing seemed real.

"You're going to love this." He beamed and sat down two steaming bowls and another basket of bread.

"Frank, your pea soup is delicious." Mildred stirred hers and sniffed appreciatively.

Florence picked up her spoon. It hovered over the bowl while she shook her head, trying to wake up from this strange dream.

"I knew it was your favorite. When you and Hattie played in the snow, your mother always had a pot of pea soup ready to warm you up. Remember?" He pointed to the window. "It's too late in the year to expect snow, but you and Hattie loved it year-round."

Of course. She stirred the soup. It looked like her mother's soup. The texture and color were right. She sniffed. Something smelled different. "Is this her recipe?"

Frank nodded and looked hopeful. "Taste it. Tell me what you think."

She blew on the hot liquid and took a small taste. It was a wonderful soup, the best she'd had in a long time. Dipping her spoon in, she took another sip and shook her head. "This isn't her soup."

"What?" Mildred's spoon stopped midair, and she gave Florence a warning look. "This is excellent."

Frank studied his daughter with a serious expression. "It's your mom's recipe."

Across the street, a man heaped dirt into a window box, then planted a yellow begonia. It was the same color as Hattie's hair. She remembered after a sledding trip, helping Hattie take her snowy mittens and hat off. They spread their clothes near the stove and went into the kitchen. Mom stood at the counter slicing bread. "Florence, check the soup. What do you think it needs?"

"What do you think it needs?"

Florence startled and looked up, expecting to see her young mother, but she saw her old father, who seemed to have shrunk. "Mom said that recipes were guides. Real cooks have to add their own special touch."

He pointed to the kitchen. "Can you add her special touch? Figure out what's missing?"

She followed him to the kitchen. On the stove, a pot of pea soup bubbled. Scanning the nearby spices, she added a few dashes from a couple of bottles. Then she found a clean spoon, stirred, and tasted.

"Well…" Her dad leaned his head toward her.

She ladled some into a nearby bowl and handed it to him.

He tasted it and smacked his lips. "That's almost it."

With a grin, she nodded. "You should have added more celery in the beginning. Mom always added more than the recipe called for."

"You're hired."

She looked at him in confusion.

"You can add your mom's special touch. This was always supposed to be a family restaurant. I want you, Howard, and your kids in my life. I'd do anything to have you in my life. Even if it's only for a short time. If it's okay with Howard, I want you to—"

"Howard's not here." She slammed the ladle onto the counter and ran from the kitchen, across the dining room, and outside. She recalled Hattie's laughter when she tried to catch a snowflake on her tongue. Her giggles mixed with Howard's boyish voice, "Throw it harder, Flo, it'll make you feel better."

But it wasn't snowing, and it wasn't winter. The day was warm, almost hot. All the businesses had bright flowers out front. Across the street, the bright yellow flower taunted her. She couldn't work for her father, not after what she'd done. Plus, he was a liar. He wouldn't do anything to be with his child. He'd left her. He'd retreated into himself and hadn't given her a second thought. Just like Howard, he didn't care about her and never had.

Chapter 19

Florence slung clothes into the suitcase. Mildred stood behind her with her hands on her hips. "What are you doing?"

"I'm leaving." She snatched her dresses from the closet, but Mildred blocked her way.

"Why? What are you going to do back there?"

"You don't understand. I have to get a job, and the kids have already missed too much school. Jane's surgery will need to be scheduled next year. I have to go back. Maybe I can work at one of the schools."

"Stop telling me I don't understand. Do you think you're the only one who's ever had something hard going on in their life? We all have hard times. Stop feeling sorry for yourself."

Florence paused, flabbergasted at her sister-in-law's outburst.

Mildred grabbed the dresses from her arms and rehung them. "You can have a job here doing something you love. Henry and I want to help you. We have plenty of room. The kids can go to school here. Peggy loves having you all." She gave her an unexpected peck on the cheek. "I love having you. Stay. Do what's best for your kids and everything else will fall into place. It doesn't have to be permanent. Just try it. Sometimes we get unexpected blessings when we stop trying to control everything."

Mildred left without waiting for an answer.

Florence sat on the bed next to the open suitcase. What was best for her kids? They missed their friends, but back home, the rumors would be starting. They both seemed to love the farm and their family. William had been playing catch with Henry, something Howard never seemed to have time for anymore.

Jane and Peggy were already inseparable. Maybe this would be best for all of them. It could be their fresh start, but what about the restaurant? Ever since her parents had dreamed about Annabelle's, she'd longed to work at a restaurant. Nothing relaxed her or energized her as much as cooking. But working with her father?

"Mom?" William stood in the doorway. "Do you know when Uncle Henry will be back? He had to get a tractor part in town, but he's been gone a long time."

She patted the bed next to her. "Do you like it here?"

He sat down. "Sure. I miss Dad and my friends, but you were right. It is fun. And you know what Aunt Mildred says about farm air?"

She studied his face. Dirt streaked one cheek. Maybe here he wouldn't have to be so mature. And maybe she wouldn't have to keep things so neat and orderly now.

Jane's crutches sounded in the hallway. Her head peeked in the door. Someone had French braided her hair. "What are you guys doing?"

"Talking." William scooted closer to her and patted the bed.

She hobbled over, putting a little weight on her sprained ankle. "Peggy says she has to go to school on Monday. She says I can't go. But I miss school. How come I can't go?"

"Well, what if you did?" Florence looked at her children, thinking that they might beg to go home, but they smiled.

"Uncle Henry says a lot of the guys play baseball and they have a sandlot for pickup games." William rose and mimed throwing a ball.

"Can we really?" Jane bounced up and down on the bed. "I could go to school with Peggy."

"Well, you wouldn't be in the same class. She's a year older than you. And it's only a few more weeks until summer vacation starts."

"That's okay. She was telling me all about the school and I can't wait." She rose and hugged her mom, then noticed the suitcase. "Are you going somewhere, Mom?"

"Just unpacking." She started putting the rest of her clothes back in the drawers. "I think we'll stay for a while."

The children left smiling, but dread shrouded Florence. Could this be the fresh start they needed, or had she made another mistake? Her mother's blanket lay at the foot of the bed. The lilac smell beckoned her to stay.

The day was already warm when she and Henry left to take the kids to school. Green shoots dotted the fields. He'd borrowed the neighbor's roomy sedan, so the kids wouldn't have to ride in the back of the pickup and dirty their school clothes. The three youngsters crammed into the backseat.

Florence turned and studied their freshly washed faces. "William, you'll need to help Jane on the bus when it's time to go home. It might rain, which will make it slippery." Was Jane ready to go back to school in another state, away from everyone she knew? Kids and teachers could be mean.

Jane, dressed in one of Peggy's old dresses, gave her mother an annoyed look.

Peggy said, "I'll walk with her down the hall, so she won't slip. Her teacher can help her too. I had Mrs. Jones when I was her age. She's nice." Peggy, scrunched between the two siblings, peered out the window. "I don't see any clouds. It won't rain."

"I hope it does." Henry gazed into the mirror.

"What's that little house by that farmhouse?" Jane asked.

Peggy giggled. "It's not a house." She giggled again, and William joined in.

"Don't laugh at me." Jane's voice sounded like she might hit or cry.

Florence scanned the area to see what they were talking about, but couldn't figure it out. Was it a hen house?

Choking back another giggle, Peggy said, "It's an outhouse. You know, a bathroom outside."

"Eww. Do they have that at school? I don't want to go in there."

Florence suppressed her own laughter. "No, dear. I'm sure the school has indoor plumbing. Only a few houses and the church have an outhouse."

Jane breathed a loud sigh of relief.

Henry slowed down and turned. The school flag waved in the distance. Two boys walking along the road waved at them, then ran as if to race them.

"Jane, remember to look out for rugs and uneven surfaces. Be careful. We don't want any more sprains now that you're almost healed." Florence marveled that Jane hobbled on her bandaged ankle like nothing had ever happened.

Jane sighed. "You already told me. I'll be careful."

"She'll be fine, Flo. Everyone here is nice and understanding. She's not the only student who's had polio." Henry pulled into the parking lot near the entrance and got out before Florence could ask who else at the school had had polio.

When they entered the front office, the white-haired secretary greeted them. "Oh, a new student. And you have polio, dear?"

"I had polio, but I'm all better." Jane stepped up to the desk. "I'm in first grade."

"I see." The secretary coughed and shuffled some papers on her desk. "I have just the class for you. Your mother needs to sign these."

After filling out the forms, Florence turned to kiss Jane goodbye, but the secretary and Peggy were already escorting her down the hall.

"She'll be okay." Henry motioned her out the door to a covered walkway that joined the elementary to the junior high and high school. "William's school is this way."

Glad that the buildings were connected, she followed Henry and William.

"Don't worry, Mom. They know where I am if something's wrong with Jane." William patted his mom on the shoulder. Then he trotted ahead of his uncle and into the junior high's main office.

After another quick form signing and no wave or kiss from her son, Florence stood outside with Henry, feeling almost as bereft as when Howard left. All alone again. She swiped a tiny tear. Henry gave her an awkward side hug. "Let's go. I've got a lot of work to get back to."

In the car, she sniffed. Feelings swirled inside her like the ingredients in a cake without the promise of a sweet outcome.

"The kids will be fine at school. William and Peggy will keep an eye on Jane. The bus will drop them off afterward and Mildred will be there to greet them." Henry patted her leg. "You'll be okay too. Work will do you good."

They rode in silence. Everything here seemed different from what she had left. No tall buildings or pollution. Instead, the county had sturdy farmhouses and the bright newness of spring. Yet, the dangers here loomed taller than any building. William might be teased. Jane might fall. Howard had left them lost and adrift. They drove toward her father, who had left her years ago, not physically, but emotionally. How could she spend her days with him? But working at a restaurant had always been her dream.

Henry fiddled with the radio knob, but failing to find a station, he turned it off. "I'll be glad to get my truck back. I just fixed the radio. It gets more stations than this car."

She'd never noticed her brother-in-law during their school years. He started dating Mildred, who always overshadowed him, after high school graduation. His quiet, hardworking presence faded into the background.

"If you need anything, call Mildred. I'll be working all day, but she knows how to get ahold of me." His smile reassured her as he parked in front of the restaurant. "Spring's here. Anything can happen in spring."

She swallowed her fears and opened the door. Mildred and Henry always seemed so positive and hopeful. Maybe some of it would rub off on her.

"I'll wait a few minutes after you go in if you want me to, just to make sure you're okay."

"Thanks." She saw him for what he was, a friend, just like Mildred. Glad she wasn't alone, she spoke with borrowed assurance. "I'll be okay. You go home and get your work done."

When he drove away, she faced the building and reread the sign over the restaurant, Annabelle's. She pushed against the door. It didn't move. She hadn't noticed that the interior was dark.

Muttering, anxiety rising, she glanced down the street. The car turned a corner, then disappeared. Why had she told Henry to leave? She pounded on the door, then studied a small sign on the window. The restaurant didn't open for another hour. She pounded again and peered into the window. Lights came on inside and someone walked to the door.

The lock turned and the door opened. "Florence? Come in. Sorry, I didn't know you'd be here this early." Her father ushered her in, then shut the door behind her.

She searched the nearby counter for a phone. "I'll just call Henry to pick me up. I don't want to impose." She shouldn't have come. Hopefully, a nearby business would be hiring. Why did she think coming unannounced would be a good idea?

He stepped back, hurt clear on his face. "Stay. Mildred told me you were coming. I just didn't remember what time. You have a job here anytime you want one. That's why I opened this place. I always hoped you'd work here. You're so like your mom. Both of you are talented cooks."

"Well…"

"We can discuss the day-to-day business over coffee. I just put a fresh pot on. I'd love to hear any ideas you might have. Recipes. Improvements. Anything. The workers won't be here for a while. Farmers are busy this time of year, so I expect a slow morning."

Her stomach rumbled. She'd been in such a rush to get the kids ready, she'd only nibbled on a piece of toast. "Coffee sounds good. Thanks Dad."

He smiled at the name. "I can fry us up some eggs too, if you'd like."

There was something so different about him. He was polite, happy, at peace, not the moody, grieving man he'd been before. She followed him through the dining room and into a neat, clean kitchen. The metal counters gleamed. Pots hung from hooks. Pans and utensils lined the shelves. Rows of spices and ingredients urged her to cook.

In the back corner, an opened door led to a set of stairs.

"My apartment's up there." He closed the door, poured them each a cup of coffee, and motioned to a small table in the back. "This is for staff breaks. Sit and I'll get the cream and sugar. Then the toast and eggs."

She poured in cream and sipped the hot brew while watching him move comfortably in the professional space. He faced the stove, which eased her nerves because he wasn't studying her reactions to his comments.

"Tell me about your family." He heated a skillet on the stovetop, then cut two slices of bread for toast. "I've missed so much."

Her cup midair, she gaped at him. Who was this man? "My family?"

He nodded and began frying the eggs. "Mildred told me you and Howard had two kids, a boy and a girl. I was wondering how they're doing. I'd love to get to know them." Humming, he sprinkled the eggs with pepper, toasted the bread, and slathered butter onto it.

Setting her cup down, she watched him, confused at the stranger he'd become. "What's happened to you?"

He placed the plates on the table and pulled out a seat. "What do you mean?"

"You're different. You never cared about me before. I know I've made mistakes but—"

"I'm sorry." His worn hand snaked out to hers, but she wrapped hers around her warm mug. "You're right. I have changed, and I didn't treat you well in the past. I understand that you're mad at me."

His words sounded rehearsed, but his tears made her stomach flip flop. Maybe she had misjudged him.

"When your mother and sister died, I shut down. I felt I'd come apart if I let myself feel, so I didn't give you the care and attention you needed."

"I was sad too. You never even noticed." Maybe all of this was her punishment because she'd broken her promise to her mother. Her inaction had ruined not one, but two families.

"I'm so sorry I failed you, Florence. There's no excuse for that. Will you forgive me?"

She gulped her coffee and burned her tongue but said nothing. She didn't want to forgive him or herself. Too much time had passed for anything to change. But he seemed sincere.

"You don't have to say anything right now. But I want to tell you about the change in me. I—"

The door in the corner opened. "Hello."

Florence rose and stared at the slim gray-haired woman, then at her father. Color rose in his cheeks. His mouth opened and moved, but no words came out. Did he have a girlfriend? Had she spent the night?

"Oh, you must be Florence. I've heard so much about you. I'm excited to meet you finally." She rushed to the table and hugged her.

All her breath left her, and she felt limp in the sturdy arms. The lady's dress was soft and smelled like lavender. Finding her breath, Florence pushed away from the stranger. "Who are you? Are you his girlfriend?" At least the children didn't know about their grandfather yet.

Her dad stood and stepped between the women. Again, his mouth opened, but no words came out. Had he been meaning to keep the mysterious lady a secret?

The gray-haired woman squeezed his shoulder familiarly and laughed. "Girlfriend? Of course not. I'm his wife, Bertha." She held her hand out. "Your stepmother."

"You're not my mother."

Her father wore two rings on his left hand. A gold one she recognized from her childhood and a shiny silver one that matched the one the woman wore on her outstretched hand. Why hadn't Mildred warned her? Being here was a mistake.

Bertha lowered her hand. "Of course not, dear. I only meant—"

"No one's trying to replace your mother. I was going to tell you, but—"

"You forgot." Florence glanced from her dad to the older lady. She didn't care about him anymore. She only needed a job to support her children and start a new life. Another business had to be hiring.

"I told you in the letters, but I guess you didn't read any of them." He ran his hands through his thin white hair.

"When I left, I said I was finished with you, and I meant it. Of course, I didn't read the letters." She scanned the room for her handbag. Had she brought her handbag?

Frank shook his head. "You always were stubborn. If you would have read—"

Bertha cleared her throat. "Stubborn? Wonder where she gets that from."

"I never read your letters because I didn't want to hear you blaming me for Mom and Hattie's deaths." Florence crossed her arms over her chest.

Frank's mouth dropped open in confusion. "Blame you? I didn't blame you for anything. Is that what you thought? How could I ever blame you for that?

Florence shook her head as if it could negate what he had just said. Of course, he blamed her. He must be lying for Bertha's benefit.

"I always wanted you in my life. When I was thinking about courting Bertha, then later when I proposed, I wrote to you. I invited you to the wedding. I wanted you to be a part of my life and I wanted to be a part of yours. Fifteen years, Flo. I didn't hear from you for over fifteen years. I sent so many letters. What was I supposed to do?"

Guilt washed over her. She had been a terrible daughter to her mother and now to her father. But he hadn't stopped her when she left, or said he loved her and wanted her to stay. "You let me move out of your house when I was sixteen. You never even missed me." Anger surged. His watery eyes wouldn't change how she felt.

"You're mistaken. I did miss you, but I believed you'd be better off there, where sorrow didn't live in every room. It was a mistake."

"I have to call Henry." A phone lay on the cluttered corner desk. She picked up the receiver.

"The pay's good here." Bertha wasn't as tall as she first appeared. Her long hair was coiled into a bun and she wore no makeup. Her face was lined and plain, like the homespun sweater she wore, but she carried herself like a city socialite. Head up, shoulders back, the way Florence had told Jane to stand. "If you need a job, Frank will treat you right. No one else in town is hiring. He's flexible. You can have whatever hours you'd like and as much or as little interaction with him and me as you want. Now that you're finally back home, let us help. What do you think?" She held out her hand. "Is it a deal?"

Florence lowered the phone receiver. She had to put her children first, and how could she do that if she didn't have an income? She couldn't rely on Henry and Mildred's generosity forever. "Can I cook and fix what I want?"

Her dad nodded. "Of course."

She shook the outstretched hand. "Thank you, Bertha." No way was she going to call her mom.

Chapter 20

Florence rubbed her back while she peeked out the window. Every part of her ached. Cooking all day was harder than she'd imagined. When the old farm truck parked in front of the restaurant, she left without a backward glance. Surprised that Mildred was in the driver's seat, she climbed in. "I thought Henry was picking me up."

"He's still out in the field." She shifted into gear, and they rattled down the street. "I guess now you're going to let me have it."

Florence massaged her neck. All day she'd imagined what she'd say to Mildred and Henry, but she was so tired that her well thought-out words evaporated. Instead, she leaned back and let the air from the window cool her. "It would have been nice if you had at least warned me about her."

"Bertha's a good person."

She couldn't argue with her sister-in-law. While Florence cooked, Bertha refilled coffee cups and mopped up spills. She worked seamlessly with the waitstaff and chatted with customers, calling them by name and asking about their families. While Florence's father played host and answered telephone calls, Bertha spent much of the time on the cash register.

"How long have they been married?"

"They didn't tell you?" Mildred raised an eyebrow.

"I didn't ask." Florence closed her eyes, longing for sleep. All day customers had streamed through the door. Glad for an excuse to keep her distance, Florence stayed busy, only speaking to her father and his wife when necessary. They had kept their distance too.

"A little over a year or two. They courted for a few years. He kept hoping you'd contact him or come for a visit. He really wanted you and your family at the wedding."

"You could have told me," Florence said, opening her eyes slowly. Her feet ached. What she wouldn't give for a long soak in the bathtub.

Mildred shot her a pointed look. "He made me promise not to tell you. You could have read his letters. You're both stubborn old goats."

Florence had put the letters into a box and pushed them under her bed. They started right after her wedding and arrived the first week of every month. The last one had shown up a week before she left for Iowa.

"They go to church with us."

She tried to imagine her dad in church. He stopped going after her mother died. He never enjoyed wearing a tie or listening to the preacher. Florence took Hattie a few times until her sister became sick. Then Florence had stopped going. Church attendance hadn't seemed to make a difference.

"You should give him another chance. He's—"

"Are the kids home from school?" Florence didn't want to give him another chance, and she was tired of Mildred acting like she had all the answers.

Mildred sighed and nodded. "They'd just gotten home when I left. William went out to help Henry, and the girls were doing homework on the porch."

She craned her neck to see the farmhouse in the distance. The day had been so busy, she'd forgotten about Jane's first day of school. Maybe Florence should have waited until tomorrow to start work. "They're by themselves? Do you think they'll be okay?"

"Yes, they'll be fine. I haven't been gone that long." She turned down the long drive and squinted. "I think I see them."

Near the house, two small figures were visible. Florence gasped. One girl was on a bicycle and the other one was climbing on. "Drive faster." She slapped the dashboard, her heart beating a tune in her ears.

Mildred laughed.

"Don't laugh. She's going to get hurt again."

The distance to the house seemed miles long. The girls zoomed across the yard and out of sight. When the truck reached the farmhouse, Florence shot out and toward the direction the girls had disappeared. Mildred jogged behind her. "Calm down, Flo. They're kids."

They rounded the corner and spotted the bicycle. Peggy steered and pedaled, while Jane clutched her cousin's waist, her braced legs sticking straight out from either side. The bike stopped smoothly in front of the women. Both girls giggled.

Florence screamed. "What are you doing?"

The giggles halted, and the girls looked at her in confusion. Before they could say anything, Florence tried to pull Jane off the bike, but her daughter was heavier than she remembered, and they both fell over onto the grass. Mildred looked down at the two, grinning. "Flo, they were doing fine until we came along."

She glared at her sister-in-law, then focused on Jane, who scowled at her mother.

"We were having fun until you made me fall." Untangling herself from the bike, her mother, and cousin, Jane took her aunt's outstretched hands and stood.

Florence picked herself up, dusting off her dress. "You can't ride a bike. I don't want you to get hurt. You already twisted your ankle."

While Jane held onto her aunt, her face started turning red. "You told me I was stronger than I thought. But you don't believe that. You don't want me to have fun."

Peggy had gotten Jane's crutches. Jane took them from her cousin and walked across the yard, with Peggy following.

"You can't keep controlling every movement she makes. You have to let go sometimes," Mildred said.

Anger rose in her. "I'm not controlling, I'm protecting. And if I don't, what will happen? I've already let her get polio. Then she twisted her ankle. I'm her mother. It's my job to look out for her."

A sad look filled Mildred's face. "You can't always protect everyone. Sometimes you have to let them live their own lives so you can live your life."

Florence glared as Mildred followed the girls toward the house. It was easy for her. She hadn't lost what Florence had lost. She didn't know what it was like to have a crippled daughter. Picking up the abandoned bicycle, she pushed it toward the porch.

Flowers and bushes lined the wrap-around porch. She walked the bike up the steps and leaned it against the fresh white exterior Henry had recently painted. The farm was neat and orderly. Even the boots next to the door had been cleaned of the usual manure. Henry and Mildred were born farmers and worked tirelessly to make their life successful. If only her life could be so wonderful.

Loud laughter interrupted her thoughts. She opened the door and followed the noise into the kitchen. Jane leaned against the counter, stirring a pot. Peggy stood next to her, retelling the bike ride adventure. Mildred, Henry, and William watched Peggy's exaggerated movements and laughed with the girls.

Discomfort settled in the pit of her stomach. Then William saw her standing in the doorway and said, "Mom, Uncle Henry let me drive the tractor. He says I'm a natural."

She nodded even as the taste of bile rose in her mouth. "How was school?"

"Great, I can't wait to go back tomorrow," William said. "We only have a week or two more, but the guys told me where they meet during the summer." He went to the sink and washed his hands, whistling. Henry joined him at the sink, taking the bar of soap William offered.

"My school was great too." Jane continued her even strokes. "Auntie, should I stir more?"

While Mildred leaned over her niece, Florence backed out of the doorway and retreated to her room. She lay down on the bed. Suddenly, she knew the answer to all of her problems.

It was in the kitchen. The image of contentment seared into her mind. Mildred and Henry had wanted more children to fill the large farmhouse. Years ago, they'd talked about adopting, but they didn't have enough money. Maybe if she worked a few more weeks at the restaurant, she could leave most of the money. It would be a start for them. Mildred and Henry would be the perfect parents for her children. Her upset stomach made her nauseous, but she knew it was the only answer. Families weren't forever. Mildred was right—she needed to let go.

"Wake up." Florence nudged Jane. "It's time." Somehow Florence didn't need an alarm clock to wake her. The past month on the farm had reset her inner clock. Her eyes flew open every morning as though her father hollered for her and her sister to wake up. Except that her father was in town with his wife.

"Don't go back to sleep," Florence said as she turned the light on and dressed.

"I'm not." Jane picked up a rumpled dress from the floor and put it on. "I haven't done that since last week." Her fingers flew as she buckled her braces over the long socks. The speed with which she'd adapted to the braces and farm life amazed Florence.

The bedroom door opened and Mildred's head peeked in. "Ready, Jane?"

Florence handed Jane her crutches. "What should we have for breakfast?"

"We haven't had griddle cakes for a while." Mildred pointed to the dresser. "That's a big wad of cash. What are you going to do with all that?"

"Well, since you won't let us pay rent, I guess I'll just save it for a rainy day."

Peggy peered around her mother, yawning, and rubbing her eyes, then smiled mischievously. "Jane and I need more doll furniture."

"Those eggs won't gather themselves. Let's go girls." Mildred left the house, with Peggy and Jane following her.

When the door banged shut, Florence added the bills to the money in the dresser drawer. After working full time for a few weeks, she'd accumulated a tidy sum, more than her bakery fund had been. Her father paid her more than the going wage. It would all go to Henry and Mildred when she left. Then, she'd find a new job and send back as much as she could.

In the living room, William's blankets lay heaped on the couch. She folded them, then placed them in the corner, knowing he'd already left to help his uncle with the morning chores. Neither of the children complained about the early morning work, although it had taken them a few weeks to avoid falling back asleep after she woke them. With school out, the farm's routine comforted Florence and gave her time to plan. She'd miss it when she left.

Florence started the coffee. While it perked, she squinted out the window, trying to see Jane. The ever-present knot of tension grew. Mildred told her that the chores were good for the children, but Florence still worried. Accidents were a big part of farm life. Cows and chickens weren't the most predictable animals. She didn't want Jane to get hurt again.

Florence poured a cup of fresh coffee, swallowed some, then got out the ingredients for breakfast. Following the cookbook instructions, she beat the egg whites separately, then folded them into the batter. It made for lighter griddle cakes, which her father had preferred. Dropping the batter by spoonfuls onto the hot griddle, she wondered why she still made them the way he liked them. But it didn't matter. Soon she would be free of him. She would put both families behind her and they'd all be better off.

She held the spatula ready while the edges of the runny cakes set, and her mother's voice returned. *Wait for the bubbles to form. Be patient.*

Now she waited. From her best guess, she'd leave in a month or so, right before school restarted and after she taught Mildred to do the exercises. William knew the process and he could show his aunt.

She flipped the cakes, pleased with the light brown edges. They were perfect. The screen door banged shut. She called over her shoulder, "Just in time. I'm almost finished with the first batch."

Setting the warmed syrup in the middle of the table, she returned to the cakes and put them on a plate. Strange that everyone was quiet now. Every morning after chores, the kids rushed into the kitchen, talking loudly, and rooting around for breakfast. Farm work made them all ravenous. With the plate in her hand, she turned and saw why the kitchen was so silent. Her father stood in the doorway, his hat in his hands.

"I was passing by, and Henry said that I should come in."

She raised an eyebrow. No one just passed by this early in the morning.

He laughed. "You have the same look as your mother when I lie. She always knew."

Not knowing how to reply, she placed the plate on the table, then returned to the griddle, ladling more batter onto the hot surface.

"I wanted to see my grandchildren and you. I saw Henry at the restaurant, and he said that mornings were usually best. But I can go if you don't want me here."

When she left town, she wouldn't be able to keep her children from him. She might as well let him stay. "There's plenty. Help yourself to some coffee."

His presence unnerved her when he moved next to her and filled a mug from the percolator. She'd kept her distance from him at the restaurant, even though he tried to get close. He used every opportunity he could to ask her a question or comment on her cooking.

After pouring a dash of milk into the coffee, he handed the mug to her. "Why don't you sit down?" He took the spatula and turned the bubbly cakes.

"Dad, you don't have to do that." A memory returned unbidden. She and Hattie crowded around her father as he made hot, round griddle cakes. They were so happy back then.

He dropped the batter onto the griddle and pointed to a large lump in one. "Remember how you hated the lumps? You argued with your mother that you needed to make the batter smooth." He laughed.

Years ago, she would have given anything to hear him laugh, but now it made her angry.

He flipped the cakes over. "Do you remember what your mom said?"

Of course, she remembered, but to reply would only encourage him. She sipped her coffee.

"She said that the lumps didn't matter. Not everything has to be perfect." He took the plate from the table and piled more on top. "Can't we start again?"

She glared at him. "Why are you trying so hard? You didn't care about me then and you don't care about me now."

A frown filled his face. He opened his mouth to speak, but the front door opened, and the house filled with voices.

"Mr. Stephens?" William placed the milk buckets onto the counter, then glanced between Florence and her father.

"How do you know him?" Florence asked her son.

Peggy swung the egg basket and giggled. "He goes to our church, and he owns the restaurant. He always has butterscotch or peppermints for us on Sundays. What are you doing here, Mr. Stephens?"

"Go wash up." Mildred took the egg basket from her daughter and tried to herd her toward the bathroom, but Peggy remained rooted to the spot.

Why hadn't Florence realized they would see him at church? Mildred mentioned that they all went together, but when she started letting the kids go with their aunt and uncle, she'd forgotten. "William, Jane, Mr. Stephens is your grandfather."

Their eyes grew wide. William scowled at her. "You told us he was dead."

She should have warned the kids. "No, I didn't. I never said he was dead. I just didn't talk about him. I'm sorry."

Henry and Mildred bustled around the kitchen, getting drinks and utensils for breakfast. Peggy hugged Frank. "Wow! Mr. Stephens is your grandfather. I wish he was mine. I don't have any grandparents."

The children eyed him anew. William pulled out a kitchen chair for him. "Mom said that your mother got kicked by a horse? Can you tell us about that?"

Jane leaned against her grandfather's chair. A slow, sly smile spread across her face. "Do you have any candy today?"

He laughed and pulled out a handful of peppermints. Frank raised an eyebrow in question at his daughter. "After breakfast, if your mom says it's okay."

She nodded in surrender, then went to make more pancakes, but Mildred stood at the griddle, already flipping a new batch, and whispered, "It's not as bad as you expected, is it?"

Florence scowled at her. She'd hoped to avoid all of this, but at least the kids didn't seem too upset that she'd never told them about him.

Her father leaned in close to Peggy and his grandchildren. "My mother was quite the horsewoman. She was much better than my father."

The phone rang.

"I'll get it," Florence seized the reason to leave the kitchen. Her father seemed to be a better grandfather than father.

In the hallway, she picked up the phone. "Hello."

"Flo?"

At the sound of the familiar voice, she reached out to the wall for support. "Howard?"

"I messed everything up."

Her heart hammered and her throat went dry. Laughter came from the kitchen and her head spun. Was he really on the phone?

"I spent one night away, and I knew … I came back and you weren't here. I can't do life without you anymore."

His words echoed inside her. *He came back.* A flutter of hope filled her.

"Florence, are you there?"

"Yes," she whispered. Another thought dawned on her. *One night away …* He'd left. He said he didn't love her. And what about the time he'd spent with this other woman? Could she even believe him anymore? Even if it was only for a brief time, he'd found love and companionship with another person. Someone who was more beautiful than her. Someone who knew how to keep families together.

"I want you to come back. Will you? We can try again."

Florence imagined what the woman must be like. Even if he wasn't with her now, he'd go back to her. No one in her life ever stayed.

"Please, Flo. Every day is worthless without you."

Without a word, she hung up the phone. She stared at the receiver until it rang again. She unplugged the phone. The only sounds in the house were those of her father talking and her children laughing.

<h1>Chapter 21</h1>

Florence held her iced tea glass against the back of her neck and sighed. There was no breeze. Heat shimmered across the freshly cut lawn. She sat on the rocking chair next to Mildred, who rocked with her eyes shut.

Through closed lids, she said, "You should take a nap with your daughter."

"I'm not tired. I'll just sit here awhile. My shift starts soon."

Mildred opened her eyes and narrowed them at Florence. "I thought today was your day off."

She shrugged and turned her head to study the tall corn. "I picked up another shift."

"What are you going to do with all your money?"

"Maybe get a car?" Florence had joined Mildred on the porch with one idea in mind, but her nosy sister-in-law was taking the conversation in another direction. How could she redirect her?

"You don't like using Henry's pickup?"

"He's going to need it, eventually." She picked up her mending basket and took out an old dress of Peggy's she was altering for Jane. "Besides, I can't keep taking your charity."

"You're acting strange. What're you up to?"

Florence accidentally pricked her finger with the needle and her voice came out sharper than she expected. "I'm mending."

"You're always mending. Or working. And you don't spend any of your money." Mildred stopped rocking and studied Florence in the uncanny way she did, as if she could read her thoughts. "Have you heard from Howard lately?"

She hadn't told Mildred about any of Howard's calls, and she hoped that no one else had intercepted one. Howard had called a few times, always telling her he loved her and that he'd made a mistake. "Why are you asking about him?"

At the hurt look on Mildred's face, she realized her words had again come out sharper than she'd intended. She didn't want to hurt her feelings or lie to her. She needed her help.

"You know, Flo. Sometimes when you hang so tightly onto something, you risk losing it all. Sometimes you have to let go. It might not turn out how you want it to, but with God, it will be good."

Florence swatted away a bug. Wasn't that what she was doing? Letting go. And she wished Mildred would stop with all the God stuff. Having her family together would be for the best, even if she was absent. Following a deep breath, she forced out the words she'd been planning so she could let go. "I want to ask you a favor, but I'm nervous."

Mildred sipped her tea and wiped her forehead with Henry's blue handkerchief. "Why are you nervous? You know I'd do anything for you or your kids."

She'd counted on that, but she needed to be careful how she proceeded. "William knows how to help Jane with her exercises, but I'd feel better if someone else knew."

Mildred narrowed her eyes and pursed her lips. Florence continued. "In case I got sick or too busy with work, it would ease my mind if someone else could help."

Mildred nodded, still looking suspicious, and answered slowly. "I'll help you with whatever you need."

"Thanks. I oil her braces every couple of days so they don't squeak. And she has to have time every day without them. The doctor told me it helps strengthen her muscles and increases the blood flow." Inside the house, the phone rang, but Florence continued, knowing William and Peggy were inside playing cards and would answer it. While she had Mildred to herself, she needed to take full advantage. "I can show you how to do the massage and stretching when Jane wakes. She doesn't mind anymore because it helps reduce her muscle cramps."

Mildred rested her hand on Florence's arm. "I told you I'd be happy to help. But are you going somewhere on a trip? Why are you telling me all of this right now?"

Florence giggled to hide her nervousness. She'd always been a horrible liar. "No, of course not. I just—"

The front door banged open and Jane squealed. "Daddy's coming to visit."

She whirled around. "What?"

"Daddy's on the phone. He says he's coming to visit, and he wants to talk to you."

Charging into the house, Florence rushed down the hall and yelled into the receiver, "I told you not to keep calling. And what do you mean by telling her you're coming?"

"What was I supposed to do? She answered the phone and asked if I could come. I want to see her and William, and you. I have something I need to tell you."

"You want to see her now? You were the one who wanted to put her away. Why don't you stay—?" A sob made her turn. Jane huddled against the wall, mouth open, tears streaming down her face.

"Florence? Are you there? I'm so sorry for what I did. Let me…"

Ignoring Howard's voice, she reached out to Jane, but she gripped her crutches, walked across the hallway and into their room. She slammed the door shut.

Without another word, Florence hung up and retreated into the kitchen. She collapsed into a chair. What could she say to Jane? There was no way she could fix this. Why hadn't she left sooner? Everything would be better once Henry and Mildred were in charge. Once she was out of the whole situation.

"I guess she heard you yelling." Mildred sat in the chair across from her.

Head in her hands, Florence nodded. "I messed everything up. Again."

"You made a mistake, just like Howard did."

"You're comparing what I did to what he did?" She lifted her head to glare at Mildred, who riffled through a drawer.

"Want some bread?" Taking out a knife, Mildred set a loaf on a cutting board and sliced thick pieces. "You make great bread, Florence. I know you learned from your mom. I'm sure she taught you that if you make one mistake in baking bread, you mess everything up." She slathered butter on two portions. "If you let it sit too long, it won't turn out right. If you don't let it sit long enough, it won't come out right. Life is like that. One minor mistake and everything messes up. But we don't have to do it all alone. God wants to help you. He's good at fixing messes."

Florence sighed. "I'm not in the mood for a sermon. Besides, I'm not the one who needs your little lecture. Howard's the one who was kissing someone else. He's the one who stopped loving me."

Mildred placed a hand on her shoulder. "Slow down. Relax. If you'll stop trying to control everything, you'll see who you're really mad at."

Florence left the kitchen and went into the bedroom she shared with Jane.

"You lied to me." Jane lay across the bed, glaring through red, puffy eyes. "You said that Dad didn't leave because of my polio, but he did."

"He didn't leave because of your polio." Sitting down on the bed, Florence tried to rub Jane's back, but she scooted away.

Jane crossed her arms. "But you said he wanted to send me away."

"Let me explain." She leaned against the headboard next to Jane. "At first, he thought we wouldn't be able to take care of you. He thought if you went somewhere else, the doctors and nurses there would help you more than we could."

"Where?" Jane's eyebrows scrunched, and she sniffed.

"It doesn't matter." The screaming and white-clad figures filled her mind. She shook her head, trying to shake the images away. "But when we visited the place, we realized it was a mistake. We had to have you home with us. It's why your dad built the ramp, and we set up the den. We both wanted you home with us. You're our family. We belong together." Guilt about what she planned to do flooded her.

"Really?" Wiping her nose, she snuggled against her mother. "Then why were you yelling at Daddy? And why don't you want him to come here?"

Jane's innocent, tanned face peered into hers. How could she explain Howard's deception? She inhaled, searching for the right words, any words that would help her daughter understand why she couldn't see her father. "I shouldn't have yelled. I made a mistake. But your dad made a mistake too. And he can't visit."

Jane tilted her head to one side. "Why not? I forgive you for yelling. I'm sure Daddy does too. And you can forgive him for what he did, can't you?"

"Well…" No, she couldn't. Her marriage was nothing like bread. Marriages couldn't withstand affairs, even if it was only a kiss. Marriages needed love. Besides, how could she ever trust him again? But how would she explain to Jane that some things were unforgivable? "It's difficult, you see…"

Jane wasn't listening. She opened the drawer next to the bed and pulled something out. Florence rubbed her palms on her dress and a sour taste filled her mouth. It was Jane's framed picture. She hadn't seen it since they left home. Since Florence hadn't packed it, she assumed it hadn't made the trip.

Jane ran her hand over the glass. "The preacher said that we all make mistakes, and that's okay because Jesus forgives our sins. And since he does, we can forgive other people." She thrust the picture toward her mother. "When I'm sad, Jesus helps me. He can help you, too."

With reluctance, she took the picture. Through the fingerprints on the glass, she saw the cherubic face, but only felt hopelessness. If Jesus cared, he'd help her explain how things really were to her daughter. If he cared, polio would never have ruined their lives. Her sister and mother would still be with her.

"Can you forgive Daddy? Then he can visit. Farm air will be good for him too."

As she looked into Jane's hopeful eyes, she nodded. What else could she do? Jane hugged her.

The door opened. Mildred held a plate with thick slices of buttered bread. "How about a snack?"

"Daddy's coming to visit," Jane said.

Mildred raised her eyebrows in question to Florence, who looked away.

Jane grabbed her crutches. "I guess we need to eat in the kitchen, so we don't get crumbs on the bed."

Sitting beside her, Mildred held the plate out to her niece. "This one time we can eat here. Sometimes we have to relax our control over everything. Then you can show me the exercises your mom does with you."

Giggling, Jane took a slice of bread. As Florence watched her eat, a plan took shape in her mind. Anyone could see that Mildred was an exceptional mother. When Howard came to visit, she would convince him of that. William and Jane needed two parents who loved each other. Sure, she would miss her children, but she had to put their needs before her own. Howard would understand. He'd already wanted to give their daughter away. He could go back and find a better wife than her.

Pushing the framed picture under Jane's pillow, she reached for a slice of bread. She would have to give up control of her marriage and her children.

Chapter 22

The children, as well as Mildred and Henry, had asked her every week to go to church with them. Now, clambering into the neighbor's sedan, Florence searched for a new excuse, but she had used them all. Since the restaurant was closed on Sundays, she could only have so many pretend headaches or do so much cooking. The icebox was full. Casseroles were ready for when she was finally gone. Scrunched in the backseat with Jane and William, her stomach tensed, and she regretted her decision to attend. She consoled herself by planning to take the time during the service to figure out how to convince Howard to accept her plan.

On the other side of the bench seat, William rolled down his window. "Uncle Henry, how come we're not taking the pickup? I'd much rather ride in the bed. There's more room. Besides, you can feel all the bumps and potholes. It's like a carnival ride. Ouch, Jane, stop poking me with your bony elbow."

Jane nudged him with a crutch. "You're on my side."

Florence scowled at them. They'd been sniping at each other all morning.

Wedged between her parents in the front seat, Peggy pushed her hair off her sweaty forehead. "This car smells funny too. I think Mrs. Yates had her dog in here."

Henry laughed, started the car, and drove down the drive. "I prefer the truck too, but this way, our hair and clothes stay nice. You don't have to keep plucking straw off your best Sunday clothes during the sermon."

As they merged onto the road and the wind blew into the interior, Florence leaned against the seat, holding her hair back.

She wasn't so sure if the car was any better for her hairdo, but it had been nice to have another vehicle to take to work while Henry drove the truck.

"The smell will go away. We're lucky Mrs. Yates traded it to us. And we're even luckier your dad is a talented handyman who could fix her plumbing in exchange for it." Mildred grinned at her husband and he winked back.

Catching the exchange, Florence's stomach settled. Over the past week, she'd become more certain of her plan. Henry and Mildred never argued. They held hands and stole kisses when they thought no one was looking. Howard would have to agree that they were better parents.

When they pulled into the church parking lot, Jane squealed and pointed. "There's Grandpa and Gramma."

The knotted feeling returned to Florence's stomach. She hated the names William, Jane, and even Peggy had adopted for her dad and his wife. The endearments and the closeness of the relationship made her uncomfortable. The kids only saw them on Sundays, but her dad kept inviting her and the children over and hinted at a dinner invitation every chance he could.

As soon as Henry parked, the kids jumped out and hurried toward the church.

"It's nice Peggy has surrogate grandparents," Mildred said, as the adults exited the car.

Florence scowled and wanted to remind her that Bertha was no one's grandparent.

Mildred returned the scowl. "Just because you won't forgive your dad doesn't mean that you should deprive your children and mine from a meaningful relationship with Frank and Bertha. You know Peggy doesn't have grandparents."

Without a word, Florence strode ahead of her. She wouldn't come back to church, but if her plan worked, she'd only be here a week or two more.

Sunday school had been dismissed for the summer. Children ran in circles around the adults who crowded the church steps or lingered under the trees in front of the building. Bertha, Peggy, and her children were nowhere to be seen. Frank fell into step beside her. "Jane told me her dad's coming to town tomorrow."

She nodded.

"You and Howard should have lunch at the restaurant. Just the two of you, my treat." He clutched his Bible to his chest.

"That's okay. We'll probably eat at home." Why couldn't he leave her alone?

"I know marriage is hard. But you both can work it out."

She stopped walking and studied him. His hat sat at an angle on his head, a light layer of perspiration on his face. She remembered how he and her mother had looked at each other. They had held hands and kissed like Mildred and Henry did, just as she and Howard had once.

He took off his hat and wiped his forehead with his handkerchief. "You should do it for your kids."

She narrowed her eyes. "You're giving me advice?"

A shadow passed over his face, and he frowned. She walked away. He'd never known what was best for his children, but she knew what was best for hers. Summoning a plastic smile, she shook hands with the greeters at the door. Then she slid into the pew next to the children.

From the row in front of them, Bertha turned around. Her yellow pill box hat and matching dress reminded Florence of an ear of corn. Holding a handful of butterscotch that almost matched her outfit, she asked, "Candy?"

The children eagerly took one each, but Florence shook her head. Her father slid into the row, smiling at her before he sat down next to Bertha. Florence jerked her gaze downward, pretending to study the bulletin resting on her dress, although not a single word registered. When Mildred and Henry took their seats next to her, the pastor welcomed the congregation.

His words jumbled in her head while flies buzzed in through open windows. Cornstalks outside stood at attention, as if listening. A teen boy crept from the church, probably to use the outhouse. Up and down the aisles, men took off their suit coats. Paper fans flashed. The soft swish of Bible pages turning during the sermon came and went. In front of her, the gray heads of her dad and his wife leaned together as she whispered to him. Her pulse quickened. That should be her mother next to him. Her sister should be between them. Wrong. Everything was wrong.

Jane elbowed her. The congregation had stood and begun singing *Amazing Grace*. When she joined in, the words registered. Memories flooded her mind. She lay in bed with a fever. Her mother rubbed her back and sang the comforting words in low tones. She and Hattie had stood in this same church, sharing a hymnal.

Amazing grace how sweet the sound

That saved a wretch like me

Florence fanned herself with the paper fan. The image of Jesus that flashed back and forth before her was similar to the one in Jane's framed picture. Heat swept over her, and she felt like she might faint. Across the years, her sister's high, squeaky voice sounded.

I once was lost, but now I'm found

Was blind, but now I see

The hymn recalled her mother's soprano voice as if she were sitting behind Florence. Mildred rubbed her arm and brought her back to the present. Florence took her hankie from her sleeve and dabbed the tears on her face. Her mother and sister weren't really singing. They were gone. She pushed past Mildred and Henry and hurried from the building. Still feeling warm and faint, she headed for the cemetery. She collapsed onto their graves and let her sorrow flow.

After a while, a hand rested on her back, a soft and reassuring touch. She assumed it was Mildred, but when she turned, her father squatted next to her. An old man in dress pants and a collared shirt with a loosened tie. He looked out of place with the fields that extended behind him.

With a grunt, he settled himself on the grass next to her. "It's okay to cry."

Anger surged inside her. She wanted to shove him over and run away. Instead, she screamed, "No, it's not. You never let me cry. I had to hold everything together. Take care of Hattie. Take care of you and the house. But I did nothing right, did I? I let Hattie die. Then after she died, you couldn't even look at me. Nothing I did could ever fill the hole they left." She pulled her knees into her chest, not caring if she dirtied her clothes on the ground. She no longer felt hot, just tired.

Deep lines crisscrossed his sad face. So different from the muscular man who used to carry her on his shoulders. "It wasn't your fault that Hattie died. It wasn't your job to keep our family together. It was mine, and I failed. I'm sorry."

"Right there at the end, Mom told me to keep the family together." She bowed her head. "I failed. If only I had—"

"No, you didn't fail. It wasn't your job. Your mom made a mistake in asking you. That was never your responsibility to bear. You were so young. I made a mistake when I stood by and allowed you to shoulder those burdens."

He stroked her hair. "Being a parent is hard. You try your best, but we all mess up."

She sighed, all too familiar with mistakes. She expected him to lecture her like Mildred, but to her surprise, he plucked a wildflower from the grass and held it out to her. "You know your mother wanted to name you Violet."

Studying the delicate flower, she shook her head. She hadn't known. Violet was a better name. Maybe if she had a different name, her life would have turned out differently.

"I was the one who wanted to name you Florence." Tears filled his eyes. He studied the oat field across the road. In the distance, a bird sang. "Before you were born, your mother left me."

She looked at him in surprise. He plucked another violet and twirled it between his fingers. Her mother would never do that. Unless he had done something to deserve it. Had he behaved like Howard?

"I thought she'd never come back. She was gone for months. One day I came in from the fields. She was in the kitchen cooking, as if nothing had changed. When she turned around to greet me, I saw you growing there."

Something in her head buzzed as she tried to make sense of what he was saying. Her mother had left? Then she came back pregnant. Did that mean…

He smiled at her. "She always loved the name Violet for a girl. But I told her if you were a girl, the name had to be Florence." Setting the flower down, he took a folded piece of paper from his pocket. "Florence means—"

"Blossoming," she said. What he was saying made little sense. Her mother had an affair?

He nodded. "But more than that. It means prosperous, flourishing. In the winter, everything dies. No one knows what the next year will bring. A farmer's entire livelihood depends upon the crops. But in the spring, things start to blossom and flourish. It's a new beginning. All the hardness of the winter fades."

The sound of the preacher's sermon reached them. Not the actual words, but their cadence. Strong and steady, like her mother kneading dough, pounding it until it was just right. The breeze blew the long grass that was dotted with the purple wildflowers.

"Our marriage was reborn because of you. You brought your mother back to me. And when you returned to the restaurant, you brought your mother back a second time. You are so like her. You blossom and flourish wherever you are planted." He handed her the paper in his hand. "Your mother wrote this for you, and she told me I was to give it to you when you needed it. Maybe I should have given it to you sooner."

Still in shock from what he had said, she clasped the yellowed paper. If what he said was true … "I'm not your daughter?"

He grinned and stroked her hair. "Of course you're my daughter. You'll always be my daughter." He kissed her forehead, stood, and walked away.

She stared while his retreating form grew smaller until he disappeared back into the church. Had he made it all up? But why would he make something up like that? She unfolded the paper. Fresh tears formed at the sight of her mother's slanted penmanship. She could almost see her bending over the page, her brow furrowed in concentration as she formed each letter.

My dearest Florence,

I wanted to write this letter to you a long time ago, but your father didn't want me to. He doesn't want any of us to live in the past. He says that the winter is over, and we don't need to remember its harshness. Yet as I've watched you and your sister grow, I've learned an important lesson. Our pain and our mistakes teach us. They help us grow. They form us into who we need to be. Without winter, we'd never enjoy spring.

You see, I made a horrible mistake when your father and I were first married. We got on well enough, but after a couple of years, I didn't feel the same about him or our life. I didn't like the uncertainty of the crops or the long hours of farm work. The routine made me tired, but it also bored me and with your dad working from sunup to sundown, I was lonely. Then, a man kept coming to our farm stand. He was dashing. He reminded me of a movie star. I still don't know how it happened. He showed more interest in me than any other man had. He convinced me to leave your father. I thought being with him would be easier, that it would be an adventure. I'd always wanted to go on an adventure. So, I packed up my trunk and went. And at first it was everything I hoped it'd be. A fresh start, a new beginning.

But he was not who he said he was, and the adventure was not what I thought it would be. He beat me, and I told myself that I deserved it since

I left your father. I thought it was the punishment for the mistakes I had made. But when I felt you growing inside me, I knew I had to choose the best for you. Even if I didn't deserve a good life, I knew you did. So, I returned to my farmer and the life we once had.

He welcomed me back. He didn't ask for an explanation, and he didn't punish me. When you were born, your father was overjoyed. He couldn't stop talking about you and looking at you. He said that you looked just like me. We had the same nose, the same smile, he said. While that might be true, I know you are most like your father, your real father, Frank. You have the same heart. I saw it when you were a small girl. You love so big, and it doesn't matter if the other person deserves it. Hold on to that, Florence. Because love isn't a feeling, love is a choice. Family is a choice. We choose who we will love and how deeply we will love them. You taught me that, you and your father.

You were the bloom that brought me back to him. The bloom that made me stay and build our family. You held our family together and I think you always will.

Keep loving, Florence, even when you don't feel like it, even when those around you don't deserve it. Even when you've given everything. You'll find that there is still love left to give. Because it is love that holds us all together.

Love,

Your mother, Annabelle

Tears fell on the paper as she ran her hand over the words. It felt as if her mother was once again stroking her back and humming into her ear. But Florence didn't know what to do with her feelings and thoughts. Her mother was different than she had thought. And her father? He was different too. Nothing made sense. What could she believe? If the letter was true, she wasn't even who she thought she was.

She refolded the thin paper. When people started streaming out of the church, she rose and met her family at the car. No one said anything when she approached them. They all filed into the vehicle and drove home silently. Back at the farmhouse, she laid down on her bed and attempted to sleep, hoping a nap would help her make sense of everything.

Chapter 23

Florence opened her eyes to the sunlight streaming into the room. Oh no, she'd overslept and missed morning chores. Why hadn't someone wakened her? Jane's side was rumpled and empty. Strange, her daughter was usually loud in the morning. The picture frame peeked out from underneath Jane's pillow. She pushed it back, then turned over. On her bedside table was a piece of folded paper. The words from the letter returned. She closed her eyes. Her head ached. Maybe if she stayed in bed, she could forget what the letter said.

"You're not dressed? You have to be at the station to pick Howard up. His train will be in soon. Remember? He had to spend the night in Chicago."

At the sound of Mildred's voice, she pulled the cover over her head. "I can't get him. I don't have time to fix my hair or do my makeup. He can find his own way here."

Mildred jerked the blanket off her head. "His train will be here in an hour. Just enough time for you to dress, then drive into town. Get up. I'll help you." She began brushing Florence's hair, then fanned her own face. "It's hot in here."

Still groggy from sleep, Florence remembered she hadn't ironed her dress. "I need to—Ow! That hurts." She placed her hand on the tender spot where Mildred had yanked the brush through a tangle. Was Mildred this rough on her own daughter's hair?

Mildred swatted the hand away and placed some pins in it. "The girls are picking berries for me and William's out with Henry. You don't need to do anything except pick up your husband." She crossed to the window and opened it wider. "Why is it hotter in your room than anywhere else in the house?" Taking the pins, she poked them roughly into Florence's scalp.

Florence bit her bottom lip and stood still. She wasn't needed here after all. Though she'd already come to that conclusion. Nobody would miss her when she was gone.

Mildred sighed. Florence turned to see the sweat that ran off her sister-in-law. "It's not that hot in here. The fan's working. Are you going through the change?"

Ignoring the comment, Mildred stood back and eyed Florence's hair. She nodded. "Looks good. Put this on and you'll be ready."

Florence took the freshly pressed dress from her sister-in-law. It wasn't the plain one she'd chosen, but the floral one that was Howard's favorite. She dressed, then put a light layer of powder and a quick swipe of lipstick on. Without glancing in the hallway mirror, she grabbed the car keys. She wasn't trying to romance her husband, just convince him that her plan was the right one. When she pulled out of the driveway, she checked her reflection in the side-view mirror. She adjusted a stray strand of hair, tried out a possible smile of welcome, and admitted that Mildred had done a decent job.

As she sped to town, she tried to practice what she would say to Howard, but no words came. The revelations from her mother's letter crowded out other thoughts. Her mother wasn't the person she thought she was. In her memory, she'd been flawless. An ideal she could never become. Her father had been the villain in her life's story, but now she didn't know what to think or believe. She'd been mistaken about so much. When she pulled into the train station parking lot, she still hadn't figured out how to broach the subject with Howard or what to do with her dad.

A crowd had gathered on the small platform waiting for the train. She glanced at the clock. It was five minutes late. Her father stood on the sidewalk in front of the car and waved to her. He was the last person she wanted to see. She wasn't ready to talk to anybody about anything, much less to him. With a huff, she got out of the car and managed a wan smile.

"I thought I'd wait with you. The train should be here soon. A lot can happen between here and Chicago." He studied his pocket watch, then tucked it back into his trouser pocket.

She nodded, not trusting herself to speak. Shading her eyes, she squinted into the distance and caught sight of the train's headlight on the horizon.

He pointed to the willow tree. "Let's stand over there out of the sun's heat."

She followed him while the train approached. "How did you forgive her? I thought affairs were always grounds for divorce. How could you ever trust her again?"

"Affairs can be grounds for divorce. You have a good reason to turn your back on Howard. I had a good reason to turn my back on your mother." His smile puzzled her.

She remembered the father he had been when she was small. She and Hattie had followed him down to the pond on Saturdays. Hattie on his shoulders and her hand in his. He taught them how to swim and fish. Their laughter had filled the air.

"But you didn't leave her, and you didn't make her leave. You seemed so happy."

"We were happy, but it took time."

The horn blared for the nearby street crossing. When the train squealed to a stop, she moved closer to her father to hear his next words. He smelled of bacon with a faint whiff of strawberries.

"Every day I made the choice to forgive and trust. And she made the choice to stay and work on us. That's what marriage is, what family is. You make a million choices every day and the most important ones are to love. Love isn't a feeling. It's a choice. And …"

Hadn't her mother said the same thing? A handful of passengers streamed off the train and into the parking lot. The conductor yelled, "All aboard!" to the milling crowd.

Frank leaned his head close to hers. "Sometimes the hardest person to love and forgive is yourself." He kissed her cheek. "If you want to come to the restaurant, I'll have a special meal waiting for you and Howard." He replaced his hat and strode off.

She stared after him. What had happened to him? Had she ever known him before? Could it be possible that she was wrong about him?

"Florence?"

Howard had stopped a few feet away. He looked thin and in need of a haircut and shave. She wanted to run into his arms. She missed him more than she liked to admit. Her feet started moving, but she stopped herself, haunted by the remembered smell of perfume and the lipstick stain. "Hi."

He shifted his suitcase to his other hand. "I'm—"

She held up her hand. "We can talk later. Let's put your luggage in the truck. We can walk to Annabelle's for breakfast."

Following her to the truck, he asked, "Annabelle's?"

"Dad's restaurant. He and his wife, Bertha, opened it. They serve Mom's recipes. I work there."

Howard slung the case into the truck bed, then faced her with wide eyes. "That's a lot of information. I'm not sure what to think of all that. Sounds like you've had an eventful trip."

"That's only part of it. There's more." She laughed. "And I'm not sure what to think about it, either."

He fell in step beside her as they walked down Main Street. "What do you want to talk about first?"

His intense gaze made her feel uncomfortable. Despite her best intentions, she still felt attracted to him. "The kids love it here. William helped Mildred butcher a chicken. She said he's a natural. He didn't throw up the first time like I did."

Howard chuckled. "Sounds about right. And Jane?"

"She twisted her ankle, but that hasn't stopped her. Nothing stops her. She goes everywhere and does everything. She named all the barn cats. Last week, I found her playing with the neighborhood kids in the barn loft. Not sure how she got up there."

He grabbed her hand and squeezed it. "I missed you. It's good to be here."

Surprised by the gesture and her racing heart, she squeezed back, but then quickly dropped his hand. Uncomfortable, she pointed to the restaurant sign. "There it is." Then she remembered that the restaurant wasn't open this early. Why had her dad told her to come by? Maybe he was getting confused in his old age. She tried to recall if there was another place open now. She was hungry and wanted to talk to Howard privately before they returned to his former home.

Ignoring the closed sign, he opened the door. "Looks like we're the first ones here."

She walked into the empty restaurant. The tables were clean and bare, except for the one in the middle. A lit candle was centered on the lace tablecloth.

Her father greeted them with a smile, then locked the door behind them. "Glad you made it here safely, Howard."

"Nice to see you." He shook hands with his father-in-law. "It's been too long."

Frank ushered them to their table, then disappeared back into the kitchen.

"He's different," Howard said. "Marriage must be good for him. Do you think that's the difference?"

She shrugged. But she knew it was more than Bertha, more than the forgiveness he had extended to her mother. Something had changed in her dad since she had left town. He wasn't the same person. She poured them each a cup of coffee from the carafe on the table.

Her father appeared with a tray. He laid down two plates loaded with food. Florence smiled, remembering that the meal was one of the suggested ones in her mother's cookbook: strawberries, hominy with sugar and cream, bacon, fried eggs, baked potatoes, and a plate of rye muffins.

Howard stared at the food. "Wow! I'm glad I didn't eat breakfast on the train." He took a bite of bacon. "I'd love to meet the new Mrs. Stephens. Is she here?"

"You two talk first. There'll be time later." He patted Florence's shoulder and left.

Florence realized that his affectionate touch hadn't made her feel uncomfortable. She took a bite of the crispy bacon. It would be hard to leave all this behind.

Howard grasped her hand. "Can you forgive me?"

She pushed his hand away. "Forgive you? You made me feel like I was going crazy. I was cleaning and doing things to help our family. You only made excuses so that you didn't have to deal with me and the kids. You left long before you moved into Don's house."

"You're right. I'm so sorry. I understand if you can't forgive me. But I'm here to win back your trust, Florence. I've quit my job. I'll work—"

"What? You quit your job? How could you do that?"

"I thought if I worked with Henry on the farm, we would have time to get to know each other again. Spend time with you and the kids. Jane told me that farm air is good."

He couldn't ruin her plan, not now. She shook her head. "You can't stay here. You've always wanted to live in a big city."

"But I love you and it doesn't matter where we live, only that we live together. I've thought it through. A slower paced life will be good for us. Life without you was unbearable. That's what I've been trying to tell you for the last few months, but you keep hanging up on me. Do you remember our chipped bowl? You know, your parents' bowl."

Eating a strawberry, she broke eye contact with him. An old bowl she should have thrown out. Was he here to tell her about another mistake she'd made? She reached for the bacon, knowing she needed to steer the conversation away from chipped bowls and mistakes.

"I was eating soup in the bowl, your soup, and that's when I remembered what you told me and suddenly everything made sense."

"What are you talking about?" Her words had never made a difference in how he behaved. Why would now be different?

"The bowl has one imperfection, but it's still useful. You held onto it because it was meaningful to you and it still served a purpose."

Florence nodded, wiping bacon grease from her mouth. Her father peered out from the kitchen door, but she turned her attention back to Howard. She remembered all the tomato soup she'd had out of those bowls when she was a child and all the soup she'd served her children. Lunch on Saturday had always been grilled cheese and tomato soup when she was a child and when she became a mother. "What does that have to do with anything?"

"Something inside me broke when Jane got sick. Then it split farther apart when that police officer came up. I thought it was me breaking apart. But those breaks were only cracks. And cracks aren't a reason to throw something away. One imperfection doesn't make something useless. Jane's sickness wasn't a reason to give up on her, but a reason to fight for her, just like you did. You tried to explain it to me, but I couldn't see it. I do now. It's the same reason you never gave up on me or our marriage before. My farm injury isn't something that should hold me back, but something that should make me fight harder. Don't give up on us, Flo. I made a mistake, but we have to use it to strengthen our marriage. The cracks just show us the parts of ourselves that we need to work on."

How could he change his tune now? It was too late. He didn't love her, and even if he did, it didn't matter. Sickness and disaster followed her like a black storm cloud.

"I can't. I'm leaving the kids with Mildred and Henry. You can go back to your mistress and your job. Or start over in the construction business. That way, everyone wins." She sat back in her chair with her arms crossed. She hadn't meant to blurt out her thoughts. From the stunned look on Howard's face, she should have waited, but she couldn't take the words back.

"Let me get this straight." He swallowed. "You want to leave the kids with my sister and brother-in-law? Here? Without us? Then we go our separate ways, without them and without each other?"

"Yes." How could she convince him? "Mildred and Henry are great parents. They've done a wonderful job with Peggy. They love each other and our kids. You know they wanted more children. It's a perfect plan where everyone wins."

"No one wins. I love you and you love me. Our kids belong with us. We'll work this out. We're a family."

Tears formed, and she blinked to keep them at bay. "You didn't want to work on our marriage before when you gave up."

"I made a mistake, Florence. Please forgive me. I've always loved you. And I do want to work on our marriage."

She turned from his pleading eyes. Her father could take back his wayward spouse, but she couldn't, wouldn't, take back hers. "I can't forgive you. I want a divorce." The plate of food no longer seemed appetizing. Her stomach revolted, and she tasted bile in her throat. She rose from the table, then after fumbling with the deadbolt, she fled the restaurant.

Howard followed close behind. "Please. Can't we talk about it?"

She said nothing, but continued walking. When they reached the truck, she considered driving off without him but waited instead. It was too hot and too far for him to walk home.

After she shifted into gear and pulled into traffic, he said, "You drive really well."

Remembering Olive's lessons, she accelerated, driving faster than normal on the country roads. She thought that smoke might come out of her ears. Patch everything up now? It was too late.

When they approached the farmhouse, her anger began to melt away. She had to make him understand. She glanced at his white knuckled hold on the door and slowed as she drove down the lane. "Watch how they interact with the kids and each other. It's the perfect solution."

As they exited the car, Howard said, "Our kids belong with us. They need us and we need them. I see that now. You tried to tell me before, but I didn't listen."

Ignoring him, Florence went inside. Mildred lay on the couch, asleep. She put her finger to her lips as he set his suitcase by the door. They tiptoed into the kitchen. A bowl of blackberries sat on the table. From the aroma in the air, she knew a roast and vegetables were in the oven. Dirty dishes lined the counter. Mildred didn't ascribe to Florence's clean while you cook routine.

Howard looked out the window. "I wonder where the kids are."

"William's probably with Henry. He's always with Henry." She gave him a knowing look as she put on Mildred's apron. He'd understand soon. "Jane and Peggy are most likely playing somewhere. They're like sisters."

"I know what you're doing." He kissed her on the cheek before she could protest. "But our kids need us. I'll go find Henry and William." He strode out of the house, letting the door bang behind him.

She hoped the sound hadn't disturbed Mildred, who seemed especially tired this morning. After rinsing the berries, she found the pie crust already rolled out on the counter. Strange that Mildred hadn't finished making the pie. She must have been exhausted.

As she stewed the berries, she remembered all the summers she had wandered the fields, picking berries with her sister, Mildred, or Howard. Howard had taught her to make an old Crisco can into the perfect berry bucket. Her spirits lifted as she cooked. Humming, she finished the pie and thought of strolling the fields and pastures with Howard, kissing behind the bushes. All thoughts of her past would need to be banished. This new life would be better for her children, and that was what was most important.

With the kitchen clean, the roast cooling on the table, and the pie in the oven, she surveyed the kitchen, wondering what to do next. Then the front door shut with a soft click, followed by girlish giggles and the unmistakable sound of her daughter's crutches on the wooden floor. She'd been a mother long enough to recognize the sound of someone, or two someones, sneaking home. What had they been up to?

In the hallway, the girls stopped at the sight of her. Water puddled around them. Their wet hair plastered to their heads.

"Where have you been?" she asked, though the sight and smell of them told her all she needed to know.

The girls looked at their muddy feet. "At the pond."

Anger and fear rose inside her. Images of empty pools from previous summers flashed through her mind. Surely polio couldn't have followed them here, but you couldn't be too cautious. Remembering that Mildred was asleep on the couch, she lowered her voice. "I told you not to swim in the pond."

The girls nodded. Peggy looked at her aunt. "But after we finished picking the berries, Mom said we were too loud and we should go outside. Her stomach felt funny, and her head ached. She said she was going to rest for a bit. It was so hot out, and …"

The anger fell away and panic flooded Florence. Upset stomach, headache, fatigue. Then she remembered how hot Mildred had been that morning. It couldn't be, could it?

Chapter 24

Florence felt Mildred's forehead, though she didn't need to. Despite the fan aimed at her, sweat beaded her sister-in-law's face. An image of her mother on a different couch and the smell of burned brownies made her heart skip a beat.

"Mildred." Florence shook her. How could she have overlooked the symptoms this morning? The sweating, the fatigue.

Shivering under a blanket, Mildred moaned in her sleep.

"Wake up, dear." She continued to shake her shoulder.

Her eyelids fluttered open. "Did you get Howard? I'm sorry, I just laid down for a minute. Let me get up." Grunting, she tried to sit up, but collapsed once more. "Let me just rest and my strength will come back." She closed her eyes. "My legs feel funny."

Florence's heart raced and tears fell. This couldn't be happening again. Outside, boots stomped up the steps and male voices sounded. "Howard, Henry," she called.

The chatting stopped. The front door flung open. Three ashen faces rushed in. "What's wrong?" William asked.

"Mom's sick," Peggy said. She and Jane had perched on the end of the couch. Their hair continued to drip.

"Mildred," Florence said. "Can you bend your chin to your chest?"

She raised her head an inch, but then it fell back. Mildred groaned in pain and Jane screamed. Florence froze, remembering, but then Howard pushed her aside.

"Henry, start the truck." Howard picked his sister up, staggering under the load.

"Shouldn't we call the doctor first?" Still in his manure caked boots, Henry started toward the phone.

"No." Howard pushed the door open with his hip. "If it's polio, the faster we act, the better. I don't know how long it'll take an ambulance to arrive."

At the dreaded name, Henry changed directions and sprinted out the door. In minutes, the truck tires squealed away, then silence settled on the living room. Florence's hand rested on the warm cushion where her sister-in-law had just been. The doilies, once centered on the back of the couch, now hung crooked. Polio had followed them. Why wouldn't sickness and disease leave her alone?

Peggy and Jane clung to each other and cried. William stared into space as if in a trance. Florence wanted to hide under the blanket that had just covered Mildred, but she knew what she had to do. Hadn't she fought this beast before?

"William, go outside and start the burn barrel. Do you know how?"

He nodded and left the house.

"Jane, Peggy, we need to get you both in the bath. Then we'll start the cleaning."

After the girls' bath, they scrubbed for hours, burning what they thought they should. Florence quieted her worries by constantly moving. The children picked at the roast and pie. Eventually, she wrapped up most of the food. William scrubbed the soot from his hands and face, then all three youngsters trudged off to bed.

Night had fallen when Florence went out to the porch. She rubbed her back, then collapsed onto the rocking chair, putting her feet up onto the porch railing. Her body hurt, yet her mind wouldn't shut off. She'd watched the children all night for polio symptoms, while planning out what and how to clean. Now her mind whirled with worry over Mildred. Sleep was out of the question until she got some news.

Peering into the darkness, she yearned to see the light from the truck with the three sitting on the bench seat. Howard and Henry would lead Mildred up to the house, explaining that it had all been a mistake. They had misread the signs. She was overworked and needed to rest. The round trip to the hospital would take a while. It was an hour or more away. But no lights appeared in the darkness. No sound of an approaching truck interrupted the night's silence except for the croaking of the frogs.

Then a light in the distance shone. She rose as the headlights bumped on the drive and grew brighter. Shading her eyes from the glare, her heart sank. It was a car, not a truck. As her father got out of the sedan, she sat down.

He climbed the steps. "Howard called me at the restaurant."

"It's polio, isn't it?"

He nodded and sat in the chair next to her. "I'm going to close Annabelle's for a bit. I heard on the radio that another outbreak may be brewing. The hospitals are full. Luckily, she got a bed. Howard said he and Henry would be home soon now that she was settled."

Under the sliver of the moon, she rose from the chair and peered into the distance. Where would she go now? How could she outrun all this? She couldn't go through all this again. To her horror, she began to sob. Her father embraced her, and she wept into his arms. She hadn't even cried like this when her mother died.

He smoothed her hair. "I know it's hard."

She pushed away from him. "You know? You don't know. How could you possibly know what I've done?" Pacing to the end of the porch, she rubbed her hands together. "I messed up my first family, then I messed up with Howard and the kids. I was going to leave the kids with Mildred and Henry. Now that's ruined." She checked his expression to see if her admission shocked him, but his mouth was set in a straight line, giving no emotion away.

Returning to the chair, she sat and rocked. Then an idea bloomed in her mind. "If Henry takes them, you and Bertha could help. Mildred will probably recover quickly, like Jane. Then, you—"

Her dad leaned against the porch railing, studying her. Then he laughed.

"Why are you laughing?" Heat rose in her face. "This isn't a joke. I keep messing everything up. Everyone will be better off without me, just like you were. You're different now. Since I left, you've changed for the better. You can help Henry raise them, even if Mildred stays sick for a while."

He sat down, still chuckling. "You're wrong. No one would be better off without you, and like I told you before, none of this is your fault." His face grew serious. "But you're right about one thing. I am different. But I didn't become different because you left but *despite* your leaving."

When he placed his hand on the chair's armrest, she noticed how fragile his skin was. Veins crisscrossed the back of his palm. On his ring finger, the two wedding bands moved slightly. His fingers were thin, thinner than she'd remembered. A long scar ran down his forearm. She'd never asked how he'd gotten it.

"When I hired Bertha at the restaurant, I didn't think I could love again, but the love grew slowly, and I kept thinking about her. I was smitten."

Florence groaned. She didn't want to hear about her father's love life or the woman that replaced her mother.

"But she wouldn't have anything to do with me. She told me she wouldn't be interested in someone that didn't go to church. So, I went to church."

"You went to church. You're telling me that's the difference. If I went to church, everything would work out." She gritted her teeth. "Why didn't I think about that?"

He chuckled again. "No, it wasn't church. It was who I met at church."

"Bertha? Well, I'm not marrying Bertha."

"No. Him."

"Oh." Realization dawned on her and she rose from her chair. "Jesus." She thought of Jane's picture and anger seethed in her. He had made no difference in her life before.

"Yes, Jesus. I had a hole in my heart. I never got over losing your mother and sister. Then you left. I felt like I was drowning and barely getting by. But I encountered Jesus in that little church, and he made the difference. He helped me to deal with the loneliness and grief."

She swatted away a mosquito, and the fatigue weighed on her body. What would it be like to not carry around the burden of her misplaced guilt and grief? "I've got to go to bed, Dad. I'll need to get up early for the chores."

He faced her and placed his hands on her arms. "Jane showed me her picture. You know she doesn't love the picture because it's beautifully painted. She loves it because of who is in it. Jesus didn't heal her, but he helped her to keep going. He helped her in ways we may not understand. Ask her about it. Jesus is love, and love doesn't always look like what we think it should. Love doesn't control and hold on, but lets go. When we release our plans and our hurts, we give him room to take them up and to take control of our lives." He kissed her forehead and walked toward his car.

Inside the house, she saw William curled up on the floor in a heap of blankets. In the lamplight, she watched his chest move up and down. She turned off the light and went into her bedroom. In the darkness, she stumbled into her nightclothes. Jane turned over in her sleep and mumbled something. When she slipped under the covers, she snuggled up to her.

"Good night, Mama," Jane mumbled.

She kissed the back of her daughter's head, thinking about what Mildred had said, that Jesus was good at cleaning up messes. Could he help her? "Jane? Can you tell me about your picture? Why do you like it so much?" What was she doing? Waking her child up in the middle of the night to ask her a ludicrous question.

Jane turned over. "When I close my eyes, I see his face just like it is in the picture. He talks to me."

"What does he say?"

She laughed and snuggled next to her mother. "He doesn't say actual words. But he speaks to my heart. When the pains wake me up in the middle of the night, he tells me it's okay and I know he's next to me."

"Does he make the pain stop?" In the darkness she couldn't see her daughter, but the sheets rustled, and she knew Jane had shaken her head.

"No, he doesn't make the pain in my legs stop, but he makes the pain in my heart stop, and I know that no matter how much pain I have, I'll be okay." Jane yawned and put her arms around her mother. "He really loves me."

Florence was tired of controlling and worrying. Tired of carrying all the guilt. Tired of being in a game she could never win. She enjoyed the warmth of Jane's small body. Could it be possible that her own child knew something she didn't?

Maybe she could trust this Jesus of Jane's. Just let it all go and give everything to him, as Mildred had said. Could it be that simple? When Mildred returned home, she would find the strength and help her friend just as she had helped Jane.

She listened into the darkness for the sound of the truck so that she could get an update on Mildred and talk to Howard. Maybe they could try again. Jesus could repair her family. Couldn't he? The chorus of the crickets and frogs made her eyes grow heavy. She fought to keep them open but finally succumbed to sleep.

Florence blinked awake as sunlight crossed the room. The events of the previous day flooded back. She'd fallen asleep and Howard had never wakened her. Jane snored while Florence slipped out of bed, put on a robe, and padded out of the room. The house was quiet. She'd slept through morning chores, but no animals protested, so she assumed the men had done them. William lay curled on the living room couch, fast asleep.

The front door was open. Through the screen, Howard and Henry climbed the steps, then took off their manure-crusted boots. Henry passed by her without a word. His unshaven face and bloodshot eyes made her take a step back. She wanted to tell him that Mildred would get better in time, but she thought maybe it was too soon. Recovery would be a long road.

Howard wore one of Henry's denim shirts and his face had the same haunted look as his brother-in-law. He embraced Florence. She sunk into him. He smelled a bit like the barn-yard, but a faint whiff of pine quieted her.

"How's Mildred?" Florence began making a mental list of the exercises she would do with her. She'd start earlier than she had with Jane and maybe the recovery would go faster. Maybe Jane would even like to help. She visualized her friend's return to health.

Howard put a hand on her arm. "We need to talk, Flo."

Startled by his immediacy, she looked into his tired face. "We can talk about us later, don't you think? We need to focus on Mildred and getting her through this. When are visiting hours? I'll go as soon as they let her out of isolation."

"Sit down." He led her into the kitchen and motioned to a chair.

Someone had perked coffee. Her stomach rumbled. "Can't we talk later? I need to make breakfast. I'm assuming you took care of the eggs and milk?"

Howard shook his head. He opened his mouth to speak, but no words came out. Tears rolled down his cheeks.

She caressed his arm. He'd never cried in front of her before, not even at his father's funeral. "I know it's hard to see someone we love in pain. But we'll get through this. When, she—"

"No." He held her hand in his and shook his head again. "We thought she was safe in the isolation ward. I assumed it would be like it was when they took Jane away. We were leaving the hospital, when we saw a doctor running down the hall. We followed him. She was having trouble breathing."

Images of the iron lungs flashed in her mind, and the rhythmic sound of the artificial breathing returned. The boy with wavy hair had haunted her for the past year, his sad eyes peering at her while the machine breathed for him. It seemed so long ago. What had happened to him? She didn't want to think of her dear friend in one of those horrible contraptions.

"They put her … in a …." Howard placed his hands palm down on the table as if to steady himself.

She put her hands over his and nodded. "I know. But she'll be okay. People survive those."

The tears continued to fall down his face, and he shook his head again as if telling himself that what he had seen hadn't really happened.

Her previous optimism faded away, and dread replaced it. Coldness seeped into her limbs. She knew what Howard had so much trouble saying.

"It didn't help." He wiped his eyes. "She didn't make it."

Florence covered her mouth and drew away from him. Numbness spread through her. Her best friend, who had always been so strong and wise, hadn't made it. The faceless enemy of polio had claimed one more life.

Chapter 25

After the graveside service, the mass of people in black left the cemetery and piled into their vehicles. Even though Howard and her father had offered to stay, Florence insisted that the walk back to the farmhouse would be good for her. Now, she sat in the short grass, next to her sister's and mother's graves. The violets had disappeared, making way for fall. At the other end of the cemetery, a fresh mound of earth covered Mildred's final resting place. Feeling drained, Florence leaned back, listening to the birds, and trying to find the energy to leave.

A car pulled into the church parking lot. Someone got out and strode toward the cemetery. As the figure came closer, Florence saw the woman in a black and white belted dress carrying a bouquet of mums. She rose, suddenly feeling self-conscious that she was a grown woman sitting in a graveyard. Dusting off her black skirt, a spark of recognition flashed when the woman opened the gate. But it couldn't be, could it? She blinked, not quite believing what she was seeing.

The woman stopped a few feet away and gasped, mirroring Florence's stunned expression. Thinner and paler than before, she was the red dress lady from Jane's hospital. "Paula?"

"It's you. What are you doing here?" Paula shaded her eyes from the noonday sun.

"My sister-in-law's funeral." She pointed to the mound of dirt. "What are you doing here?"

"Jenny, my daughter." She indicated a small gravestone near her, then shot a confused look at Mildred's plot. "Are you related to the Wrights? Henry Wright?"

Florence nodded, thinking that this was getting stranger by the minute. "Yes. Henry's wife Mildred was my husband's sister. She's the one who just passed away."

Recognition dawned on Paula's face. "Oh, you're Frank Stephen's daughter, right? You were always sweet on Mildred's brother, Howard."

"Yes. Howard and I married. You're from around here?"

Paula laughed. "My maiden name is Neil."

Florence tried to place the woman with the stylish blonde bob. "Neil … Neil …" She faintly remembered a small girl, a few years younger than her, that had always trailed after a bunch of rowdy siblings. Then she remembered what Mildred had told her when she first arrived in town. "You all just sold the family farm, didn't you?"

Paula nodded, looking down at her pumps. "Junior talked us into it. My husband passed away at Normandy and I didn't think Jenny and I could handle it by ourselves. So, I agreed to the sale, thinking I'd never move back. But when Jenny died, I felt like I needed to come home. I'm staying with my aunt and uncle. They run the hardware store. It's good to be near her." She bent down and placed the flowers on the marker.

Florence joined her and searched for a helpful comment, but all comfort had left her. Paula stood, wiped her eyes, and pointed to the graves where Florence had been. "Are those your people?"

"My mom and sister. They died from the Spanish flu. Many years ago."

Paula cleared her throat. "I'm sorry. My aunt mentioned that Mildred died from polio. If only they had a way to stop all these horrible diseases."

"If only," Florence said as she made her way toward Mildred's grave. Paula fell in step with her. No stone had been set yet, only a mound of dirt marked the place where she rested.

"In my nightmares, polio is a black mass that chases me," Florence said as she kneeled next to the dirt. "Its blackness has invaded my life. It crippled my daughter, ruined my marriage, and now it's taken my best friend from me. I keep wondering if it's the same darkness that killed my mother and sister and drove my father away."

Ashamed that she'd just confided her fears and life story to an almost stranger, Florence put her hand on the solid mound that covered Mildred's body. Why did she always say the wrong thing? She continued kneeling, hoping Paula would leave. A nearby bird chirped, filling the silence. Florence's knees complained, and she stood.

Paula flashed her a thin smile, tears glistening in her eyes. "There is a darkness, a blackness in our world that is out to get us. But I'm glad that God is bigger than that. After Jenny died, I was mad at God. Mad he'd let her die, that he'd let the blackness overtake her."

The leaves on the oak tree in the middle of the graveyard had begun to turn colors. Paula picked up a yellow one from the ground and twirled it.

Mildred had asked Florence who she was really mad at. Now Florence realized that she'd been mad at God all these years. It had been God who had allowed heartache to enter her life. He had taken those she loved most from her. "How did you get over your anger?" Florence asked.

"It took a while. But I told him how I felt. I screamed at him." Paula kept twirling the leaf. Overhead, the sun had disappeared behind a dark cloud.

"Did that help?"

"I still hurt. I miss Jenny and my husband, Gary. But when I talk to God, it gets a little easier." Paula grabbed Florence's hand and squeezed it. "I wish I could say something that would make it all better. But I don't think there's anything I can say or do. Let God speak to you."

Florence remembered what Jane had said about her picture. God didn't stop the physical pain, but he stopped the pain in her heart.

In the distance, thunder rumbled. They looked into the darkened sky. "I can drive you home. Looks like it's going to storm."

Following her new friend to the parking lot, Florence said, "I'd rather walk."

"Walk fast, or you'll get wet." Paula hugged her and drove away.

Florence followed the country road toward the house. The thunder rumbled. The dark clouds resembled the layers in a cake. Lifting her face to the gray sky, she screamed, "Why do you always take those I love? Why do disease and sickness keep following me?"

The first drops of rain hit, cooling her forehead. Out of the corner of her eye, a purple speck caught her attention. A flower where the road and grass met. She bent down and plucked the bloom from the ground. Then the rain started to fall. She ran with the violet clutched in her hand.

By the time she reached the long lane, the rain stopped, and she slowed to a walk. Her heart beat fast and her breath came out in gasps. Vehicles filled the lawn. At the farmhouse porch, she knocked on the door. It felt good to be there, feeling the heaviness of her wet hair and dress. The fatigue in her muscles. She felt alive, truly alive.

William peeked his head out. Muted voices and the clinking of silverware came from inside. "Why are you knocking? You look like a mess, Mom."

She smiled. She knew someone who was good at cleaning up messes.

Jane peered around her brother. "What's in your hand?"

She handed the wet flower to Jane. "It's a promise."

After an emotional day, Florence felt drained, but marveled at Jane's speed and agility mounting the stairs. Was it possible that polio had made Jane stronger? A newspaper on top of the Candy Land board game caught her eye, and she remembered the list of polio victims from almost a year ago. Despair had filled her then, but now hope filled her. Death and disease didn't have to be the end but could be a beginning.

She opened her mouth to praise her daughter, but then closed it, not wanting to disrupt the quiet that had settled on the house. Henry had put Peggy to bed an hour ago, then disappeared into his room.

Jane paused outside her cousin's door. "I don't understand why Aunt Mildred had to die. Polio only hurt my legs."

She'd expected the question at the funeral or afterward when people crammed into the farmhouse eating casseroles and whispering, but Jane had spoken little. She had become Peggy's shadow, letting her cousin use her hankie and patting her back.

"Your aunt had a different type of polio than you did. It affected her lungs." Florence leaned against the banister, saying a silent prayer that she would have the words to comfort her daughter. "We don't know why sometimes polio affects only the legs, or why some people only have flu-like symptoms, or why some die. But we know none of it is your fault or mine. Bad things happen. We trust God is still in control and will help us get through our sadness."

She kissed Jane's forehead, hoping that her daughter would begin to internalize the lessons just as she was doing. Jane hugged her mother and slipped into Peggy's room, where her cousin slept.

Florence descended the stairs. She wanted to help Jane get ready for bed, but knew that Jane could handle that by herself. Mildred had taught her to not hold on too tightly to those you love. Loving doesn't mean controlling. Hearing William's soft snoring floating in from the living room, she went out onto the porch.

Still dressed in his Sunday suit, Howard sat on the porch step whittling. Without turning to her, he said, "I'll sleep on the couch again. Willie doesn't mind."

She sat next to him. "What're you whittling?"

He handed her the object. A wooden rose. He'd whittled a stem with thorns and a single leaf. "I started making it on the train. It won't wither like a real one."

Running her hand over the wooden leaves, she thought again of the violet from earlier. This flower was a hard copy of a delicate original. Real flowers and real life weren't as sturdy.

"Going to the hospital made me feel like polio had reinfected Jane. I remembered all the mistakes I made and how I messed up our lives. If only I was as strong as you and Mildred."

"I'm not strong." She took his hand. "I thought I'd messed everything up too, but Mildred helped me realize I didn't. I made mistakes, just as you did. But life is made of a thousand letting gos." She laughed.

He turned his head and pushed a strand of hair out of her eyes. "Why are you laughing?"

"We're so similar. I can't believe I'm just now realizing how similar we are. We both felt responsible for our pasts. Do you think that's why we've had trouble? Our past hurts keep bumping up against each other."

"Maybe." He rubbed a finger against her cheek. "You think we were doomed from the start?"

She leaned closer to him, inhaling his scent of pine and aftershave. "My mom told me that love is a choice. Family is a choice."

He scooted closer to her, their lips almost touching.

Could she trust him again? What if he strayed again? But she knew she wanted to try. Didn't she owe that much to her mother, her sister, Mildred? Life was short.

"I choose you, Howard."

He kissed her. "Good, because I choose you too. And sleeping on the couch is uncomfortable."

A few weeks after Mildred's death, Howard, Henry, and the children trudged outside to do the chores. Florence went into the kitchen to begin breakfast. Finding Mildred's apron, she put it on and went to look in the fridge, but the phone ringing stopped her.

Shutting the refrigerator, Florence made her way into the hall and picked up the receiver. "Wright residence."

"Florence, is that you?"

Surprised by the clearness of her friend's voice, Florence felt overcome with emotion. "It's me. Olive?"

"Oh, Florence. I've missed you. We've all missed you."

"We?"

"We just had the coffee group and everyone's wondering when you're coming back. And Alice wants to know when Jane and William will be back. I think she has a little crush on him."

Surprised by Olive's show of emotion, Florence filled her in with all that had been happening in Iowa. Howard's return and Mildred's death. "We're planning on staying for a little while longer until Henry and Peggy are settled in. We hope to be back soon, before winter sets in. Howard is helping with the farm now, but he's set up an interview at a construction company back home. I think he'll enjoy that even more."

"I'm so sorry for your loss. But I'm glad Howard and you worked things out and that you'll be home soon. We're really busy at the bakery. Think you'd be able to help?"

"I already have some new recipes."

After they said their goodbyes and Florence hung up, she went into the bedroom that she and Howard had been using. Jane had moved into Peggy's room. Florence had given up her worry about the stairs. She rooted around on her dresser, locating some of Mildred's recipe cards for cookies and candy. Once she returned to Michigan, she knew the customers would love the new treats. In the mirror, Florence saw the reflection of her mother's faded quilt on the bed.

Even though she'd washed the quilt, it still smelled like her mom. Florence spread it out on the bed she and Howard shared. She had mended the blanket, using parts of Jane's outgrown dresses and even one of Mildred's old shirts. She could still tell where the holes had been, but that was okay. She'd been learning to let go of perfection. Imperfection was the hallmark of a life that had loved to the fullest and sometimes love got messy.

The front door opened. The chores were done, and she hadn't started breakfast. Turning off the bedroom light, she peeked into the living room. Everyone sat. "What do you all want for breakfast? Sorry, I'm a little behind."

No one said anything or moved. If she didn't know better, she'd assume they were aliens and didn't understand her. But their grief still weighed on them. Returning to the kitchen, she decided to make biscuits. She mixed the dry ingredients, then sifted twice like the recipe called for. She'd always hated the extra work, but her mother said it was one of the secrets for perfect biscuits. They needed something light to lift the heaviness of their grief. She worked in the butter and lard with her fingertips. The work helped with her anger, but the ache remained. She missed her friend and struggled with the same questions. Why had polio struck Mildred, of all people? And why had it taken Mildred and not her delicate daughter? None of this made sense. But life rarely turned out how she thought it should.

Slowly, she added the liquid, mixing it in with a knife. When she first started making biscuits, it had been difficult to determine how much liquid to add. Her mother said that it was another biscuit secret and one day she'd stumbled upon the correct consistency. *Trust the process*, her mother coaxed.

Then the memory of how she'd perfected the biscuits surfaced. It wasn't until after her mother had died that she had succeeded. To give Hattie something to do besides cry, Florence taught her to make biscuits. They read the recipe so many times they had it memorized. Experimenting with various amounts of liquid and different techniques, they'd finally stumbled upon perfection. They had presented the batch to their father.

After he bit into the flaky biscuit, he grinned for the first time in months. "It's perfect, just like your mom's." He hugged them and they cried together. But the tears were happy tears, thankful tears for what they still shared.

She had lost so much, but she hadn't lost everything. Even though her mother, Hattie, and Mildred were gone, their lives had blessed her. Jane had undergone a terrible ordeal, but she had survived. Now Florence would survive. Her father had grieved, forgiven, and thrived. She could do the same. Despite the ache in her heart, she thought of Jane's picture and a peace settled on her.

"Help me blossom," she prayed. "Help me show my family how to blossom when so many weeds threaten to choke our growth."

As the dough reached the desired consistency, she knew what her family needed and how she could help everyone. Finally, a battle she could win.

Wiping her hands on her apron, she went into the living room. Peggy lay curled on her father's lap. William and Jane leaned against their father. They all sniffed and stared into space.

Summoning up her last bit of courage, she readied herself to do what she knew Mildred would do. Putting her hands on her hips, she pushed her shoulders back. "Breakfast isn't going to make itself. Peggy, Jane. You girls need to roll out the biscuits. Henry, you're on bacon. Howard, get some jelly from the basement. William, set the table. I'm hungry. Hurry."

With dazed expressions, the group rose and followed her directions. Jane found her crutches and asked, "What are you going to do?"

"I don't know how to make bacon." Henry stared at the stove in confusion.

"Good thing I'm overseeing," Florence said.

Soon, the kitchen became a hive of activity. Florence didn't think she'd ever seen so many cooks, but everyone moved carefully, and no one bumped into anyone. When Howard reappeared from the basement, carrying multiple jars of jam, he took over setting the table while William showed his uncle how to fry the bacon. They made a bigger mess than she would have, but she didn't clean, only watched from the corner, thinking how proud Mildred would be.

The girls quickly rolled out the biscuits and got the drinks. Peggy spilled juice and halfheartedly wiped it up. They spoke only necessary words, but a smile or two peeked out from time to time.

When they gathered around the table, Florence said, "Mildred would be proud of how we all worked together."

Everyone stared at her as if she had broken an unspoken rule.

Florence reached for a warm biscuit, as light and fluffy as her mother's. "We have to talk about her. We can't forget her, can we?"

All heads shook.

Howard gave a small chuckle. "Like we could forget her. For a little sister, she sure was bossy."

Henry laughed, then sniffed. "We forgot to pray." They all bowed their heads as he said, "Thank you, Lord, for my wife, and bless this food."

Peggy let out a single sob. Henry patted her arm and Jane rubbed her back. Slowly, everyone filled their plates. The sound of clanking silverware and a buzz of quiet chatter floated around the table.

Florence waited until almost the end of the meal to say, "We should celebrate Mildred."

The former silence settled on the room. All the utensils stopped moving, and everyone stopped chewing.

Howard pushed his plate back and took a sip of coffee. "What do you mean? Didn't we already do that? We've had the funeral and the wake. What's left?"

Florence swallowed her bubble of anxiety. She didn't need to worry. She was in the middle of those who loved her. "I think we need something else to celebrate Mildred's life and bring us together. After Hattie and my mother died, my father and I went our separate ways. We grieved apart. Grieving needs to be done together as a family. It will help us grow stronger. It will help us learn. Most importantly, it'll honor Mildred."

"I think we should throw her a party," Peggy said, a faint tinge of excitement in her voice. "We could have her favorite foods."

Henry nodded. "That's a good idea."

Florence got out a piece of paper and pencil to begin the list. "I'm sure my dad and Bertha would help. They'd probably let us use the restaurant."

"Can we have balloons?" Jane asked.

William elbowed his sister. "Don't forget cake."

Chapter 26

Annoyed at the delay, Florence shuffled through the pile of mail for the second time. With so many party preparations and so little time before they left, she didn't want to waste another moment. But she couldn't go into town if she couldn't find the keys. Could they be under the table? Only a partially dressed doll lay on the floor. Where were they? That morning, Howard had told her he'd take the kids to school, then be right back to help Henry in the fields. She parted the curtains. Strange. The truck wasn't there. The sedan that had once belonged to the neighbors was gone too. Henry must have sold it, like he'd planned. After Florence and Howard left, he wouldn't need a second vehicle.

Thinking that the truck might be on the side of the house, Florence put on her coat, got her handbag, and stepped outside. Maybe Howard had left the keys in the ignition like Henry usually did. She peeked around the side of the house. No vehicle and no sign of Howard or Henry. Where was her husband?

An old feeling of dread threatened to close around her. Trying to shake the feeling off, she tightened her coat against the morning chill. She shouldn't expect the worst from him, but his absence made her doubt. At the sound of vehicles, she turned.

The truck drove down the driveway, with Henry waving to her, grinning like he'd won a blue ribbon at the county fair. Howard was in the sedan behind him. When they exited the vehicles and approached her, Howard's grin swallowed his face, making Florence nervous. Could he be hiding something?

She exhaled her worries and managed a faint smile, not wanting to jump to conclusions. "Was something wrong at school?"

In his excitement, he bounced on the balls of his feet. "Nope. We just had an errand in town."

"Oh?" Florence peeked at Henry out of the corner of her eye.

The smile on his tired face reassured her that all was well. He winked at her. "I'd better get started on the day's work."

When Henry left, Howard pulled a key from his pocket. "Do you want to know what the errand was?"

"Well …" She really didn't. She'd started packing their belongings yesterday, but she had more to pack and lots to do for Mildred's life celebration. "Okay. What were you doing in town?"

"I went to Henry's bank and gave him some of our savings. Not a lot. He wouldn't hear of me paying more. I think it's worth—"

Florence put her hand on Howard's arm to quiet him and to process what he'd just said. Their savings? Of course, she'd do anything to help Henry and Peggy. But why hadn't he …

"I know I should have talked to you about it. But I wanted to surprise you." He pressed the key into her hand.

"We already *have* a car."

"No, *I* already have a car."

For a second, anger knotted her stomach, but quickly evaporated. After being in Howard's palm, the key felt warm in her hand. She let the warmth spread throughout her.

He put his arm around her and led her toward the car. "If you're going to be baking for the bakery, you'll need a car. Besides, who knows what else you might get into."

"It's mine?" She smoothed her hand over the glossy red paint. No bugs or grime marred the round headlights. The chrome had been buffed to a shine. "How long did it take to get the car this clean?"

He opened the door. "Henry and the kids helped. Don't worry about that. I'm just sorry we couldn't afford something new."

"I don't know how to thank you." She kissed him.

"I'm the one who needs to thank you for all you've done. Now, go do your errands."

She climbed in the car and was about to thank him again, but he shut the door and walked toward the barn, limping ever so slightly. When she pulled out of the driveway in *her* car, Florence thought how lucky she was to have the car and a healthy, happy family. *Lucky.* Linda, the sour-faced girl from the hospital, had called Jane lucky. Florence had doubted that her family was lucky, but now she knew the truth. Her family had *not* been lucky. God had blessed them. Even through their losses, God had continued to look after them and provide for them.

While she drove into town, she prayed God would bless Linda and she would have the eyes to see who her blessing came from.

Florence parked on Main Street between the grocery store and the restaurant. Getting out of the car, she tried to decide which building to go in first when her father walked out of Annabelle's, whistling. She waved at him.

"What brings you to town?" Frank was dressed in soft gray trousers and a matching sweater. Florence assumed Bertha had a lot to do with his wardrobe. He'd always had trouble matching clothes after her mother passed away.

"Howard and I are going to try again, and I'd like for you and me to give it another chance too. Can we start again?"

He enfolded her in his arms. "I'd like nothing better."

After a minute, she pushed away. Frank's eyes shone with tears. Florence sniffed, not wanting to cry publicly. "And we're having a celebration for Mildred. I was wondering—"

Across the street, Paula, with a downcast head, exited the grocery store and walked toward them. Florence waved her over. "What's wrong?"

Paula sniffed. "No one is hiring. I hate to keep living off my aunt and uncle's goodwill, and I don't want to move. But if I can't find a job …"

Florence raised an eyebrow in question at her father. He nodded. "Well, we'd love to hire you at the restaurant."

"What?" Paula looked in confusion at Florence. "Hire me?"

"First, I should introduce you to my dad, Frank Stephens. He owns Annabelle's. I'm the cook, but we need some extra help. Don't we, Dad?"

"It's a family business, and we'd love to welcome you into our family." Frank beamed at his daughter. "We have a special meal coming up to honor one of the town's finest women. We could use your help."

On the day of the celebration, the restaurant shone with cleanliness. The silverware had been polished. The floors gleamed. William, Jane, and Peggy had even scrubbed the walls, only complaining a little. The aroma of golden cake, Mildred's favorite, scented the air. In the dining room, balloons and streamers hung from almost every surface.

"William, put the table here." Florence pointed to a space next to the door.

Grunting, William set the table down, then rubbed his back. "I think it's time to take a nap. That was heavy, and my arms are still sore from all that scrubbing."

Florence gave him a skeptical look, then draped a white tablecloth over the table. "Girls, do you have the pictures?"

Peggy placed a picture of her mother on one side. Then Jane added her picture of Jesus. Florence put an arm around each girl. "Mildred would love it." She wiped her eyes. Mildred's small gesture, giving her niece a picture, had affected all of them.

"Is it time to open the door, Auntie?" Peggy looked outside where a long line of people waited, holding covered dishes.

Florence nodded. The girls opened the door. Men and women dressed in their Sunday best filed into the restaurant. The party goers placed casseroles, fried chicken, and side dishes on a long table at the back of the dining room. The dishes weren't organized, but Florence had learned to focus on more important things. She crossed to the back corner, where Paula leaned over a table. "Do you need any help?"

Paula straightened the edge of the tablecloth on one of the restaurant's drink and dessert tables. "I think everything's running smoothly."

People had taken glasses of punch from the table and chatted in groups around the room. Florence rubbed her hands together, trying to get rid of the nervous energy. "I feel like I should do something. I thought I'd need to be more involved in planning the event, but there hasn't been much preparation required. The party seems to have organized itself."

Paula handed punch to a small boy, then turned her attention back to Florence. "Just relax. After your father went to buy ingredients for the party at the store, word of the celebration spread. Instead of an intimate dinner, it's now a community luncheon. I never met Mildred, but I'm thinking she'd like seeing everyone working together."

Placing cups on a tray, Paula went around the room, handing out punch to the partygoers. Howard sidled up to Florence and placed a warm arm around her shoulder. "Is something wrong? You look like you're about to cry."

The celebrants formed a line and served themselves. Florence sniffed and leaned into her husband's embrace. "Mildred would be happy with this, wouldn't she?"

He kissed the top of her head. "She was happy when her family was happy."

Henry waved to them, then accepted a glass of punch from Paula. He sat with Frank, Bertha, and William at a table in the middle of the room. Meanwhile, Peggy and Jane scanned the area, and not seeing one of their parents, they snatched cookies from the dessert table. They sneaked off into a corner to eat them, their brown braids bouncing on their backs. Peggy leaned down to her cousin and whispered. Both girls laughed. Florence smiled at the loud sound of the two healthy children. Then, she remembered the last ingredient to make the event a success.

"I'll be back in a minute," she said to Howard. "I need to get something."

"Let me help you."

She patted his arm. "Not right now. This is something I need to do myself."

In the parking lot, she opened the car door. She took the cookbook from the floor and held it to her chest. Closing her eyes, the worn weight filled her arms. Time seemed to stop, and she heard the laughter of her and her sister as they danced around the kitchen. Mom stirred something on the stove. Dad leaned over her mother and kissed her cheek.

Opening her eyes, she watched a yellow leaf fall from a tree. A willow tree swayed in the breeze as if it were serenading this next great adventure in Florence's life.

Fall was a time to celebrate. Now that the harvest was in and the barns were full, it was time to rejoice in all that had happened, the good and bad. She thought of her mother's quilt. All the stitches were like the lives that had weaved in and out of her own life. Grace's mom, Carol, had said that God put people in our paths to help us and now Florence could see that so many random acts in her life were too perfect, too wonderful to be coincidence. Polio almost tore her family apart, but instead it became another thread that held them together.

Entering the kitchen through the back door, she placed the cookbook on the shelf, not because she needed it, but because she wanted to know it was there, in the home where it belonged. Then she went in to finish the meal with her family. The family she had chosen. The family where she would blossom and grow.

Author's Note

I hate the word crippled. To me, it means something that is broken and less than. Something that can't measure up to the world's standards. Dictionary.com defines the word as impaired and weakened. When I hear the word, I cringe inside

I remember the first time I heard it. My mom and I were standing outside a school building, chatting and waiting for my dad to pick us up. A teenager hung his head out of the window of a passing car. He hurled the insult, and it landed at my feet. The word confused me. I looked at my two healthy arms and legs. Was he talking about me? No, it couldn't be.

The only other person anywhere near me was my mom, and it surely couldn't be her. But then I took a second look at my mom. She was different. Of course, I'd seen the crutches she'd walked with before. I knew she'd contracted polio as a child. I knew her legs looked different from the legs of my friends' moms, but the difference to me had been neither good nor bad. The difference had always been neutral. She was my mom. She took care of me and that was enough.

When that person hurled that word at my feet, I felt an anger that I'd never felt before. Others viewed my mother's difference as a weakness, an impairment. But I never did. I viewed my mother's differences as her strength and her power.

In a world where polio had been almost conquered, the disease faded from so many minds. I grew up in the shadow of polio and my mother's story. I could never forget. Though this story is fictitious, my mother's faith and resilience, shown through the character of Jane, are real.

In this book, I've tried to leave my readers with an important message that my mother taught me. Our trials don't need to define us. Our trials can make us stronger. Our trials can point us to the one true source of strength.

My mother is now in heaven. She's dancing on her two perfect legs with her precious Jesus. And I'm here on earth, marveling that God used someone the world considered crippled to leave a legacy of faith and wholeness for those she touched.

Here is my mother's story in her own words:

On a hot August night in 1952, my life changed forever. Before that, I was a normal child who had turned seven in April and finished first grade. My mother's cousin said I was pampered, but I know I was very loved, the third child behind two older brothers, one ten and one fourteen years older. I was my parents' late-life, big surprise.

I loved playing outside where there was so much to do. We lived on a dirt road with many neighbors. Everyone had a big yard with a garden and clothesline. Our yard also had a big sandbox my dad made, a board swing hanging from our clothes pole, and a wonderful willow tree. There were other trees, flowers, and even a rock garden—a child's paradise. I spent a lot of time outside. My mama would pack me lunch in a paper bag some days so I could sit on the back stoop and eat. There were dirt pies and cakes to make. I had sour rhubarb to munch on, our big front porch to play house, complete with a doll buggy and dolls, jacks, marbles, a jump rope, and anything else I could smuggle out of the house.

That day Paula, a little girl from across the road, came over to play. Mom offered us two Dixie cup ice creams, the kind with the little wooden spoons, one vanilla and one chocolate. Because we both wanted chocolate, Paula ended up going home, and I ate both. From then on, I rarely ate chocolate ice cream.

After I went to bed that night, I began to feel sick with a terrible headache and high fever. I had to be carried to the bathroom because I was so weak. A wall calendar had a picture of the holy family—Mary, Joseph, and Jesus as a boy with a white dove above them. I often looked at the picture and said I wanted a doll like that baby Jesus. My brother, Dean, wanted to run right out and get me one.

The first doctor my mom and dad took me to said I had the flu, but Dad didn't believe him, and they took me to another doctor. He only touched my skin and then told my parents, "She has polio." He arranged for me to be admitted to the Sister Kenny Polio Hospital in Pontiac, Michigan rather than the other polio hospital, Herman Kiefer in Detroit, Michigan. He insisted the one in Pontiac was where I should go.

I don't remember the doctor's office or the trip to the hospital, where my first memory was lying on a bed or stretcher in the hallway. There was no room for me when I arrived. The rooms were full and additional patients ended up in the hallways. Recently, I realized I got a bed in a room because someone died. The hallway was quite noisy with so many sick and so many medical people coming and going. I don't know how long I stayed there.

The ward I went to had many people, both young and old. It was scary when I realized I was on my own. My parents had to leave and only visited twice a week. Mama came by way of two buses once a week. They both tried to make the trip on Sundays. I am so thankful for their presence because they kept me from giving up. Mama brought me little toys and green olives, which I craved for the salt. And she brought me love. My illness was very hard on her. She cried a lot and blamed herself for me getting sick. Of course, it wasn't her fault.

When I first arrived, I was paralyzed from the neck down from paralytic, not bulbar, polio. When my fever and headache went away, I began to regain strength in my hands and arms. They treated me with hot packs. Big barrel-like metal containers filled with hot burlap wraps were rolled in. The rough fabric was folded over my arms and legs and covered with a rubber sheet to help retain the heat. We got salt tablets because of fluid loss. After the hot pack treatment, my limbs were moved and stretched to prevent atrophy and to make them work again, always a painful workout. Once I bit a therapist because of the pain. The hot packs were applied while I was in bed, but the therapy was done in another room.

A constant memory is hunger. Breakfast was oatmeal, toast, and milk, but I didn't like the oatmeal. The heavily buttered toast was cold, but I ate it except for the crusts, which I buried in the oatmeal. I was a picky eater and ate very little. My high point of the day was the evening snack, which consisted of a four-square saltine cracker and a glass of milk. I often asked for another cracker and usually got it, making that the highlight of my day. I still like to have treats and plenty of food on hand. I don't want to be hungry or have those I love hungry. It hurts to remember that hungry little girl. I really missed mashed potatoes. When I went home, Mom made them for me often and I still love them.

The hospital was a boring place for a once-active little girl. When I could use my hands, Mama brought me a dollhouse and other toys to play with. I told her that other children had no toys, so I gave some of mine away. I don't think she minded.

Nights were the worst. When they turned off the light, I was afraid in the dark. I called for Mama, but no one came. Now, at sixty-three, I'm still afraid to be alone in the dark. When it stormed, I could see the lightning through the big windows and hear the thunder, which frightened me, but I made peace with the storm and learned not to be afraid of it. At least it provided light. One night I fell out of bed and could not get up from the cold, hard floor. I was afraid. I called and cried, but no one came for a long time. I remember someone finally came and picked me up.

The nurses and aides must have been overworked with so many sick people, but one nurse or aide tried to make life interesting by dyeing her hair pink or blue. She was nice and her colored hair made me smile. I don't remember the nurses being friendly or loving, but they probably didn't have time. They did yell at me for not eating, for hiding my food in other food, and for concealing the vitamins I didn't want to take under my pillow. A very old tutor came to help us with schoolwork, but I don't remember learning anything.

I spent thirteen months in the hospital—a long time. I got very lonely. I recall a Christmas home visit planned for a day and a night, but I don't remember exactly how long. It seemed there were fewer polio patients left at the hospital. As time passed, I worried that my parents weren't coming. I waited and waited, probably crying, and then felt so relieved when they showed up. Being home was wonderful to see my family and have nice food. I don't even remember getting presents, but I'm sure I did. As an adult, I don't care about presents. Just being with my family and seeing them happy is so much more important.

I still remember the smells, the oatmeal, cold buttered toast, and hot burlap. On my eighth birthday, I was still in the hospital. I have a picture of myself with another patient and a birthday cake. I was very thin. While in the hospital, I grew taller and lost my baby teeth. When I was discharged, I used Canadian crutches with a full leg brace and a lock at the knee that I had to push up and down when I wanted to sit. Quite weak at first, I spent a lot of time resting on the couch. My folks had gotten a TV, but there were few shows to watch.

When I finally got a wonderful homebound teacher, I was anxious to learn. I wanted more work to do because I'd missed a year of school. I was glad I learned to read in first grade and had somewhere also learned phonics. When I finally went back to school, I rode a handicapped bus and attended a class for handicapped children. No mainstreaming there.

Our teacher had all the students with special needs. We did little woodworking projects and some written assignments. Two of us who had polio and one girl who had cerebral palsy were anxious to do real school work. After a time, we got to go to normal classrooms for math and eventually for all subjects. Praise the Lord. I was on a mission to be a regular kid again.

About the Author

Sarah acquired her love of stories as a child when she created adventures to help herself fall asleep. Many nights, you can find Sarah asleep with a book on her face, mumbling to her husband, "one more page…"

Traumatic events from her early life haunted Sarah for years. Now, she desires to share hope and healing with her audience. Drawing from life experiences, Sarah writes truth infused fiction, devotions, and blogs. An award-winning author, she has been published in Mature Living, Whispers of Grace, Macaroni Kid, Inkspirations Online, ChristianDevotions.Us, Refresh Bible Study Magazine, and Asbury University's Alumni Publications. Mentor and online chapter president for Word Weavers International, Sarah is a graduate of Asbury University and regularly attends writing conferences. A speaker with Stonecroft Ministries and a guest speaker for Enlightened Bible Study, Sarah speaks on Biblical lessons and her healing from abuse.

With a background in teaching and tutoring, Sarah homeschooled her two sons and is ready for the next stage of her life: encouraging others with her writing and speaking. She enjoys hiking, traveling, and going on mission trips with her husband. Sarah is always on the lookout for a new lesson to be learned, a new setting to discover, or a new character to write about.